Granada

Paul S. Bradley

Paul S. Bradley is a pen name.
© 2021 Paul Bradley of Nerja, Spain.
The moral right of Paul Bradley to be identified as the author of this work has been asserted in accordance with the Copyright, Design, and Patents Act, 1988. All rights reserved.
No part of this publication may be reproduced or transmitted in any form or by any means, electronic or mechanical, including photocopy, recording, or any information storage and retrieval system, without permission in writing from the publisher.

This is a work of fiction. Any resemblance of characters to actual persons, living or dead, is purely coincidental.
Editor: Gary Smailes; www.bubblecow.com
Cover Illustration: Jill Carrott; www.virtue.es
Cover Photo: Stock Image from www.pond5.com
Layout: Paul Bradley; Nerja, Spain.
Darkness in Granada is the fourth volume of the Andalusian Mystery Series.
Publisher: Paul Bradley, Nerja, Spain.
First Edition: January 2021.
Contact: info@paulbradley.eu
www.paulbradley.eu
Available in eBook and Print on Demand. See the website for details.

ISBN: 9798606501786

The Andalusian Mystery Series

Andalucía is wrapped in sunlight, packed with history, and shrouded in legend. Her stunning landscapes, rich cuisine, friendly people, and vibrant lifestyle provide an idyllic setting for a mystery series. The first four books are linked, the others are standalone cases. The author recommends reading them in numerical order.

1- *Darkness in Málaga.*
2- *Darkness in Ronda.*
3- *Darkness in Vélez-Málaga.*
4- *Darkness in Granada.*

The series will continue with *Darkness in Córdoba*. See website. www.paulbradley.eu

Dedication

To Maggie Parker, for keeping me going.

Acknowledgments

My heartfelt thanks to Jill Carrott, Elizabeth Francis, Fran Poelman, Renate Bradley, and editor Gary Smailes.

Paul S. Bradley

1

Valentina looks exhausted, thought Phillip appraising his former spouse as she draped her bare arms over the white metal gate to his villa. Her pale skin reflected the dying pink rays of the late December sun as it sunk from view behind a distant mountain ridge. The rolling countryside surrounding Phillip's villa was speckled with white buildings, olive groves, and fruit trees. Long shadows merged slowly into the gathering twilight gloom. On the Mediterranean coast, three kilometers below, the halogen street lights of Nerja flickered on, lending an orange glow below the ever-changing kaleidoscope of heavenly color. Another stunningly beautiful Andalusian sunset closing out what had been, until this moment, a wonderful idyllic Sunday with dear friends, excellent food, and vino tinto.

Valentina's ice-blue eyes glared hard into his. He stood transfixed with his arms around the slender waists of his dark-haired fiancée, Amanda, and her best friend Salome, the famous Flamenco dancer. He stared right back.

"You needed two women to replace me?" said Valentina finally in English. Her Russian accent still oozing seduction as she rolled her tongue languidly around the r of replace, but her sad expression belied her attempt at humor. Her magnificent long blond hair had lost its former gloss, her face looked thinner, still beautiful, yet vulnerable.

"Your cooking skills left much to be desired," said Phillip. "Too much borsch. What do you want?"

"I need a bed for me and my son."

"We're not a hotel, especially for ex-wives," said Phillip.

"I don't care where I sleep but the little one needs a bath, a proper bed, and some healthy food."

The rear window of the small grey saloon buzzed and slid downward. A boy with shaggy blond hair stuck out his angelic face, yawned, and rubbed his eyes. "Mama, why have we stopped?" he said in Russian.

Amanda gasped. Phillip gulped.

The boy's face was a mini version of Phillip's.

"Now you understand," said Valentina.

Phillip nodded and looked at Amanda, his pulse racing.

What does my love think of all this? He thought. And why does she seem so happy? I'd have thought ex-wives turning up unannounced with a boy that could be my son would have infuriated or at least concerned her.

"They will stay here," said Amanda. "I'll go and prepare the remaining guest room. Salome," she added indicating her bandaged arm. "Come and help."

The two women went inside whispering. Salome walking stiffly with her bad back. Phillip clicked the gate control and watched as it slid back to reveal

Valentina's slimmer but still shapely curves dressed in baggy jeans and a loose blouse.

Valentina smiled to herself. Her culinary skills might have been rubbish, but she could see instantly that Phillip hadn't forgotten the intensity of their lovemaking. Men, she thought, they are so easy.

"Your women appear to be injured," said Valentina. "I trust that was nothing to do with you?"

"Of course, not," said Phillip. "But that is none of your business."

Valentina regarded him. "Very well," she said turning then opening the rear door. "Come, Sasha, and meet your real father," she said in Russian.

Sasha climbed down, walked over to Phillip, stopped before him, and held out his hand. "Hello, Papa," he said in unaccented English.

Phillip looked him up and down. A tall, skinny boy with steely blue, curious eyes, shaggy blond hair, and a missing bottom front tooth. He reminded Phillip of a photo of himself in the family album. It was even the same missing tooth. Emotion welled over him.

Valentina watched him like a hawk, aware of what Phillip must be struggling with. It's not every day unknown flesh and blood turn up out of nowhere.

Phillip squatted, returned Sasha's inquiring gaze, took his hand, and shook it. "Welcome, my son," he said in Russian. "Forgive me if I seem a little shocked. But you have to be the most wonderful surprise of my life."

Sasha threw himself into Phillip's arms. Phillip hugged him. He'd only just met this boy but the certainty that he was his son was never in doubt.

Valentina climbed back into the car and maneuvered it into Phillip's drive. She stopped then watched them for a moment, tears streaming down her cheeks.

Phillip released Sasha and stood, his knees creaking. He continued holding the boy's hand as he opened the driver's door. Valentine climbed out, went to the rear of the car, and opened the trunk. She removed one of two large suitcases. The tears continued to flow. Phillip and Sasha had immediately bonded. She'd been confident that Sasha would but wasn't sure if Phillip had changed; perhaps resentment after the acrimonious divorce had twisted him against her. But he was still the same. Soft and trustworthy. A brief moment of regret made her shudder. She'd been stupid and was paying the price. If only she hadn't been so impulsive, they could still be together. But she shook it off. It was, how it was. Finally, Sasha was with his father. And whichever woman was Phillip's partner would make a fine stepmother. Perhaps both of them, anything went nowadays. More importantly, Sasha would be safe here; safe and loved.

2

Detective Inspector Leon Prado parked next to the many trucks and vans in front of his regular café on the outskirts of Ronda. He climbed out, but then remembered his wife's parting words from under the cozy warm bed covers at their home in the old town.

"Wrap up warm," Inma had insisted. "In your mid-fifties, you need to worry about your circulation."

He buttoned his thick winter coat against the hard frost, made sure his tweed cap was on tight over his thick silver hair and at the preferred angle, then headed toward the steamed-up entrance.

The place was buzzing with drivers enjoying their early Monday morning infusions. He nodded at several acquaintances and took his customary seat by the window. He unbuttoned his coat, shifted the Christmas tinsel and fairy lights draped across the glass, then wiped away the condensation with a serviette to check his car as more vehicles arrived. He didn't want to be blocked in, as often happened at this time of day.

He scoured the bar area looking for a waiter, nodded to Pepe, who hardly acknowledged him he was so busy but that was all Prado needed to do. They knew what he wanted. While he waited for his breakfast, he watched the barista take down another Serrano ham suspended from the rail over the bar, remove the conical fat collector, mount the leg into a stand, and attack it with a razor-sharp carving knife. Once the outer skin had been removed, revealing the succulent dark pink flesh, he began slicing wafer-thin bite-size pieces at an unbelievable speed. Minutes later, Pepe served his toasted mollete, with local olive oil, and a café solo.

"Buenos días, Pepe," said Prado frowning as he wrestled with the aluminum lid of the prepackaged clear plastic container. He hated these stupid European Union health and safety laws. Fine olive oil should be served in glass or ceramic bottles, where it could breathe and be easily poured without spilling. Customers should be able to use as much or as little as they preferred to minimize waste.

"Hola, Inspector," said Pepe clearing the next table then almost running back to the kitchen.

This was the time of day when Prado did his best thinking. He ignored phone calls, the regulars left him alone and he could chew the delicious bread roll, in as much peace as forty men chattering over jaunty seasonal music would allow. But he was acclimatized to that and was able to shut it out completely.

His mind meandered back to the lunch at Phillip's yesterday. He wished he could barbecue meat as well as that, then perhaps his family might come around more often. His burnt burgers and half raw sausages were avoided like the plague. Perhaps he'd ask Phillip to help him master the art of the grill. The possibilities of a terrace packed with family enjoying his culinary masterpieces flashed through his mind while he enjoyed his breakfast.

One day, he thought, as he bounced back to reality.

It had been an interesting seven months since heading up a new department in the National Police. It had been an eye-opener. In his previous position, as head of the serious crimes squad throughout Andalucía, he'd been buried in the sordid world of drugs and associated gang busting. The vile things these greedy animals did to each other for ego, power, and money had depressed him, but he was determined that Spanish streets should be rid of the scum and had become obsessed with catching them. However, his relentless drive to arrest such delinquent fools had kept him away from his family. He'd ignored his wife's yearning for company and missed his boy's important milestones. Eventually, Inma had enough of the endless broken promises to be home and had thrown him out. He'd found solace in the whiskey bottle in the loneliness of a tiny, rented apartment located near his office in the comisaría in central Málaga. On occasions, he'd slept at his desk. Then the kidnapping of a teenage Danish girl had gone dreadfully wrong. He'd been pushed sideways into what he and everyone had presumed was a dead-end job to prevent him from committing yet more carnage.

As the sole member of the new department for crimes involving foreigners, he'd been given an office next to the station chief on the top floor under the pretext of it appearing to be a promotion. However, he and everyone knew that he was being watched like a hawk. It made him feel like a naughty schoolboy.

But it hadn't turned out so badly after all.

The job was far less physically demanding, most of it cerebral, and much could be done by teleworking.

He'd found time to reconcile with his wife and now grown boys away at university in Sevilla. Life was sweet once more.

He finished his coffee and resumed the ninety-minute journey down to Málaga center. His first task was to review the Crown case with el jefe, his boss. He mulled over the details as he drove.

It was a grey morning as Prado joined the tail end of the morning rush hour on the tree-lined Avenida de Andalucía. The stop, start, gradually untangled as he crossed the bridge over the currently dry Rio Guadalmedina where he turned into the maze of narrow streets of the Casco Antiguo, old town. He passed the Teatro Cervantes, turned into Calle Ramos Marín, and arrived at the comisaría. He returned the pool car to the underground garage, went up to the top floor in the lift, knocked on his boss's door and went straight in.

He found Jefe Superior, Provincia de Málaga: Francisco Gonzalez Ruiz, standing at the picture window gazing over the bustling Plaza de la Merced. Office workers scurried across the former medieval marketplace to their respective buildings. Language students ambled in small groups from the several cafes to their daily lectures chatting animatedly.

Prado noticed his boss's uniform jacket was hanging over the back of his desk chair. Almost unheard of, thought Leon, half-naked at work. There must be something special cooking. Prado couldn't help but notice that his chief was staring at the statue of the artist Pablo Picasso. He was sitting on a bench at the opposite corner of the tree-lined square in front of his birthplace. Two attractive women were perched on either side of his bronze likeness, sitting on the bench having their photo taken by a young man.

"Are you watching the pretty girls, or is the statue inspiring you?" said Prado.

El jefe turned and indicated that Prado should take a seat. "You were right," said el jefe frowning. "The great man has stirred my grey cells into action. Not that you'd notice."

"Wasn't he a bit of a womanizer?" said Prado grinning.

"He was an artist," said el jefe. "Form, shape, and texture dominated his life."

"Especially the female of the species."

"And it's precisely his skills at representing them on canvas that might help us resolve the Crown case," said el jefe sitting down. "But before we lose ourselves in that, I'd like to review progress since forming your new department."

"Where would you like to begin, Sir?" said Prado.

"Frankly, Leon, after leading the fast-paced serious crime squad for nearly twenty years, I was skeptical that you could adjust to working on your own on more dreary cases, but I'm pleased to say that you have surprised me. I'm impressed by how you have compensated for your lack of linguistic talent by surrounding yourself with excellent voluntary translators."

"Phillip and Amanda are far more than just interpreters, Sir," said Prado.

"Remind me why."

"When I met Phillip Armitage at the Guardia Civil in Nerja, he was a lonely, ex-British soldier in his early forties licking his wounds after an acrimonious divorce. He ran an internet guide to Spain which, at the time, he was finding somewhat tedious and his considerable language talents were underutilized. Now, after helping me solve my first three cases, he has rediscovered his lust for life and proven himself an asset to our police force. He not only helps with English, German, and Russian speakers but provides amazing insight into their culture and knows how they think. His assistance in the Crown investigation has been invaluable."

"I agree, and Amanda?"

"Amanda Salisbury is thirty-three years old, American by birth but has lived here since she was seven. Her father was stationed at the joint Naval base in Rota, near Cadiz. Her mother is of Moroccan origins and insisted her daughter grew up with equal exposure to both parental cultures. She speaks Arabic, French, English and her Spanish is better than mine. Her videography skills contributed to solving both our first two cases and her feminine intuition is amazing."

"And now they are engaged to each other?"

"Yes, but they don't let that interfere with the help they provide."

"Does that mean you wish to continue working with them?"

"Yes, even if I had full time assistance but I think we should consider giving them some sort of recognition for their services. They do after all work for nothing and relish giving something back to their adopted country."

"For which we are grateful. What do you suggest?"

"We could at least pay their expenses promptly and a word of encouragement from you in front of the team here would be well received. Most know them by now and all show respect despite them being foreigners."

"I'll give it some thought. Now, where are we with the Crown case?"

"Four adults working together seeking retribution against Marquez, their former headmaster, and abuser when they were teenagers at school, is a conspiracy, not a case," said Prado.

"Call it what you like, but where are we?"

"After thirty odd fruitless years hunting down Marquez, I believe that something occurred two years ago to reinvigorate their campaign. It prompted them to commit serious crimes to flush out their adversary. Risking their liberty in such a fashion suggests desperation. It's as if their lives will be worth nothing unless they can exact their own form of justice."

"Perhaps they were concerned old age might kill Marquez off before they could find him," said el jefe.

"Possible, but I'm inclined toward an unforeseen event of some sort. Worrying about Marquez dying before they could find him wasn't anything new."

"You could be right," said el jefe. "I have to say that I was impressed by their inventiveness. I've not come across anyone trying to flush out their adversary using his favorite hobbies as bait. But what a weird mix of preferences? I can only assume that Marquez must have had one hell of a fucked-up childhood to become obsessed by perverted sex, illegal bullfight gambling, religious artifacts, and a penchant for Picasso paintings, especially his muses. What do you propose to do next?"

"We have Malcolm Crown in jail awaiting trial for setting up a sex trafficking ring and dark web voyeur website that included abducted underage teens," said Prado. "Patrick O'Reilly established an illegal bullfight gambling service. Sonia Augustin used her restoration workshop as a front for stealing precious religious artifacts and auctioning them off online. It leaves us with one victim, still out there hunting for Marquez. We have no idea who he or she is, or where Marquez is hiding. My instincts tell me that we shouldn't wait for the fourth victim to call the shots. We need to be proactive in flushing them both out and I suggest that we use the one remaining passion of Marquez that has not been exploited."

"Picasso?" said el jefe.

"Correct, Sir."

"Have you seen this?" said el jefe sliding over a small pamphlet.

Prado picked it up and speed read both sides. It advertised a Christmas exhibition at the Parador Hotel located in the Alhambra Palace in Granada. 'Picasso and his Muses' was the title of the event. The inauguration was due at lunchtime on the coming Friday, the day of the El Gordo Christmas Lottery draw; in four days. It would close the day before Los Reyes Magos, on the afternoon of the fifth of January. The chief executive of the state-owned Parador Hotel chain would introduce the mayor of Granada, who would officiate. He was to thank Anne Pennington, the American owner of the collection for allowing these rare paintings to be moved from her private gallery at home in Granada city to a high-security conference room in the hotel. The American Ambassador to Spain would also be attending from Madrid along with several distant relatives of the Picasso family.

"Big guns for a relatively small event," said Prado.

"If you knew your Picasso, this is no minor happening," said el jefe. "These paintings haven't seen daylight for over thirty years. Every Picasso lover in the world won't be able to resist this and it's been promoted heavily through art connoisseur media."

"May I safely assume that you want me to hijack this event to flush out Marquez?"

"That's exactly what I'm thinking and with luck, the fourth member of the conspiracy. They are just as desperate to locate Marquez as we are."

"I'm not sure if the paintings on their own would be enough for Marquez to risk revealing himself," said Prado.

"That's exactly why I was gazing at the great man," said el jefe. "Seeking some kind of signal from him."

The mid-morning sun chose that moment to illuminate the square. Something metallic flashed on the hand of one of the women by Picasso as the sun faded quickly behind a cloud.

"That's it," said Prado. "Do you remember the religious artifacts that Amanda and Phillip discovered in Vélez-Málaga when they were helping the Flamenco dancer Salome Mendosa look into her birth family background?"

"The Las Claras treasure, of course," said el jefe. "What about it?"

"Have you considered adding it to the exhibition?" said Prado. "With his favorite paintings and artifacts all under the same roof. Marquez should be wetting himself."

"That should do it," said el jefe. "But there is just one tiny complication."

"Several complications, Sir. Salome, our beloved Flamenco dancer, and owner of the treasure might not cooperate. The hotel won't have a spare room near the paintings, and can we arrange all this and publicize it in time?"

"I'm sure all those can be dealt with, Leon. But how the hell do we do it without an obvious police presence?"

"I know exactly how," said Prado. "And there won't be a cop in sight."

3

"What are we going to do with Sasha and his mother?" said Amanda, as she and Phillip huddled around the island in the kitchen eating slices of locally grown fresh mango waiting for the coffee machine to warm up. "They can't stay here indefinitely."

It had proved impossible to extract Valentina's plans from her the previous evening. After picking at left-over ribs and salads from the barbecue, Sasha and his mother were both so dog tired, they couldn't or wouldn't talk and had gone to bed early where they were still.

"I agree," said Phillip stroking her shoulder. "But until we know what their plans are, we can only speculate. However, I will say this."

"What, my love?"

"You are amazing."

Amanda stood, wrapped her good arm around him and they kissed.

"Whatever happens here," said Phillip. "We are getting married at the end of February. Anything else has to fit around that."

"I agree," said Amanda returning to her stool.

"Then let us promise each other that whatever stress or challenges this may present, we solve them together."

Amanda poured her coffee, raised the cup to her mouth, and nodded. "Promise," she said. "But it won't be a smooth ride."

"No, darling. With this Russian drama queen, it will be a rollercoaster."

They both heard the noise as a guestroom door opened and bare feet pattered on the tiled floor heading in their direction. Their hearts beat faster as they both stared at the kitchen door, anxious to see who it was.

"Morning, both," said Salome still dressed in her sleep shirt. "Any spare coffee?" She gestured toward the guestroom. "Any developments?"

"Still sleeping," said Amanda sliding over the plate of mango. "How's the back?"

"Still twinges, but I've taken an anti-inflammatory. Give me five and I'll be fine."

Phillip fetched another cup from the cupboard and poured Salome a coffee.

"Thanks," said Salome. "What are you going to do about Valentina?"

"Await an explanation," said Phillip. "What else?"

Another, lighter set of bare feet pattered toward the kitchen. Everyone watched as the door opened and in walked Sasha dressed in jeans and a striped T-shirt.

"Any breakfast?" said Sasha in English. Phillip laughed, ruffled Sasha's hair, and lifted him onto a stool.

"Fresh mango?" said Phillip.

"Yummy," said Sasha.

"I like that," said Phillip. "A young man that knows

what he wants. What do you prefer to drink?"

"Water, please."

"Then water it is," said Phillip taking a plastic beaker from a cupboard, filling it from the water bottle, and serving it to Sasha. "How did you learn such good English? You have no accent at all."

"On TV."

"Amazing," said Phillip resting his arm on the boy's shoulder as he tucked into his fruit.

"I see he's teaching you what to feed him," said Valentina coming through the door, still dressed in the same clothes as the previous evening.

"You've brought him up well."

"Thank you but he'd prefer white bread and sugary rubbish."

"How about you? The mangoes are fresh," said Phillip picking up another one and beginning to peel it.

"That would be great. I guess you'll be wanting to know our plans."

"When you're ready, no hurry."

"I need to return the rental car this morning and do some shopping," said Valentina. "I'm out of decent clothes and the cases are full of dirty laundry."

"Where do you have to take the car?"

"Málaga airport. Afterward, I'll catch the train into the town center, shop, then bus it to Nerja and grab a cab back here. Would you mind Sasha? I won't be that long. Perhaps you could introduce him to your sister's girls. He's been a bit short on children's company for a while?"

"Good idea but they are at school until this afternoon. The bus delivers them back around four."

"Where do they go?"

"It's an international school in Rincón de la

Victoria, they speak English and Spanish."

"Sounds perfect."

"My nieces love it. What do you propose after you've returned the car?"

"Don't worry Phillip, I won't be disturbing your life."

"That's considerate, but now Sasha and I have found each other, we would both like to spend time together. Will your plans allow for that?"

Valentina looked down and chewed on a slice of mango. She finished it, swallowed then looked directly at Phillip. "Yes," she said. "That was the point of coming here. Now if you'll forgive me, I need to get off to Málaga. Come and say goodbye to Mama, darling."

Sasha burst into tears. His mother rushed to him, picked him up, and hugged him. Tears streaming down her cheeks. "Be brave, my son," she said in Russian. "Remember what we discussed?"

"Yes, Mama. Love you."

"Love you too."

Valentina handed the distressed boy over to Phillip and headed for the bedroom. She came out with a shoulder bag a few seconds later. "Can you see me out the gate?" she said. "I've driven all this way without scratching the paintwork, I'd hate to ruin it at the last minute."

As he opened the front door, still carrying Sasha, Phillip noticed the Spanish plates. "I thought you said, you'd driven nonstop from Berlin."

"I did but switched cars at the borders. Easier on the insurance."

Phillip nodded, followed her out, and zapped the electric gate.

As it began to slide open, Valentina turned and kissed him on the cheek. "Take good care of him," she said, climbed in the car, reversed out perfectly, and drove off.

***

Phillip closed the gate, shut the front door behind him, carried Sasha back into the kitchen, and sat down with him on a stool at the island. The poor boy was so distressed, Phillip was at a loss what to say or do. He looked up at Amanda. She came over and stroked both their heads.

Phillip's phone rang.

Amanda answered it.

"Thanks for a great barbeque yesterday?" said Prado. "Inma was most impressed. Now she's prodding me to beef up my grilling skills."

"Sorry to cut in, Leon," said Amanda. "How can we help? Only we've had an unexpected development here that needs Phillip's attention."

"Can you tell me?" said Prado.

"Later," said Amanda.

"Then I'll come straight to the point," said Prado. "It's urgent and involves Salome and the Las Claras treasure."

"Hold on, Leon, Salome is here. We'll go into the next room."

Amanda and Salome went into the lounge and closed the door gently behind them.

Sasha sobbed pitifully.

Phillip watched them go. Grateful for the solitude. At least he wouldn't have to expose his parental inadequacies in front of the ladies. He hugged Sasha tightly and rocked him gently.

***

"Hola, Leon," said Amanda as they settled onto the sofa. "Salome and I are on speakerphone; how can we help?"

"I'm in Málaga with el jefe. We're discussing a forthcoming exhibition at the Parador Hotel in the Alhambra Palace; Granada. It's called 'Picasso's Muses.' The paintings are from the private collection of an American lady called Anne Pennington. It's being inaugurated this Friday."

"Really," said Amanda. "I've been trying to meet her for ages. She has an interesting story to tell as well as an amazing art collection. I'm surprised she's agreed to show her paintings though, she's a bit of a recluse and rumored to be suffering from onset Alzheimer's. Why are you telling me this?"

"We think Marquez may well risk coming out of hiding to see such rare works of his favorite painter but just to make sure, we want to spice up the temptation by adding the Las Claras Collection to the exhibition. Our thinking is that two out of four of his passions in one place would be strong enough motivation for a final burst of pleasure. He's not getting any younger. Salome, would you mind helping us out, I assure you that your treasure will be secure."

"I'll need more than security, inspector," said Salome. "These are ancient and precious items that need delicate handling. If you can rest my mind on that issue, then I'll be delighted to make the collection available."

"Then you choose the moving team, and we'll pay,"

said Prado.

"I'd prefer that," said Salome.

"How were you thinking of setting this up?" said Amanda. "Surely, Marquez will sniff out the faintest hint of any police presence."

"I agree," said Prado. "That is my next request. Could you and Phillip front this on our behalf? We'll foot the bills of course."

"Sorry, Leon but Phillip is out of the loop for the moment," said Amanda. "But don't worry Salome and I will handle it. We need to be out of Phillip's hair for a few days anyway until he's resolved his current challenges."

"Sounds intriguing," said Prado "Did something happen after the barbecue?"

"You could say so," said Amanda. "We'll head off for Granada shortly, but we need to ensure that the hotel will cooperate with us. Any help you could lend in that direction?"

"It's a state-owned business," said Prado. "El jefe will make a few calls and I'll text you with the name of the hotel manager. I'll also be sending a surveillance expert to meet you there. We need facial recognition cameras installed to discreetly monitor all visitors. I'll also arrange for you to drive straight up to the hotel entrance and park the car outside. One of the benefits of the hotel's location is that there is only one way in and one way out. And for exhibition visitors, access is by foot only."

"OK. We'll be leaving in about thirty minutes. We should arrive at the Parador around eleven."

"Thanks for helping out," said Prado.

"It's a great idea," said Amanda. "Let's hope Marquez rises to the bait."

4

In the traditionally decorated lounge of a grand townhouse located in a narrow street not far below the Alhambra Palace in Granada, Silvano Furlan, a medium height chunky man in his mid-sixties with curly grey hair was helping his elderly wife out of her armchair.

"Aren't you worried about your paintings?" he said in accented English. He was Italian but had lived in Granada since a holiday there in his early twenties.

"What paintings?" said the frail Anne Pennington in her American twang putting her hand over her mouth to cover a yawn.

"The Picasso muses," said Silvano, concerned that her oncoming Alzheimer's seemed to be worsening.

Anne looked at him puzzled for a moment, then it twigged. "Not at all," she said. "The hotel security arrangements were most impressive. Is your outfit ready for Friday?"

"The cleaners are delivering it on Wednesday. When are the exhibition organizers picking up the paintings?"

"Thursday evening."

"You'll need to turn off all the alarms into the gallery."

"Of course."

"Can I ask you a question?"

"Of course?"

"Over the last four years, you've had all seven muse paintings cleaned by some restorer in Málaga, yet you wouldn't let me help you. You took the heavy pictures down yourself, disappeared for three days with our driver, then rehung everything while I hovered outside the gallery door not allowed in. I felt like a redundant idiot."

Anne reached out and gripped his hand. "There were good reasons, Silvano, and please be assured that there was no affront to you intended. It's just something I had to do alone."

"After three years of marriage you ought to be able to trust me by now, and my love, perish the thought, but what if you die? What would I do with this house and your precious artworks?"

"My darling Silvano," said Anne resting her frail head on his shoulder. "It's not an issue of trust but you're right, you need to know. Make us some tea and bring it to the veranda where I'll explain."

Five minutes later, Silvano placed a tray laden with a silver teapot and fine porcelain cups on a small round table between two cushioned cane chairs. The veranda overlooked the long beautifully manicured garden bordered by oleanders and magnolias. Further up the hill, some six hundred meters beyond the tree line at the end of the steeply sloping garden could be seen the red brick towers of the Alhambra Palace. The gardens were similar to the original seventeenth-century design but after Anne had purchased what was an old ruin over thirty years previously, the house had been built from scratch behind the original façade.

Silvano waved at Angelo, the gardener, who looked up from pruning the roses as he took his seat. Angelo nodded and returned to his secateurs.

"Do you remember when we first met?" said Anne pouring the tea for them both and adding a slice of lemon.

"How could I forget? I'd spent years wondering what you were like as a person. Occasionally, I'd watch you from my restaurant as a taxi whisked you off somewhere or brought an elderly gentleman to visit you. I respected that you were a private person but the day you came into my bar for the first time, I was spellbound. You moved so graciously for such a petite lady and had a commanding allure about you, I was captivated from that very moment."

"You Italians are so charming. That's what attracted me to you. Godfrey, my late partner was so reserved with his compliments. My staff had always spoken highly of your restaurant and I'd often been tempted to eat there. But Godfrey avoided being seen in public, especially with me. While he was still alive, I felt obligated to be true to him and his memory. When he died, I needed someone to talk to who wasn't cleaning something or tending to the garden. I thought I'd come to the restaurant to see if I could meet anyone. I've always been a bit of a recluse and never dreamed to look for another partner let alone marry for the first time. I was seventy-eight, who thinks of love at such an age, especially with a man twelve years younger?"

"Why haven't you discussed this before?"

"I wanted to move on from the past and live for the moment."

"Is that why you never ask me about my background?"

"Something like that. We all carry baggage and I preferred to leave that behind and make a clutter-free fresh start. You keep your secrets and all those beautiful lovers. I'll bury mine and we'll concentrate on enjoying each other. Has it been good for you?"

"Wonderful, the traveling has been amazing. I have seen more of the world in my short time with you than in all my life, and I agree. I'm happy to leave the past alone except to say that I was working my balls off most of the time. I've hardly had any lovers, there was a mortgage to pay."

"Whatever, but I have to tell you about Godfrey."

"You don't need…"

"No, I must. As you said, should I die, there are some practical realities that you need to know."

"Then who was Godfrey?"

"Have you heard of James P Steinman?"

"Means nothing to me."

"He was one of America's richest oilmen around the middle of the twentieth century. He died in 1962 leaving everything to his only child, Godfrey, who was twenty-one and studying Law at Harvard University."

"Nice start to life."

"Not necessarily. Believe me when I say from bitter experience that wealth brings a whole bunch of responsibilities and problems you have never even dreamed of. Initially, Godfrey toed the line defined by his father's executors and trustees. He did all the right things, went to church, married into another wealthy family, and had four children with his frigid wife. He didn't join the family business but started his legal practice, climbed the Washington DC ladder, and launched into politics. Ultimately, he became the youngest Republican senator ever. That's when I met him."

"How?"

"I worked on Capitol Hill."

"Doing what?"

"You know that I'm a qualified lawyer, back then I specialized in helping politicians divest themselves of their wealth so they could make informed and unbiased decisions on what is right for the country, not their fortunes. Well, that's the theory. Godfrey consulted me, I helped him set up the Steinman Foundation and we began an affair. I lived just around the corner from Capitol Hill on C Street, South East in a rowhouse. Godfrey used to slip around when he could. The house is still mine, but I rent it out to my younger brother and his family."

"You were a senator's mistress? That's awesome."

"Mistress no. That implies a commercial relationship for exclusive sex. I prefer lover or muse. For a strongly minded feminist determined to make a career in a male-dominated world, even that was a painful concept to willingly accept and adapt to. So, I looked around for something I could latch on to, something that would help me feel OK with my new status. And then I went to the Picasso Museum in Barcelona.

"The artist's life story fascinated me. He was the ultimate chauvinist and classified women as goddesses or doormats. Yet how could such an ugly selfish little runt, paint like an angel and attract such beautiful women? I became fascinated by what kind of girl could touch the heart of such a heartless man. Naturally, I compared myself with them. Which one did I resemble, was I floorcovering or divine? It spurred me to buy as many of his muse paintings as I could lay my hands on. As you know, I love gazing at them all these years later. I still ask myself the same question. What am I? It's why I insisted this exhibition was to be called, 'Picasso's Muses'. Perhaps it might guide other women in similar situations to reconcile their inner torment."

"If it helps," said Silvano gazing into her eyes. "I only see you as a goddess."

"Thank you," said Anne stretching out her hand and taking his. "That's what Godfrey used to say but I still can't bring myself to accept that. I'll forever battle with my conscience. Was I a decorative whore, or did he worship me?"

"The paintings must have cost a fortune."

"Thirty years ago, Picasso wasn't that popular, but today's values are astronomical."

"I hadn't realized you were that wealthy."

"Silvano, darling before you start having ideas about knocking me off, nothing in this house or the weekend place in Nerja belongs to me, and I don't own the properties. They all belong to the Steinman Foundation and on my death revert to them. In effect, Godfrey paid for all this plus a generous allowance to persuade me to leave Washington, otherwise, the scandal of our affair would have ruined him."

"What is it with Americans and affairs? In most of Europe, especially the Latin-based countries such as mine and Spain, having a lover is usual and acceptable behavior, providing it's discreet."

"I've always wondered why?" said Anne.

"It's no different from the Steinman's or any wealthy dynasty. For centuries, the family, its survival, and position in society came before everything.

Getting married wasn't an individual's decision, the whole family was heavily involved. Not so much nowadays, but families obliged, particularly their eldest children, to marry for the betterment of them all rather than for romantic love. Once the offspring had been produced, the family lineage, position, and wealth secured, many couples reverted to a marriage of convenience and sourced their romance elsewhere. Both men and women took on lovers. It kept them happy and content and enabled their marriages to endure. Godfrey was simply following these ancient traditions with you?"

"Exactly, but sadly in America, it is not acceptable. You've heard of Puritans?"

"Of course, never met one though."

"America was founded by and is still run by them. Mistresses are persona non grata in their so-called polite society. Sex is something rarely discussed yet they are happy to carry guns and kill each other by the thousands. I couldn't continue living among such priggishness and hypocrisy. It's why I happily accepted Godfrey's offer to escape here, but I made him pay top dollar."

"And you were right to. You dedicated your life to him. Missed having a family of your own and had to live in exile. You have nothing to be ashamed of," said Silvano, pausing for a minute. "You must have loved him deeply to do all that for him."

Anne's eyes watered, she nodded and sniffed.

Silvano stood and wiped her eyes with his handkerchief.

"The early years were marvelous," said Anne holding his hands. "We traveled regularly, and he loved buying things for me."

"Can I ask how that worked?" said Silvano.

"Sorry, what do you mean?"

"Even back then you couldn't just splash money around willy-nilly. It had to be accounted for and tax returns completed. Surely as an investment expert, you must have been conscious of that."

"Now I understand. It wasn't difficult. At that time, the Foundation was only Godfrey with a part-time bookkeeper. However, he was obliged to spend its considerable funds on charitable concerns, not himself. So, we cooked up a mission for him to do that. It was to seek out talented artists from impoverished backgrounds and support them with grants and training courses. In reality, I was the only artist and received an extremely generous monthly grant. Also, we both had Foundation credit cards and just bought whatever we wanted. He submitted the receipts to the bookkeeper and that was that. When he died though, that all changed. The Foundation had now expanded substantially and needed to be squeaky clean with its administration. They came to me and asked me for an inventory of everything I had purchased, or Godfrey had given to me as they couldn't trace any records. I had no receipts, so was unable to help them. They asked if they could come and take stock of everything. I refused but did agree to sign a contract that defined what would happen in the event of my death. You need to read that. If you don't understand it, at least meet with my lawyer and have him explain the detail because when I'm gone, it will become your problem."

"Thank you, my love. Just what I needed to help me grieve your loss."

"It will keep you busy," said Anne grasping his hand again. "Which is more than the Steinman family, or the

Foundation ever did to help me when Godfrey passed. I only heard about it on the news. There was no contact from the family, even though they all knew of my existence. Almost the next day after he'd gone, a Foundation lawyer came here to warn me to stay away from the funeral. For my cooperation, I made the bastards pay for another painting. God, I hate them."

"That I can fully relate to. Which painting?"

"The self-portrait of Picasso as a youngster, when he still had hair, a scraggy beard, a pathetic mustache, and a hint of orange lips. Listen, dear husband, this all sounds extremely morbid and not our usual frivolous approach to life, but I am sorry to say that I am not long for this world. My doctor told me recently that my heart is dodgy, and my Alzheimer's is accelerating. Hopefully, we can enjoy a few more months as man and wife but when the time is right, you must put me in a home. On my desk, you will find that I have made the arrangements, signed the papers, and given my bank instructions for you to have control over my accounts. I have changed my will, leaving you my house in DC but you will have to battle my brother for it."

"I don't want your money, my love. I have enough from selling the restaurant and have more than adequate pension provision."

"I know that my love, but you deserve something for your patience and kindness to me. My final years have been vastly enhanced with you around. And the next time, I open the gallery, I'll show you how to deal with the alarms. OK?"

"Thank you."

"But you must promise me one thing."

"Anything."

"If you are yearning for passion and lust, don't let my presence deter you from an afternoon's pleasure. But if you run off with a young hussy, we're done. I treasure your companionship but that's all I want and have to offer."

"My darling, I'm well past all that but I will promise you this."

"What?"

"I will happily love and care for you for as long as it's possible."

5

Phillip continued to hug Sasha. The poor boy was still sobbing but less dramatically. Instinctively, Phillip knew that it was time to say something.

"Tell you what," said Phillip in Russian sitting him up and cleaning his face with a kitchen wipe. "Instead of hanging around here all day waiting for your mother to return, why don't we look around Nerja, take a run on the beach, have lunch, and maybe an ice-cream. The water might even be warm enough to paddle. Then this afternoon, we'll go and chop down a Christmas tree from my sister's farm next door and see some of their animals. By then it will be time for your cousins to be back from school."

The weeping petered out. Phillip could almost hear Sasha thinking that life when visiting Dad might not be so bad after all.

"No beach things," he sniffed.

"Sasha, my dear boy. Then we will have to buy you some. Do you like shopping?"

He shook his head.

"Me neither, so it won't take long. Can I ask you a question?"

Sasha nodded and looked directly at Phillip.

"How old are you?"

"Seven."

"When is your birthday?"

"May."

"So, you are seven and a half."

Sasha shrugged.

Phillip counted back to the last time he and Valentina had made love. It was only a few days before she ran off with Ivan, a Russian diplomat neighbor. Then he spent about two years in Shepperton on the houseboat while he sold his shares in his company, plus six years in Spain. The dates worked."

"Was it cold where you lived in Russia?"

"Yes."

"Did you live in Moscow?"

"No, but not far outside."

"What do you use for a surname?"

"Armitage."

Sasha jumped down, grabbed Phillip's hand, and led him into the guest room. The open suitcase was perched on a low stool in the corner with the lid propped up against the wall. Crumpled clothes filled the interior. Sasha went to the bedside drawer and slid it open. He picked out an envelope, closed the drawer, and handed it over.

Phillip glanced at the front. There was one scribbled word. 'Phillip.' He felt the contents. There were papers and something passport sized. He opened it and extracted everything. It was a British Passport in the name of Sasha Armitage. It had been issued by Her Majesty's Passport Office when Sasha was five. He hadn't changed that much from the photo other than less chubby cheeks and the missing tooth. The date of birth was May tenth. The only travel data was a Schengen area visa and one entry stamp for Berlin.

"Was this your first trip out of Russia?" said Phillip.

"Yes," said Sasha.

Phillip turned to the back page and was shocked to find his name, address, and telephone written as next of kin with no mention of his mother. There was a knock on the door. Amanda peeked her head around.

"Sorry to interrupt you boys but Salome and I are leaving now, Prado needs us in Granada. We're helping him set up an exhibition but will be back sometime tonight. I'll text you when."

"OK my love, take care," said Phillip.

"Bye," said Sasha.

Amanda paused, came over to Sasha, ruffled his hair, and smiled at him. "Bye, Sasha, have a great day with your dad."

"What's wrong with her arm?" said Sasha after Amanda had left.

"She had an accident," said Phillip turning back to the papers. "The stitches come out tomorrow so after that she won't need the sling."

He examined the birth certificate. It was also British, and Phillip was registered as the father but divorced from the mother. Phillip wondered how the hell Valentina had managed all this from Russia.

"Any other things to show me?" said Phillip.

"Yes," said Sasha. He led Phillip by the hand over to the suitcase and pointed inside.

Phillip started removing Sasha's clothes, piling them neatly on the floor next to the stool. They were mainly winter items in need of a wash. At the bottom was a large brown envelope. Phillip picked it up, his hands trembling. It was quite heavy. He opened it and poured the contents out onto the bed. They were photographs. He flicked through the pile. There were several of Phillip and Valentina gazing lovingly at each other but most of the remainder documented Sasha's life from when he was a baby including a few with Valentina's parents. Nice people, who Phillip had met on several occasions.

"How are they?" he said.

"Gone to heaven," said Sasha.

"Who took the photos?"

"Mama and Pieter."

"Pieter lived with you?"

"Yes."

So, this is it," said Phillip flicking through the photos and reading the notes on the back. "Your life so far."

"Yes."

"Had you started school?"

Sasha nodded.

"Did you like it?"

Sasha nodded again then looked at Phillip with the saddest of expressions. He opened the drawer again, took out a letter-sized envelope, and gave it to Phillip.

Phillip was puzzled. What is going on here? He thought as he extracted a wad of documents from inside. The top one was a handwritten letter. He scanned the first page. It was dated the previous evening.

'Dearest Phillip.

You don't know how relieved I was to find you well and with a lovely new partner. That was the last piece of my jigsaw. Now I can go ahead with my plan knowing that our beloved son is in good hands with you and Amanda.

The truth is that I am dying.

It was why I was in Berlin. A last desperate attempt at finding a cure for the cancer that is eating away at my pancreas. Sadly, I am too far gone. The German doctors have given me a maximum of a few months.

I watched my mother die of the same disease.

Phillip, it was awful. She wasted away rapidly and in great pain. There is no way that I could put Sasha through all that. I want him to remember me as I am, not a doped up skeletal wreck incapable of comforting him.

I am not coming back.

By now I am far enough away for you not to follow me.

Please do not try.

I have booked myself into a remote hospice, where you will never find me so don't waste your time searching. The quicker I become a distant memory, the faster Sasha will put me behind him and move on.

Keep him as busy as you can, he loves to run so go jogging with him. If he is occupied, stomach full, and physically exhausted, the more rapidly he will adjust to his new circumstances. He is also a capable skier so take him up to the Sierra Nevada as often as you can.

When I pass, the hospice will send you my jewelry, remaining assets, and ashes plus the death certificate. Scatter me where you like but somewhere nearby where Sasha can talk to me or place some flowers if he wants.

Sasha knows what I am doing. He doesn't like it and I am not sure he even understands it fully, but you and Amanda will give him the strength to see it through. Maybe he might have some brothers and sisters in the not-too-distant future. Don't keep Amanda waiting as you did me, she is not getting any younger.

Lastly, I want to apologize from the bottom of my heart for the pain I put you through with our divorce. I was stupid. My only excuse is that I was on my own too much and bored out of my skull. My hormones were crying out for motherhood and I was too impatient. This was dammed selfish of me when you were working your balls off trying to build your business. I should have been more supportive rather than whining.

I assumed that the child was Ivan's, our former neighbor, but as Sasha grew more like you every day, I arranged for his blood to be tested. Ivan was not the father, so I swear on my life that he could only be yours. It must have been that last time together. Remember? Ivan left me as soon as I told him. If you have any doubts, please test Sasha yourself but having seen the two of you together, there is no other possibility.

Pieter was more of a companion so you will have no recriminations from him, and I doubt he'll bother to visit. I persuaded him that Sasha would move on better if he weren't constantly reminded of the past and me.

His British passport and birth certificate are genuine; don't ask. They are more than enough to prove that you are his legal parent but just in case you have any difficulties, this envelope contains notarized legal papers from the British Embassy in Moscow granting you sole custody.

It breaks my heart to leave Sasha, but I know you will love and care for him as I did.

Your ever-loving Valentina.'

Phillip looked at Sasha. Tears continued streaming down his face. Phillip took him in his arms and hugged him. The poor boy wailed and shuddered.

"You do understand that Mama isn't coming back?" said Phillip.

Sasha nodded his head. Phillip held him tight and rocked him.

"Let me say one thing now," said Phillip when Sasha had calmed down. "Anything else can wait until you feel up to discussing it. You probably feel nervous about just meeting me, but I want you to know that both Amanda and I are delighted to have you as our son. We will never make up for the loss of Valentina, but we promise to love, treasure, and look after you as best we can. Life here in Spain is different from Russia, our weather is awesome, the beaches can be used all year round, the people love children, the food is amazing and even the beetroot is edible. You can go to school with your cousins who will help you settle in and after a while, all this pain will fade away. Does that help?"

Sasha nodded, sat up, and sniffed.

Phillip reached out and took a tissue out of the bedside dispenser, wiped Sasha's eyes, and face, and pinched his nose with it. "Have a good blow," he said. Sasha obliged. "There," said Phillip inspecting the tissue contents. "My first snotty nose."

Sasha grinned.

"Look, darling boy, I'm not proficient at this parenting stuff," said Phillip. "You'll have to put me right when I mess up. OK?"

"Fine, Papa," said Sasha.

Phillip glowed with pleasure. "Anything else you need to tell me?" said Phillip.

Sasha shook his head.

"Then let us try and put it all behind us and move on. Now, shall I show you what Amanda and I do for our work?"

"If you must."

"Oh, I think you'll like it. Come."

Phillip took Sasha's hand, led him to the study sat them both down, and turned on his computer. "We run a website about Spain. It's called Nuestra España which means…"

"Our Spain."

"Wow."

"Mama said."

"Watch this," said Phillip clicking on Amanda's Tomatina video. Within seconds, Sasha was chuckling at Amanda's antics in the tomato fight in Buñol.

"We make short videos that tell the story of Spain to the world. When you aren't at school, you can come with us to film new ones, even be in some of them. Would you like that?"

Sasha nodded.

"OK, shall we do some shopping then try the beach?"

"Yes, please, Papa."

6

Salome turned off the Frigiliana Road and down onto the coastal motorway heading east toward Almuñecar. It was a clear day with a balmy temperature. The palm trees swayed gently in the light breeze at the side of the road.

"I'm glad Prado called with this new project," said Salome as they headed into the Capistrano tunnel. "It will deter me from dwelling on the horrors of last week. How about you?"

"I agree," said Amanda touching her wounded arm. "It's not every day that I'm locked in a pitch-black crypt without food and water, surrounded by skeletons and a crazy woman trying to hang herself. How is Barbara?"

"A typical day in the life of a videographer," said Salome. "Last I heard, Barbara's OK physically but a long way from regaining her mental health. I'll be a bit more careful who I choose for a driver next time."

"Fingers crossed she makes a full recovery. Has your new status sunk in yet?"

"No, there is too much to assimilate. Adopted orphan of unknown origin to the daughter of gypsy crook turned hero is a bit much in such a short timeline. But what is exciting is that it has helped crystalize the rest of my life. At last, I know what to do and the prospect thrills me."

"Won't you miss the live performances and the Flamenco scene?"

"Of course, but if the flamenco university project flies, I'll be too busy to worry about it. I try and visualize how the Las Claras convent will look when it's refurbished. It keeps my mind off my painful back and the theaters I've let down."

"Are you sure you can afford it, especially now you're no longer earning?"

"I'll have to break the project into phases and spread them over several years but if we can obtain this EU grant the mayor is talking about, I'll be fine."

"Maybe, we could use this exhibition to ask for donations?"

"That's brilliant, how?"

"We'll set up a page on Nuestra-España and I'll send videos to the major networks. What with Picasso's granddaughter attending and Anne Pennington coming out of hiding for the first time, the media will be wetting themselves. It will draw a lot of visitors to the website."

"Wow, that would be amazing. Why couldn't I think of that?"

"Phillip taught me how to squeeze every drop from each opportunity."

"How do you think he will cope as a babysitter?" said Salome as they drove past Nerja Caves.

"Just fine, it's not as if Sasha is still in nappies. It will be just two boys playing boy stuff. We would just be in the way."

"Until the laundry needs doing."

"Phillip does that too."

"Maybe I should be rethinking this husband sharing concept?"

"What about Vincente?" said Amanda.

"Trying to be rid of me?"

"Never, just being nosy."

"I admire Vincente as an architect but I'm unsure about him as a lover. Perhaps when we start working together, he might grow on me."

"There's no hurry," said Amanda. "And there is the more pressing matter of how to transport the treasure to the exhibition, prepare a catalog and promote the event all in about twenty-four hours?"

"That's why I have you. For transport and handling, I'll use the same firm that packed them up and stored them in the security warehouse. We'll have to discuss display cabinets with the hotel. What did you think of Valentina?"

"I was sorry for her."

"She appeared troubled and was way too skinny," said Salome.

"Vulnerable was how I saw her. She's had a rough time over something."

"Has to be a man involved. She's either running from him or has done something nasty. Either way, she needed to get the boy out of Russia."

"Isn't he cute, though?"

"He's gorgeous and luckily you're about to become his step-mother. How do you feel about that?"

"Frankly, I've always been worried about parenting a child that isn't mine. Not because of the child but because of the arguments arising between two different parenting styles. I don't want to be in the middle of it or the referee."

"That can't be easy."

"We'll wait and see what transpires. Fancy a coffee?" said Amanda.

"Great idea."

"Then take the old road up from Salobreña. There's a trucker's stop I know."

For fifteen minutes they wound through a steep-sided gorge with the gushing Rio Guadalfeo to their left and spectacular waterfalls cascading down the limestone rocks to the right. Just past the road sign for the mountain village of Guájar Fondán, they pulled into a service complex nestling at the foot of stark cliffs. Salome parked outside the two-storey hotel just past the gas station with the café and restaurant on the lower floor. It was a brick building long past its best. The new motorway had dramatically reduced its turnover but inside, it was clean, cozy, and warm with a log fire roaring in a huge open fireplace. Other than that, it was the usual old fashioned truck stop. Serrano hams suspended from a rail over the timber bar. Drivers chatting about their families and favorite football teams. Old bullfighting posters on the walls and the Menu of the day chalked up on a blackboard hung between the hams offering a three-course meal with drinks for seven Euros. They ordered up the traditional Spanish breakfast and took a table by the window.

They both logged onto the café Wi-Fi and checked their messages. Amanda read the urgent text from Phillip.

'Further developments,' it said. 'Valentina has left Sasha with us and gone off to die of pancreatic cancer. Will explain in detail this evening. We are heading for

Nerja to shop then the beach. Will chop tree from next door and buy lights and decorations. We need to make a special Christmas for Sasha and of course you. Love you. X'

Amanda showed Salome the message.

"I thought she looked peaky?" she said. "Where has she gone?"

"We'll have to wait until tonight," said Amanda.

"That is cruel."

"Patience is a virtue."

They finished their coffee, paid, and resumed their journey rejoining the motorway just beyond the Presa de Rules, the dam that formed a huge Reservoir. It was an incredible piece of engineering that had taken over twenty years to construct.

To the right of the motorway were the Alpujarras mountains and beyond them the snow-covered peaks of the Sierra Nevada. Running along the tops of many ridges were ranks of giant wind turbines rotating majestically. Then to the left, the mountains flattened out to reveal vast plains of cereal crops and almond trees. Granada was drawing near.

Their first view of the ancient city was as they passed the Hotel Suspiro de Moro. Granada opened up before them in the valley below. A brown haze wafted over the center, but the red bricks of the magnificent Alhambra Palace walls and towers stood out.

"Was this where Boabdil, the last Moorish King of Granada burst into tears?" said Salome.

"His proper name was Sultan Abu Abdullah Muhammed," said Amanda. "He was devastated about leaving his beloved Alhambra Palace. The hotel marks the last point before the iconic monument disappears behind the hill. He paused here to take one final look and say farewell. The story goes that he blubbered like a child. His mother Aurora scolded him with the immortal words, 'You cry like a woman who couldn't defend like a man'. She was an accomplished artist but not maternally minded."

"Sounds like a bitch to me. Is this what you and Phillip do for your website?" said Salome.

"We explain Spain and its history to the world. We mainly use videos nowadays but Richard, a fellow American who started the site with Phillip, used to write the articles. I learned most of my knowledge from them."

"You know more about Spain than I do."

"With all the dancing you have done across the United States, you know more about my country of birth than me."

"Fair enough but you have lived here for most of your life. Aren't you ever tempted to go back to the US?"

"Only to visit. I love Spain far too much to ever leave permanently."

"And now you have Phillip."

"And his son."

"I'm sure Sasha won't be his only child."

"Not if I have anything to do with it."

"Aren't you worried that he might want to help Valentina through her dying moments?"

"We talked about her earlier. We know it won't be easy, but we refuse to let her arrival disturb our wedding plans and have agreed to thrash out any problems."

"Sounds good."

"Strangely enough, Valentina and Sasha's arrival has cleared a nagging doubt I had about having children with Phillip."

"What brought that on?"

"The men I've experienced were pretty useless when it came to sharing parental responsibilities. Having seen how good Phillip is with Sasha has relaxed me about that."

"But he's always been great with his nieces; they adore him."

"Yes, but only in short bursts."

"Fair point."

***

Alhambra, in Arabic, means the red one. The name derives from the bricks made from the red, fertile soil that covers the hilltop overlooking what is now Granada city. The site was originally developed as a fortress by the Romans. Then expanded by a succession of Moorish rulers each determined to outdo his ancestors by building larger and more luxurious palaces. Today, it's one of Spain's most treasured and visited monuments.

Salome drove slowly up the slope toward the central gate. The massive palace wall towering over them as she stopped at the security barrier under Puerta de las Carros. Prado had been as good as his word. Salome showed her ID card to the guard. He smiled and waved them through.

They turned right past the gift shops and craft studios, parked up by the Parador hotel gates, walked through the gardens to the main entrance, and went through the double doors into reception.

The Parador Hotel is located at the top end of the palace grounds. It was formerly a monastery built on the orders of the Catholic Monarchs on the site of what was a Nasrid palace. The monastery was rebuilt during the seventeenth century, but remains of the original Moorish buildings are preserved in the Nazarí Room. It was converted to a hotel in the early twentieth century opening its doors in 1945. It's an enchanting place to stay with stunning views over the palace buildings, the Generalife gardens, and the Sierra Nevada.

The women had hardly walked through the door before a distinguished silver-haired man in his sixties wearing a black morning suit and brass name tag, introduced himself.

"Welcome to the Hotel Parador, Señoras Mendoza and Salisbury?" he said shaking their hands. "I am the manager, Ildefonso Sanz. Please follow me to the room we are suggesting for your exhibition."

They followed Sanz across a covered patio furnished with sofas and coffee tables, through some double doors, and into a spacious but large empty room with parquet flooring and floral drapes. "This is where the inauguration will take place," said Sanz. "That door leads into the Picasso exhibition and we propose to use this room here for your artifacts."

He unlocked the door, turned on the lights, and led them in.

The edges of the bright room were lined with waist height glass display cases lined with black velvet covered shelving. Each case was fitted with picture lights to illuminate the contents. "Although this room is smaller than the Picasso exhibition," said Sanz. "It has no external windows. The hotel and these three rooms will be protected by armed guards during the exhibition and there is constant monitoring by surveillance cameras. Each display case will also be protected by sensors so anyone approaching close than fifteen centimeters will set off the alarm."

"It sounds fine," said Salome. "And these display cases are perfect. When can we gain access to set up?"

"As soon as you like," said Sanz.

"Are there likely to be any objections from the other exhibitors?"

"We wanted to ensure that you were happy with the space and security arrangements before inquiring. We don't envisage any problems but now we will call the lady concerned." Sanz took out a mobile from his jacket, swiped the screen, and put it to his ear. "Could I speak with Señora Pennington please?" he said in excellent English. There was a pause. "Yes, it's Ildefonso Sanz from the Parador concerning the exhibition." He waited. "Good morning, Señora, sorry to disturb you but I have a favor to ask. We've had a request by one of Spain's most renowned Flamenco dancers to run an exhibition of some recently uncovered treasure and religious artifacts in the room next to yours on Friday."

He listened.

"Yes, it would run concurrently with yours but their opening ceremony would be in the evening so there would be no conflict. Would you have any objections? Only I have their organizers here with me now and we need an urgent decision." His face dropped. "Oh, I see, very well, I'll inform them no. They will be extremely disappointed."

Amanda grabbed the phone. "Excuse me, Anne. Sorry to barge in. I'm Amanda Salisbury a journalist covering both exhibitions on behalf of CNN." She listened for a second. "Yes, it would be appearing on

American Networks."

Amanda waited for Anne to finish, said goodbye, and handed the phone back to Sanz. Then she turned and grinned at Salome. "She's thinking about it. We're to go up to her house now and discuss it. She said for Señor Sanz to give us directions."

"Good, good," said Sanz. "Parking is impossible there, so I'll have the Hotel limousine take you and bring you back. Follow me to reception please."

Sanz escorted them out the gates and waited with them until the car arrived. When it did, he opened the rear door and they slid onto the back seats.

Just before he closed the door, Sanz paused.

"I do hope that you can persuade Senora Pennington to let you join with her exhibition," he said. "The combination of the treasure and paintings would mean a lot to me and my staff. And it would be the most exciting event here ever."

He closed the door and nodded to the chauffeur.

7

"I suppose you're accustomed to this luxury," said Amanda as the chauffeur steered the sleek black Mercedes around the hairpin bends and garlanded narrow streets down to Anne Pennington's house.

"My reward for all those years of buses and tube trains banging my bulky dress cases into people's legs."

"Fair enough."

"What made you suspect that Anne might change her mind?" said Salome.

"Until his death, Anne was the mistress of Godfrey Steinman. She was forced into exile to avoid a scandal that would have ruined his almost perfect reputation as a goody-goody senator for the Christian right. It's rumored that Godfrey paid her one hell of a fat allowance, and ample funds to buy an incredible art collection. Godfrey died about five years ago and she is suffering from ill-health. After thirty years of enforced silence to protect her lover, my instincts told me she wants to make a noisy exit."

"What on earth for?"

"Revenge, perhaps?" said Amanda as the car stopped outside the ornately detailed façade of a massive townhouse. "Or just because she can." They clambered out and rang the bell next to the imposing timber door.

It was opened by Silvano. He smiled at Amanda and Salome. "I am Anne's husband, Silvano. Anne is with her paintings. Please follow me," he said in English.

They entered a spacious hallway beautifully decorated with a three-dimensional ceramic panorama of the Alhambra Palace on the wall opposite the entrance. A grand marble staircase to the left circled up to a gallery landing. A huge, blue-framed clear glass lamp was suspended from the high ceiling. Ficus bushes in giant pots decorated in glazed blue-Granada design stood between the marble columns that supported the landing. Moorish archways led off to the right and through to the back of the house. They entered a rear living room then down a flight of stairs to a basement hallway. Opposite the bottom of the stairs were double timber doors that stood open. They went into a spacious, well-lit, air-conditioned room some hundred meters square with seven paintings mounted on each of the four walls. The seven muses were hung together opposite the entrance. Anne was admiring one of them. She was dressed in a long white linen dress decorated with lace. Her silver hair was swept over her ears and pinned up at the back of her long neck with a gold and emerald brooch.

They introduced themselves and shook hands.

"My goodness," said Anne in English. "What have you done to your arm?"

"Just a cut," said Amanda. "Nothing serious. Stitches out tomorrow."

"Good luck with that," said Anne appraising Amanda. "It's not often I find myself looking down on another woman, my dear."

"I like to think that nice things come in small packages," said Amanda.

"That's generally my experience. And it's an honor to shake hands with one of Spain's finest Flamenco dancers," said Anne to Salome. "Tell me how you came about this treasure."

"It's a long story but my grandfather hid it from looting soldiers in the crypt of an old convent in Vélez-Málaga during the civil war. I acquired the building recently and found the treasure along with the corpses of my grandfather and parents."

"How fascinating but you must be devastated," said Anne.

"I was adopted as a baby so never knew them, but it was still a shock. Now I want to tell their story, share the treasure with the world, and use any funds raised to save the old convent."

"A worthy cause," Anne turned to Amanda. "Are you sure that the exhibition will be broadcast in America, CNN you said?"

"Absolutely," said Amanda. "They take all my videos about Spain. You can check them out on their website. They will also appear all over the English-speaking world including the BBC."

"Sounds perfect," said Anne looking pleased with herself. "Then I would be delighted to share my exhibition with you. We can even combine our inauguration events if you like."

"Thank you, that would be fantastic," said Amanda.

Anne turned to the painting. "Picasso had many wives and girlfriends, often at the same time. One would assume that he loved women, yet he had an outrageously macho attitude defining us as goddesses or doormats. Altogether, he created forty-six paintings, fourteen drawings, and six sculptures of his models and muses. I have seven of the paintings. This is Picasso's first muse, model Laure Germaine Gargallo Pichot. He took up with her in 1901, when he was twenty. She was the girlfriend of his Catalan friend Carlos Casagemos who committed suicide in February of the same year. Germaine went on to marry Picasso's friend, Ramon Pichot, in 1906. As you can see his abstract concepts were still in the developmental stage and look more like a child's drawing." Anne pointed to the adjacent wall. "But if you look at this self-portrait of him as a young man, you can immediately identify that he was an extremely talented artist from his youth and earned his money doing traditional portraits and paintings."

"I certainly prefer the early works compared with his prolific cubism," said Amanda. "It's too freakish for me but what do I know? May I ask what prompted you to hold this exhibition?"

"Do you know my history?" said Anne.

"Only second hand," said Amanda. "Which proves how silly it is to listen to a rumor. I'd always thought you lived in Nerja."

"We have a small place there for the summer," said Anne. "To escape the melting Granada heat. I used to hold mini art exhibitions in the lounge to support local artists, but I haven't been recently. Silvano has never seen it. Sorry, what was the question?"

"History, dear," said Silvano. "You were about to tell us your sordid past."

"Goodness was I," said Anne. "I hope you are broad-minded. Silvano and I came together late and although I try to forget it, my baggage continues to haunt me. Before we married, I'd spent most of my adult life in the shadow of a man I loved and adored. In return, he treated me as his goddess. However, we never married. He already had a wife in Washington DC. I was his mistress or 'muse', as I prefer to call it. Until now, I have kept my vow to remain quiet about our affair. But my silence has only encouraged his family to ignore my existence and forbid me to attend his funeral. Their behavior was puerile, and they made me feel like a doormat. I want to redress the balance.

"Godfrey Steinman's family run large among America's religious right. They hold themselves up as honest Christian white citizens and give generously to their select causes and favored Republican politicians. Yet they chose to ignore that the man of the house kept a mistress for over thirty years. Without me to keep him happy, he would have divorced his frigid wife and dumped his ungrateful offspring long ago. Thanks to me, he did his duty. I kept him going. Reluctantly, and with a heavy heart, he stood by them and thanks to that, the family name remained upright and pure enabling them to continue their good works with a clear conscience.

"Before I die, I want to rattle their cage by exposing their hypocrisy and at the same time send out a strong signal in support of mistresses everywhere. I want everyone to know their true value to society. Some of us may be well paid, but we forgo a normal life of marriage and children to support our lovers. We may have a few snatched moments of pleasure, but our jobs are lonely, the pain of forever waiting for the next visit is barely endurable and we are ostracized by most."

"I, er... I was a mistress for a few years," said Amanda. "Long before I met my current partner, but I share your feelings."

"Me too," said Salome. "Twice."

"I'm in exalted company," said Silvano. "Don't you worry that breaking your vow of silence will hurt Godfrey's family?"

"Frankly, I don't give a damn," said Anne. "They deserve it. Now, how shall we do this?"

"A personal interview will be best," said Amanda. "You can look straight at the camera as if staring them in the eye."

"Sounds perfect," said Anne with a gleeful expression.

"We'll also put it on the internet via our popular guide to Spain," said Amanda. "Our subscribers adore these lighthearted distractions. They're a pleasant break from the usual doom and gloom. I'm sure they'll spread it all over the world."

"Mmm…," said Anne. "I look forward to that. Could you both stay for lunch and help me prepare a script? It would be embarrassing if my fading memory chose that moment in front of the camera to let me down. I want to slay the Steinman's, not be their object of mirth. And Silvano's spaghetti vongole is to die for."

Salome and Amanda exchanged glances and nodded.

8

Málaga prison is a modern building located on former farmland at Finca la Moraga, just outside the town of Alhaurin de la Torre some twenty kilometers, northwest of the city. It was designed to facilitate the rehabilitation process rather than create a daunting ambiance of punishment. With a heated pool, gym, sports hall, football field, leisure room to watch TV and movies, and a hospital, it has received severe criticism for resembling a luxury hotel. Two prisoners, dressed in their orange overalls, were peering through the observation window from the hospital foyer into the small ward.

"Is Crown, OK?" said Sonia Augustin.

"Not really," said Patrick O'Reilly in his thick Irish brogue resting his arm on her shoulder. "He says it's just a virus, but I think it's something more serious. They're doing some tests."

Sonia a woman in her early forties, with short blond hair looked striking and much younger than her years. Patrick a tad older at forty-seven was muscular and fit having spent hours in the gym, but he still limped painfully. He'd been gored as a trainee bullfighter during his teens. Patrick held out his arms. Sonia fell into them and they hugged briefly. They'd orchestrated a visit to Crown on the pretext that seeing his friends might cheer him up and facilitate his healing. In reality, they had plans he needed to be aware of.

"Our new communication system works then," said Sonia into his ear.

"Just make sure they don't find your phone," said Patrick. "Then they can trace mine and that has been safe since the day Prado locked me up in here."

"Should we bring our plan forward?" said Sonia. "I'd hate for Malcolm to die in here."

"No. He wants us to stay put until after the exhibition in Granada," said Patrick. "If that doesn't flush out Marquez, nothing will."

"How will we know when or if Marquez arrives at the exhibition?"

"Paul will hack into the security system."

"Will he be able to monitor all the visitors?"

"In vivid HD color. He'll run the footage through facial recognition software. As soon as Marquez arrives, we'll know it."

"What then?"

"Paul will follow him home."

"What if the police catch him first?"

"Then so be it, but we are confident that they will bring him to the comisaría in Málaga. Prado isn't going to let Marquez be dealt with by Granada cops."

"Let's hope you're right."

"But how can we get at him from here?"

"Marquez will be uncooperative. After a couple of days, they'll charge him with something and bring him here. He'll be on remand. Just like us."

"And you plan to have a little chat?"

"I do, but we won't be saying much. My anger needs a stronger outlet."

"Mine too, but one or two sentences would be good."

"Then we should be able to accommodate you."

"Shall we talk to Malcolm?"

"Let's go in."

O'Reilly opened the ward door and walked in. Sonia followed.

"You are not allowed in here," said a nurse in Spanish calling out from the side office.

"We're here to see our friend, Crown," said Sonia. "Hasn't the warden warned you?"

"The warden isn't up to date with his current condition," said the nurse. "He's too sick to receive visitors."

"Any idea what's wrong with him?" said Patrick smiling at the nurse.

"We've sent some blood to the Lab in Málaga for analysis. It will take a while for the results to come back. We'll all have to wait until then."

"Can we just pop our heads around the drapes and say Hola," said Sonia. "Knowing that we care about him might improve his mood and determination to get well."

The nurse looked hard at her; her face softened. "Two minutes," she said.

Crown was lying propped up by bulky pillows. He looked pale and drawn but was awake. He perked up seeing his friends. "Where are my grapes?" he croaked.

"Sorry, I ate them while we were waiting," said Patrick.

"Bastard," said Crown.

"I'll bring wine and cheese next visit," said Sonia.

"We could go for a picnic," said Crown. "The sports field would be ideal, pleasant views of the barbed wire. Any developments?" Patrick moved close and whispered their plans in his ear. "So, Friday is the big day?" said Crown.

"I doubt if Marquez will attend the opening ceremony," said Patrick. "Too much security. He'll pick another busy time when he can lose himself among the crowds and the police surveillance team is getting bored with no action. Probably between New Year and Three Kings. That's when most foreign visitors will attend."

"Your two minutes are up," called the nurse from the office.

They hugged Crown separately and returned to the foyer. Their guards entered, re-cuffed them, and escorted them back to their respective wings.

9

Amanda and Salome hurried home to Nerja after a long afternoon with Anne. They were both tired but desperate to learn about Valentina, her illness, and how were Phillip and Sasha getting on.

They needn't have worried.

The house looked like a Christmas Grotto. Flashing fairy lights decorated the garage door. A small Santa and two reindeer were driving a sleigh across the roof with a sack of gifts on the back. Feliz Navidad in lights and tinsel under a large holly wreath adorned the kitchen window.

"Oh dear," said Salome. "Phillip's flipped."

"No, I adore it," said Amanda. "I've never really done Christmas, my mother is Arabic, so our celebrations were always muted."

"Mine too. My adoptive parents weren't bothered. Three Kings was their thing, lots of presents and food but nothing like this.

They parked up and went inside through the kitchen door.

Everything was quiet.

"Hello. Anyone home?" called Amanda.

"In here," came a whisper from the lounge.

The girls crept in and gasped.

There was a huge pine tree in the corner, the star on its top almost kissing the high ceiling. It was beautifully decorated and covered with sparkling lights. Olive sprig wall decorations with electric candle lights illuminated the room, creating a warm, cozy, and welcoming glow.

"I didn't want to disturb him," said Phillip. "We had such a hectic day; the poor thing was so tired. After supper, we both collapsed here, and I've not been able to wake him."

"It was good to keep him busy," said Amanda sitting down and stroking Sasha's cheek.

Phillip disentangled himself, stood up, lifted Sasha to his chest, and headed for the bedroom. "I'll put him to bed," he said.

"I'll pour us a glass of wine," said Salome shaking her head in wonderment as Amanda followed Phillip to the guest room. "To celebrate your tasteful decorations and our great day in Granada."

Several minutes later they reconvened around the kitchen island, picked up their wines, and chinked glasses.

"Did he settle?" said Salome.

"Not a peep," said Amanda. "And his laundry is done, and a few boy posters added to the walls of the guest room."

Salome gave Phillip an admiring look.

Phillip shrugged and went over to the fridge. He picked up Valentina's letter from the top and passed it over.

Salome and Amanda read it together then looked up at Phillip, tears in their eyes.

"That is so tragic," said Amanda going over and hugging him. "And you were so right to make him feel at home."

"That is a relief," said Phillip. "I've been wondering all day what your reaction would be?"

"Please, darling," said Amanda. "I'm not an ogre."

"I know that, silly. I was more worried that I'd done the wrong thing for Sasha. I'm not exactly the most experienced parent."

"Neither of us is," said Amanda.

"More like baptism by fire," said Salome. "Forgive me for asking but what about legal custody. Surely Valentina can't just dump Sasha here without some form of paperwork?"

"She's thought of everything," said Phillip. "Surname is the same as mine. There's a British Passport, birth certificate, and notarized custody via the British Embassy in Moscow. There's even an envelope full of photos documenting Sasha's life since birth. She's written all the names and contact details on the back and a brief note of their contribution to his life. If at any time in the future, he wants to go back to Russia, there is a ready channel of communication open to him."

"Then I better start learning Russian," said Amanda.

"Да дорогая," said Phillip.

"Don't tell me," said Amanda. "Yes, dear."

"Yes, darling, and I agree, we should help him remember his roots, even take him there when he's older and acclimatized to life and language here."

"That's a big challenge for a small boy," said Salome. "He has to learn Spanish, communicate at home in English, and keep up his Russian. Isn't that a bit much?"

"Nonsense," said Phillip. "At this age, they soak up knowledge like a sponge. Give him three months with my nieces and at school then he'll be able to talk with you in Spanish."

"Incredible, what a great start in life," said Salome. "I congratulate you both, you've adapted to a difficult situation admirably. It bodes well for your larger family."

"Sorry," said Phillip. "Am I missing something?"

"I'm not pregnant yet," said Amanda." But I have every intention of being so as quickly as nature blesses us."

"Don't you want anything to eat?" said Phillip blushing.

"We had a superb lunch with Anne," said Salome. "I'm still stuffed."

"Me too," said Amanda. "Some exercise is just what the doctor ordered. Ready for bed, darling?"

"What about your arm?"

"We won't be needing that."

10

Amanda awoke with a jerk and checked her phone on the bedside table. "Shit," she said and threw a pillow at Salome in the adjacent bed.

"What?" mumbled Salome.

"It's nine o'clock," said Amanda throwing back the covers and heading for the bathroom. "I forgot to set the alarm."

Salome joined her in the spacious shower.

"At least everything is ready," said Salome.

"What?" said Amanda stepping out of the noisy hot water spray. She grabbed a towel from the heated rail and started drying herself vigorously, gently dabbing at her scar tissue. The stitches had been removed and the wound was healing well.

"At least," said Salome. "Oh, never mind." She finished rinsing down and turned off the water. "Will we have time for breakfast, I'm starving?"

"It will have to be quick," said Amanda.

Thirty minutes later, the two elegantly dressed women walked into the busy Parador Hotel restaurant and gave their room number to the maître d. They ordered coffee, then helped themselves to enormous fruit platters each and took a seat at the only available table in the center of the spacious room.

Through the large windows, the garden shrubs and terrace furniture were covered in crisp frost. Mist wafted gently around the pine trees.

"Do you think we can take one final look before the opening ceremony?" said Salome. "Just to make sure?"

"We can only ask," said Amanda finishing her coffee. "Ready?"

Salome emptied her cup and stood.

"How's the back?" said Amanda as they left the restaurant.

"Still the odd twinge, but much better, thanks."

The doors to the exhibition rooms were firmly closed. Two burly and armed uniformed guards glared at everyone that approached them. The inauguration was due at eleven and was only for guests. The public would be admitted from midday.

The guard's expressions softened as the women approached. They'd become familiar over the previous two days while setting up the thirty-seven items of the Las Claras treasure. One unlocked the outer door, escorted them inside, and did the same to the inner door leading to their exhibits.

They turned on the lights and gasped.

Mounted on the opposite wall to the entrance was a huge photograph of the jaded Las Claras Convent. 'The Secrets of Las Claras.' was printed in large letters in the sky over the church roof. Next to it, at both ends, were posters describing the treasure's discovery in English and Spanish.

The display looked magnificent.

Each item was illuminated by the display case lighting and identified by a printed plaque in Spanish and English mounted on top of the glass, describing its fascinating heritage.

The mini golden statues of Columbus's three ships formed the centerpiece in the middle of the room. It was eye-catching and the gold gleamed dully under the lights.

"Staying up late to finish everything was worth it," said Salome. "It looks wonderful."

"I agree," said Amanda. "But it's been an exhausting three days preparing and cleaning everything. Let alone the translating and printing of all the graphics."

"Has Phillip finished the website?" said Salome.

"I'll check," said Amanda swiping her phone and opening the Nuestra-España App. She held up her phone and showed it to her friend.

"Wow," said Salome. "Impressive. Let's hope it raises some money."

One of the guards escorted a young woman, with short black hair, wearing black jeans, a black jacket, and black-rimmed glasses into their room. It was Prado's surveillance expert.

"Hola, Rosa," they said in unison. "All done?"

"Cameras and microphones installed and working," said Rosa. "Even the facial recognition system works. I tested it on you two. Every inch from the external gate, through the lobby, and into the exhibition rooms is covered. If Marquez turns up, we'll have him."

"If he does arrive," said Salome. "How will you apprehend him? We don't want any drama among all these precious artifacts."

"Don't worry," said Rosa. "Marquez is too old to be a threat. Anyway, our chunky guards will materialize quietly on either side and if necessary, carry him out discreetly."

"What if the software fails to recognize him?" said Amanda.

"Prado has arranged for live feeds to be streamed to the home of his sister, Teresa Marquez, who lives in Marbella," said Rosa. "Also, to a room set up especially in Alhaurin prison for his three victims. Dr. Anna Galvez and Eduardo, the technician who produced the aged images of Marquez, will also be looking in from the forensic lab with Inspector Prado. If Marquez were able to fool the facial recognition software, hopefully those familiar with the way he moved would be able to spot him. All we need now is for Marquez to show up."

Just before ten-thirty, the dignitaries and honored guests began assembling for coffee in the foyer outside the two exhibition rooms. Amanda and Salome stood next to Anne and her husband chatting with Picasso's granddaughter, the mayor of Granada, the American Ambassador, and the CEO of the Parador Hotel chain. Two minutes after eleven, the master of ceremonies hushed the crowd and after some brief speeches, Picasso's granddaughter explained the artist's motivation behind the works. Salome summarized the story of Las Claras Convent and what she intended doing with it. The mayor declared the exhibition open and the doors to each display were opened by the guards. Amanda filmed the event discreetly but as instructed was only allowed glancing background shots of the seven muse paintings.

The American members of the press could hardly restrain themselves. As soon as the granddaughter had finished speaking half a dozen of them surged toward Anne, microphones in hand.

"Who was the rich American who paid for the

paintings?" said one.

"Is it true that you were his mistress?" yelled another.

"Why isn't he here to share your special moment?" And then they all started screaming questions at Anne. Nothing to do with paintings, all to do with her and her secretive past.

Amanda and Salome looked on in horror.

Anne remained as cool as a cucumber. She held up her hands and glared at them until the shuffling and coughing stopped.

"I will say only this," said Anne. "I am producing a video that fully explains my story. It will be available on CNN, BBC, and Nuestra-España websites as of tomorrow. Take it and do with it what you wish."

"I apologize for their rudeness," said the mayor in Spanish as he walked beside Anne toward the painting's exhibition. "These people have no decorum."

"Thank you," said Anne in reasonable Spanish. "But it was only to be expected. They've been after my scoop for years. Now I'm ready to let them have it."

"That's brave of you," said the mayor. "I have to say though that I find them an embarrassing example of your country's intrusive media and by the look on his face, I think your ambassador would rather they disappeared down a big hole."

"I'm sure he would but he'll love the video," said Anne smiling.

"Why?" said the mayor.

"He's a Democrat."

The mayor shrugged, the intricacies of American politics beyond his understanding.

The guests assembled in front of the paintings

where Picasso's granddaughter explained the nature of his relationship with each woman. The dignitaries were then led through to the treasure exhibition where Salome expanded on the story of her ancestors and how they and it were discovered in the long-lost crypt underneath the convent.

Back in Málaga, Prado and el jefe watched the live stream in the forensics lab.

When Salome had finished speaking and after the applause faded, el jefe said. "Well, if that doesn't flush Marquez out, nothing will. Otherwise, he will die somewhere, and nobody will know who he was."

"I doubt Marquez will show today," said Prado. "If he is going to deem us with an appearance, he'll try and blend in with the expected deluge of exhibition visitors after the New Year celebrations are done."

"We have no idea when or if he will show," said el jefe. "We need to be on our toes, all day, every day. Are our officers in place?"

"They are undercover, Sir," said Prado. "Mostly, cleaners, gardeners, and security guards. One guy is even giving guided tours around the palace to visitors that turn up without a booking."

"Really," said el jefe. "Well, I hope he shares any gratuities with his fellow officers. It is the season of goodwill."

"I'll have a word," said Prado.

11

The exhibition opened to the public just after midday. The enthusiastic crowds swarmed in keen to see the paintings and treasure. Anne was bombarded with questions in English and Spanish which she answered happily. It was the same for Salome as she stood in front of the display case containing the three golden statues.

At one-thirty, the exhibition closed until three pm to give the guards a break. The three women and Silvano joined the exalted personages down in the hotel restaurant for an excellent lunch. Afterward, they returned to the empty exhibition room. Silvano found a couple of chairs. Anne sat down next to Salome. Amanda prepared her camera and pressed record.

Salome held up the cordless microphone, looked at the camera, and began. They had rehearsed this several times at Anne's house, but Silvano stood out of shot with a copy of the typed script just in case Anne's memory faded.

"My name is Salome Mendosa. I'm at the Picasso Muses exhibition that opened this morning in the

Hotel Parador located on the magnificent grounds of the Alhambra Palace in Granada, Spain.

"I'm sitting with Anne Pennington, the person who kindly agreed to allow the paintings out of her home gallery to allow art lovers to appreciate what has been hidden from view for over thirty years.

"Anne, this is a big moment for you?"

"Thank you, Salome," said Anne. "I decided that after all this time, I should share them with the world. They represent just a few of Picasso's many lady friends and provided me and my lover great pleasure during our time together."

"Why are the paintings so important to you?"

Anne paused and looked directly at the camera.

"Over forty years ago, I was a lawyer on Capitol Hill in Washington DC," she said smiling. "I gave all that up to be Godfrey Steinman's mistress. He was a senator and high-flying political figure. He used to pop out from the senate to my house around the corner for his daily dalliance. If it were even hinted that this religious family man and distinguished member of the Republican Party had a bit on the side, his career would have been ruined. Morals were still a powerful voting influence in those days. The easiest solution was for me to leave the country. That came with a price."

"You didn't come cheap, Anne?"

"You always have to pay for quality, my dear."

"Did you love, Godfrey?"

"I worshipped him, and he treated me like a goddess. Having said that, muses like me spend an inordinate amount of time on their own, waiting for their lover to make what is usually a brief appearance. Building my art collection helped fill those wasted hours. Picasso intrigued me. I never met him but through his paintings felt that I began to understand what women saw in him. They helped me come to terms with my circumstances, although I still battle with it myself. What was I? Paid painted lady or a key ingredient to Godfrey's happiness. Sadly, as his health faded, we hardly ever spoke. I only learned of his death on the TV news and I was forbidden to attend his funeral. That was his family's thanks for my thirty dedicated years."

"I can understand them not wanting you there," said Salome.

"So, can I, my dear," said Anne, "So, can I, but it is thanks to me that he was still with them. A long-term muse plays a vitally important role in the life of her beloved. She keeps him happy, content, and fortified to tolerate life at home. Mistresses all over the world understand this. Wives naturally resent us." Anne paused and the camera zoomed onto her face and held the shot. Anne looked into the lens and smiled. "After Godfrey died, I had the good fortune to meet a lovely man and fall in love again. We married three years ago, and I have to say that if I were starting life over again, I would prefer marriage to mistress. But only with the right partner. Thankfully, I found one. Many don't.

"However, I remain grateful for my life with Godfrey. It was unconventional but served us both well. These precious paintings are my treasured memories of our time together and whatever happens, they will stay with me forever."

12

Anne and Silvano sat in their lounge watching CNN and then various talk shows as her revelations sunk in, were analyzed, and commented on. The outcome was exactly as she had wished. Poisonous rhetoric from Republicans abhorring her lack of Christian values. They declared her an insult to the sanctity of marriage and insinuations about her lack of morality bounced around the studios progressively sinking to outright insults calling her a whore and prostitute. Anne laughed her head off.

The telephone rang. Silvano picked it up and pressed the green button. "Hello," he said.

It was the Foundation's lawyer calling from Washington DC. Silvano passed over the handset.

"Anne Pennington," she said.

"Sorry to disturb you," said a deep male voice.

"Nice to hear from you, Harry," said Anne. "The nonsense on TV not enough for you."

"You only have yourself to blame," said Harry. "However, I'd hate to think that you are hurting. My dear friend, Godfrey wouldn't have liked that. But you're not having another painting."

"I have more than enough. And thanks for your concern but I'm laughing my socks off. All this prudish hoo-ha only proves that Godfrey was right," said Anne. "If they are apoplectic now, just imagine how they would have been thirty years ago if we'd gone public then."

"All you've done is reawaken the puritans," said Harry. "The Christian right thinks that this reinvigorated debate on morals will win them the higher ground in the next election."

"Then they still have their heads buried in the sand," said Anne. "Most modern Americans will laugh at their outdated attitudes and vote Democrat."

"So that's your game," said Harry. "I hadn't appreciated that you were such a political animal."

"I'm not, but I do care about my country."

"Our country is great," said Harry.

"Not from where I am sitting," said Anne. "Ask any European what they think of America and you'll get a weird look and a brief reference to a banana republic, before moving quickly on to discuss something more meaningful. But you didn't call me to discuss my politics or welfare, did you, Harry?"

"No, Anne. The family just wanted to remind you and your husband about the terms of your contract with the Foundation when you die."

"That's more like it," said Anne. "I'm fully aware of my obligations. Goodbye."

Anne replaced the phone on its base.

"OK, my love?" said Silvano.

"Almost perfect, my darling," said Anne. "A strong gin and tonic, however, would set me up for a wonderful night's sleep."

"Coming right up."

13

Phillip was determined to make Christmas a memorable occasion for Sasha and to introduce Amanda and Salome to his family's seasonal traditions. His mother had been obsessed with the annual ritual, continually striving to improve on the previous year. Without fail, his father had blown a fuse when the January electricity bill had arrived.

He ordered the biggest free-range turkey from his favorite local butcher. A brandy laced pudding and cake he sourced from an English supermarket in Torrox, along with an array of table decorations and some outrageously expensive crackers. He downloaded carols from Kings College, Cambridge, and along with Noddy Holder and other old favorites spent all of Christmas Eve playing them loudly and repetitively as he cooked and set everything up on the huge terrace table. Nobody was allowed to help; everybody was banished from the kitchen.

Glenda, his sister, and her tribe would be joining them, and everyone was instructed to dress up in their finest.

At seven p.m., the festivities began. Everyone

looked gorgeous and entered into the spirit of the occasion by humming along to the music as they gathered around the tree awaiting the distribution of presents. The kids were completely overexcited, but Sasha was a little bashful with his smart new outfit.

The door from the kitchen opened, and Father Christmas arrived carrying a huge heavy sack and placed it on the floor in front of the tree.

"Ho, ho, ho," said José missing off the h sound. He proceeded to open the sack and lifted out four large square packages. He read the label on each and passed one to each child. Each was received with a shriek followed by a rapid ripping of wrapping paper to reveal four identical but differently colored electric scooters. Thankfully, all the batteries needed charging, otherwise, that would have been the end of the evening's entertainment.

Anna, the eldest at eleven passed around the remaining presents. Then they all sat down at the table and Phillip served his bumper feast. First came the popping of the crackers. Only one exploded, the puzzles didn't work, the jokes were pathetic, but the paper hats were magnificent. They lasted until the photos had been taken before joining the growing jetsam on the floor. About three seconds.

The kids hardly ate a thing.

The highlight though was the serving of the Christmas pudding and its allure of promised silver treasures. Phillip drizzled warm brandy over the top and carried it in from the kitchen singing at the top of his voice, "We all like figgy pudding," as the blue flames fluttered out to nothing. As soon as the kids had found their silver ornaments, they were excused.

Phillip passed around the port with some stilton

cheese and they talked about weddings, convents, Picasso paintings, and Prado.

The conversation started slowing about midnight.

The kids were discovered asleep in Sasha's bedroom.

Phillip helped Glenda and Jose carry his nieces back home and returned to find Amanda and Salome already in bed asleep.

He sat down in the lounge with a tumbler of Carlos Primero and watched the fairy lights twinkling with a great sense of nostalgia and love.

Then the timer clicked, and everything went black.

He went to bed.

14

During the night of January second, Anne Pennington suffered a heart attack. She died in her sleep. Silvano didn't notice until he awoke at his usual time and nudged her to serve orange juice and coffee. She didn't move. He called the emergency services, but they could only confirm her death. At least she didn't suffer, thought Silvano.

He knew what he had to do.

He called the undertakers and when they came to collect her, gave them her passport. He sent the emails to the list she had given him. Her local lawyer, the media, the Foundation lawyer, the manager of the Parador Hotel, Salome and Amanda, and her brother in Washington DC.

He went and made himself some breakfast and while he waited for the vultures to descend, he sobbed the loss of the only woman that he'd cared for since his mother.

After breakfast, and when the staff had arrived, he gathered them together in the hallway and told them the news. They shared a group hug and shed their tears silently then he fired them and gave them their extremely generous severance envelopes.

That was the easy bit.

The Foundation's lawyers would send their bully boys to try and recover the paintings and would want to place the house and contents up for sale immediately, but they would have to wait until he was ready.

He needed at least three days for the ashes to be returned from the crematorium along with the national and international death certificates. More importantly, he had to drag out the time until the exhibition was finished in four days. Then they could take the paintings.

There would be no funeral.

As his last act of remembrance, Silvano would scatter Anne's ashes over the back lawn, then pack his belongings and leave. He would go back home to Italy and live with his widowed sister in Siena city center.

After breakfast, he gathered the ring binder containing her latest will, other legal documents, and private papers from her desk. He popped them into a leather briefcase and stood by the front door as he ordered a taxi on the local app. Minutes later it arrived and took him down the hill to the city.

It dropped him outside her lawyer's office just around the corner from Calle Reyes Católicos. He left the briefcase and its contents with the senior partner and then enjoyed a long walk around the beautiful city he had come to love.

It was a cold, windy, cloudy day as he strode purposely among the early office workers. He found a café open and entered closing the door behind him. He sat near the window and sipped a strong café espresso, then popped into the restroom where he washed and dried his face and looked at himself in the mirror. He was ready.

He caught the street train back up to the Alhambra Palace and jumped off at the stop around the corner from the house.

Four of them were waiting outside.

The men wore heavy grey overcoats, trainers, and baseball hats. They were large, muscular, and sporting sunglasses despite the clouds.

"We've come for the paintings," said the eldest in American English.

"Sorry," said Silvano. "Not all of them are here but before you can have access to this house you will need a court order. As you know the courts are closed until the seventh of January, so I suggest you come back after that. If you can obtain an order, I can assure you of my complete cooperation."

"You have no authority here, Señor Furlan," said the eldest. "This house is the property of the Steinman Foundation and we have every right to enter, remove the contents and place the property on the market. Our van is arriving shortly. Now," said the man frustrated and holding out his hand. "Hand over the keys."

Silvano looked at all four of them with disdain. They took deep breaths and closed in on him.

"Are you trying to intimidate me?" said Silvano.

They backed off.

"To be reasonable," said the spokesman. "We will give you half an hour to pack your personal effects and leave."

"Most kind," said Silvano. "However, your bosses need to double-check the Foundation's contract with Anne Pennington. It clearly states that due notice to leave the premises is to be granted to staff and any other lawful residents occupying the property at the time of her death. The Foundation shall only be entitled to unfettered access when those persons have left, which shall be no more than a maximum of ten days after the death certificate is issued. And that gentlemen, will be within three days. In thirteen days, this place will be all yours. Now, if you'll excuse me, or do the police need to be involved?"

Silvano extracted the keyring from his pocket, found the front door key, inserted it, and opened the door. He stepped inside, paused, and turned. The men made to follow him in.

"I would check the contract penalty clauses if I were you. Breaking the terms would be extremely expensive for the Foundation and I am sure your superiors would be most distressed if you ignore them. Now, as we say in Italian, vaffanculo."

Silvano closed the door firmly behind him, leaned his back against it and breathed a sigh of relief.

15

Ildefonso Sanz was sitting in his office at the Parador hotel, head on hands in despair. He'd arrived late that morning after a dental appointment, had just read the email from Silvano, and was trying to come to terms with the shock of Anne Pennington's passing. His pretty assistant, Rama, brought him a cup of coffee. She was in her early twenties, born in Spain to migrants from Mali. She was bright, helpful and he could discuss anything with her without worrying about it going further.

"What's wrong?" said Rama.

"A bomb is about to go off," said Ildefonso.

"Shall I evacuate the hotel?" she said.

"No, no. I mean a proverbial bomb. The lady who donated the art to the exhibition died last night and her husband has just told me that she didn't own the items. While she was alive, she had control of them but now she's gone, the foundation that owns them may well want them back before the exhibition finishes."

"That seems fair," said Rama.

"It does to them, but if the foundation removes the paintings, those people who have paid for flights from all over the world, plus entry tickets and our hotel rooms will be disappointed and angry. It will cost us a fortune in refunds and severely damage the hotel chain's reputation. We have to delay them taking the paintings."

"Can we revert to any legal means to hold them up?" said Rama.

"I'll have to speak to our lawyers, but we didn't sign any contracts with the lady. It was just a handshake between two neighbors."

"Then I would speak to the lawyers," said Rama. "However, there is one more thing you could do to delay matters."

"Go on."

"You could say that the paintings can only be released to the foundation when they can present proof of ownership issued by a Spanish court and a receipt describing the paintings as the originals painted by Picasso."

"Sorry, I don't understand."

"Look, you accepted delivery of the paintings as originals without doubt or question, but you don't know that they are for sure. What if you return the paintings and the foundation comes back saying they are forgeries? You have no leg to stand on. At the moment, you can prove that the paintings delivered are still the ones hanging there because they were filmed being unpacked and mounted. Since then, they have been under constant surveillance."

"Now, I understand, Rama. That is brilliant but where could we find someone to authenticate the paintings?"

"Why not call Picasso's granddaughter? You spoke with her at the opening. She must know experts who can do that. You'll have to pay of course but that will be much cheaper than reimbursing the foundation for the current value of the originals."

"How much might that be?"

"At least sixty million Euros, maybe more."

"Good heavens, that much? OK, connect me with the granddaughter, then I'll speak to the lawyer to arrange the necessary paperwork."

***

The four burly men in overcoats arrived at the Parador Hotel just before midday. The long line of visitors waiting to enter the exhibition stretched outside the front door as far as the hotel gate some hundred meters from the entrance. The men barged their way through the crowd and into the reception. Nobody was in attendance. They rang the bell and waited.

The receptionist appeared through the office door and approached the desk. He was speaking English on the telephone discussing the price of wedding receptions. He indicated to the four that he wouldn't be long. Six minutes later, he ended the call.

"We are not accustomed to waiting," said their usual spokesman in English, his face white with rage.

"Then how may I help you?" said the receptionist.

"We are here to collect the Picasso paintings," said the spokesman.

"Is this a joke?" said the receptionist. "You barge in here like you own the place, demand to collect millions of dollars' worth of paintings without presenting any identification or legal documents giving you the right to do so. Sir, with due respect I suggest you go away and come back with the necessary paperwork, otherwise, I will have to inform the police."

Spokesman thumped the desk hard, glared at the receptionist, turned, and barged out through the crowd, his men following. There were many rude comments from the queue, questioning the men's parentage as they headed toward the gate.

The receptionist smiled and returned to the office.

"Well done, Jabi," said Sanz. "And everyone. Our delaying tactic has worked, but they will be back. We just have to hope that the authenticator from London arrives as promised on the afternoon of the fifth. Meanwhile, make sure that whoever is on reception knows who to watch out for and what to do if they come back."

***

Silvano had walked alone, back, and forth on the relatively flat lower rear lawn scattering Anne's ashes handful-by-handful. They had a mildly greasy texture and a faint but not distasteful odor. The smaller grains stuck under his nails and on his skin. Tears streamed down his cheeks as he recalled how often they had taken this same stroll arm in arm enjoying the beautiful gardens and each other's company.

He'd instructed Anne's solicitor to sell her house in Washington DC. He had no loyalty to her brother and his family. They had made not a single attempt to contact Anne during her thirty years in Spain and had sent no message of condolences despite the email he had sent informing them of her death.

***

In the small hotel office behind reception, the four staff were on edge. Ildefonso Sanz fought the little voice in his head telling him to chew his nails. His eyes flitted between his fingers and the main door visible through the one-way mirror. "Do you think, they will manage to obtain a court order?" he said to nobody in particular.

Then the main door opened.

But it was just an elderly couple.

Jabi went out to attend to them.

"Unlikely," said Rama. "The courts aren't open until after Three Kings, but you know that boss. Stop panicking, it will be fine."

"I'm not panicking," said Sanz. "Just sharing my concerns. We have two days to go until the exhibition closes and you know these Yanks. They are bound to flash dollars around and bribe their way to a court order."

"Of course, they won't," said Rama. "There's no one at the court but a night watchman. He'll happily take their money, but he won't do anything."

"Thank you, my dear," said Sanz. "You're right of course but this tension is relentless."

"We'll make it," said Rama.

"We better," said Sanz. "Or I'm out of a job."

***

"Is he going to show?" said Crown from his sickbed in Alhaurin prison, his eyes never leaving the monitor.

"He'd better," said Sonia looking over at Crown from her chair. "Or all this was a waste of time. My life, thrown away for fuck all."

"He will," said Patrick chewing his nails as he stared

hard at the screen. "He's an arrogant git. He won't be able to resist such a tempting event."

"So many positive waves," said Crown. "But I wish he'd hurry up."

***

"Not yet, Sir," said el jefe into the telephone at the forensics lab. "But we're confident he'll show before the end of the exhibition on the fifth."

El jefe listened to his boss ranting at the other end, blushed, and grinned sheepishly as he ended the call.

"Cracking up, Sir?" said Prado.

"I'm not," said el jefe. "But the bosses are extremely nervous about the cost of all this and are demanding a result. They were a gnat's whisker away from calling off the whole thing. But I managed to persuade them. In two days, it has either worked or not. Two days won't make that much difference to the cost, but it might make a hell of a difference to the outcome. Come on Marquez. Where are you, dammit?"

***

On January fifth, just before midday. An elderly, portly man dressed in a tweed jacket, beige trousers, and sporting a green trilby hat limped into the foyer and through to the Picasso room. The brim of his hat had prevented a clear view of his face from the cameras both in the queue outside and when showing his ticket in the foyer. He limped as he approached the paintings and stopped in front of the portrait of Marie-Thérèse Walter. Twenty minutes later, he was still there despite comments from others also attempting a straight-on view. He ignored them and continue to stare like a man obsessed.

He turned, deliberately looked straight into the security camera, and smiled. All three victims pointed their fingers at the screen.

"That's him," they cried in unison.

Sonia picked up the direct line to Prado.

"We have him too," said Prado. "Keep watching." He hung up.

Two guards eased themselves around Marquez and herded him out the door. No-fuss had been made and nobody had noticed.

In the hotel office, they danced.

In the prison, they hugged.

At the forensics lab, they shook hands. El jefe smiled and went off to call his bosses.

In a small row house in Marbella, Teresa Marquez wept with joy. At last, she could see and touch her beloved brother.

16

On the midafternoon of the fifth, Prado and el jefe sat in the Málaga comisaría observation room watching Marquez through the one-way mirror. His resemblance to one of the aged simulations was remarkable. Eduardo, the technician had been delighted.

Marquez seemed relaxed and calm. Almost as if he were happy to be there but he was saying nothing; communication had been limited to requests for water, food, or visits to the restroom.

He'd had nothing on him other than a few hundred Euros in cash and a driving license in the name Rodriguez Sanchez Sanchez.

"At least the license gives his fiscal number and name," said el jefe. "They should lead us to a vehicle and a home address."

"Hopefully, but just because he carried a license doesn't mean that he had driven to Granada," said Prado. "To see the paintings, he could have just used it to prove his identity was the same as that on his entry ticket."

"Hell of a cheek," said el jefe. "Using his real name with one modification."

"Hiding in full sight," said Prado. "First rule of survival. It's so close to his real name it could be described as a typo."

"If he didn't come by car, how did he travel to the exhibition?"

"Perhaps he lives in Granada and used the street train? But that is speculating. We need to make him tell us. I'm hoping his home could contain all the evidence we need."

"Can't we just charge him?"

"With what? There are no outstanding charges against him, and none were ever brought. Even if there were, they would have long exceeded their statute of limitations and last time I checked the statute book, Sir, visiting a Picasso exhibition was not an offense."

"You mean after all this; we have nothing to charge him with? Well, you better find something and quick, or else I'm for the high jump and that means so are you."

"Relax, Sir. All we need are statements from his victims so we can bring fresh charges against him. At the moment, we are holding him for his protection pending inquiries, which as you know can be extended to four days."

"I want his man locked up forever," said el jefe. "He's evil."

"How do you suggest we do that?" said Prado. "When we have no evidence that he has committed a crime."

"Are you saying that Crown senior reported nothing even after Marquez stole all that money from him?"

"There were no denouncements ever made against him, and I can understand why. If Crown senior had brought charges, he risked exposing his dodgy property dealings, and prison would have taken Marquez beyond his reach. Crown wanted him at liberty so he could exact his form of punishment and maybe recover his money."

"What about the children? Did Crown not want Marquez locked up for abusing his son?"

"Same logic, Sir. It would have taken Marquez out of circulation."

"I need to discuss this with our lawyers. Keep him on ice until I have consulted them. We have to find something to charge the bastard with."

"First, we need to knock him off his confidence pedestal," said Prado.

"How?" said el jefe.

"Teresa Marquez, his sister, is on her way from Marbella," said Prado. "I'd like to put them together. See what happens. She might talk some sense into him. A confession, maybe."

"I doubt it but as you said. Let's see what happens. I'll be back as quickly as I can."

El jefe almost sprinted out of the room.

Prado watched Marquez but other than scratching his balls, there was nothing to see. There was a knock on the door and an officer showed Teresa in. Prado stood and shook her hand.

"Nice to see you again," he said. "Please take a seat."

"So, you found him," said Teresa, a medium height slender woman. She had a pretty and youthful face for her age. Short dark hair framed her oval cheeks setting off her pert nose and light brown hazel eyes. She made herself comfortable but was embarrassed and avoided looking through the window.

"More like, he found us," said Prado pouring her a glass of water from the dispenser. "Did you see his arrest?"

"I did. He seemed happy to be handing himself over."

"He still does. Take a look if you are up to it. He seems comfortable, even hums to himself occasionally."

"I can't think why," said Teresa taking a quick peek.

"Look, this will be difficult for you after all this time. I'm going to leave you alone for a bit. It will give you a chance to acclimatize yourself to his presence before facing him."

"What do you want me to say to him?"

"We need to know several things. The most important is the name of the fourth victim. We have Crown, O'Reilly, and Sonia behind bars and want to prevent the fourth person from tracking him down and exacting revenge. Any hint where he is living will be helpful. His driving license application was from an apartment in Madrid. We have checked there, and it's located in a block that was recently condemned. We also don't know how he traveled to Granada or if he owns a vehicle. Don't ask him directly just chat generally and see where the conversation goes. After you've settled down and talk is flowing, tell him about your elder brother's death and your suspicions that he was murdered. It might touch a raw nerve."

Prado left. Teresa looked at her brother. It was undoubtedly him. Any trace of embarrassment disappeared. Her heart raced, at last, she could touch and smell him again. The only man she had ever loved.

Teresa sipped her water and relished the sight of Rodriguez through the mirror. He hadn't aged at all well. He might look happy and confident but there was a wariness about him, and his skin color was pale and unhealthy.

"Ready?" said Prado from the door.

Teresa nodded, finished her water, and joined Prado. Her hands were trembling.

"You'll be fine when you're in there," said Prado leading her into the corridor.

Prado opened the door to the interview room, showed her in, and left her to it.

Marquez looked up. His expression was astounded but then ecstatic as he struggled to his feet. Teresa rushed to him and they hugged. "They can hear everything," she said into his ear.

"I know," said Marquez.

"How are you?" she said.

"Tired," he said.

"You enjoyed seeing the painting?"

"One of the highlights of my life."

"I was watching."

"Really? It's amazing how technology has moved on. How are you?" he said releasing her. They both sat down holding hands and gazing into each other's eyes.

"My feelings for you are still the same," he said.

"Me too. It was nice of them to let us have some time together."

"What do they want in return?"

"To protect you from the fourth victim. The other three are behind bars."

"I know. Which prison?"

"No idea. Why?"

"I would prefer not to be anywhere near them. They hold more than a grudge against me."

"I can't blame them. Dear Rodriguez," she said

looking into his eyes. "I don't understand why you didn't share your yearnings with me. Maybe I could have helped you with them?"

"You were clear that your future husband came first."

"You could have pressed harder. When a girl says no, she doesn't always mean it."

"It's a bit bloody late to tell me that now, Teresa," he said raising his voice and turning away from her. "I might have taken a completely different course of action. All of this could have been avoided."

"That's right blame me for your depravities. Typical," she said glaring at him.

He calmed. "Sorry," he said.

"Well, that's something," she said grasping his hands. "Did you hear that our elder brother, Pablo, is dead?" He nodded and tears came to his eyes.

"How did you find out?" she said.

"I was there. Teresa, I think I killed him."

Prado leaned forward in his seat back in the observation room. This was unexpected.

Teresa drew back letting go of his hand.

"What do you mean?" she said.

"I often came to Marbella just to watch you and hear your voice."

"Why didn't you come and see me? I wouldn't have said anything. Was it you that bugged my phone?"

"I know nothing about that, but I often sat in the café where you used to meet Pablo. Once my back was almost touching yours."

"I wish you hadn't told me that," said Teresa bursting into tears. "Although that might have given you some warped pleasure, it's just another hurtful thing you've done to me. Disappearing without telling me anything was bad enough and now this."

Rodriguez stroked her arm, his face racked with remorse.

"I never meant to hurt you," he said. "But I wasn't thinking."

"Too wrapped up in your fantasies," said Teresa dabbing her eyes with a tissue. "What do you mean, you think you killed Pablo?"

"One evening, I saw him talking animatedly to an attractive blond woman. She seemed familiar. Then it twigged, it was Sonia Augustin. She was the young girl I used to, er..."

"I know who she is. Did you hear what they said?"

"No, but I was determined to find out. I watched them go outside together and say their farewells. She went one way and Pablo the other. I followed him home and waited outside until the concierge had slipped out for a break. Then I snuck in alongside another resident, found his apartment number on the mailboxes, and went up to his floor. I knocked on Pablo's door and when he inquired who it was, I told him I was a neighbor with a wrongly addressed letter that was for him. When Pablo unlocked his front door, I leaped in to prevent him from slamming it in my face. He fell, and I landed on top of him. He was winded but seemed OK. I sat him down on the sofa and he started murmuring nonsense.

"Gradually, I understood that he'd never forgiven me for taking the golf course money from him and his fellow directors. However, Sonia had enlightened him about what I had done to her and the other kids. He called me a monster and demanded to know how I could bring so much shame on the family. I confirmed what Sonia told him was correct and to this day, I don't understand why, but then I told him about us. He seemed to explode, then keeled over. I checked his pulse, but he was dead. Teresa, I made him so mad, it brought on a heart attack."

"That would explain a lot," said Teresa. "I thought that Sonia may have drugged him or something because the concierge said he spoke like a drunk."

"Extreme rage can have a similar effect."

Teresa grasped his hand again and looked at him. "The guilt must have been awful to live with."

"It gnawed away at me like concentrated acid, but it wasn't the end of that night's disasters," said Marquez. "When I tried to leave our brother's apartment, Sonia was lurking outside with a tall dark man. I assumed she must have spotted me leaving the café and followed me to Pablo's. When she saw me, she couldn't hold herself back.

"It was her rage that saved me. If she'd waited around the corner until I came out, she would have had me. Instead, she threw herself at me screaming blue murder even though there were a locked glass door and metal bars between us. I slipped out of the rear fire exit and escaped."

"What did you do next?"

"I knew that they would hunt me down relentlessly. It panicked me into a forced relocation and another new identity. I left Andorra and went to Madrid to procure new papers and buy a vehicle. I then set about keeping a watch on all four of them. After that, they cranked up their efforts to find me."

"Where's your vehicle now? Perhaps I can collect it?"

"Would you. You'll need to find a discreet place to park it."

"I'll find somewhere. Just tell me where it is."

"At the palace. Keys on top of the driver's tire, parking ticket in the glove compartment."

"Where are you living? Perhaps I can come and visit you when you get out of here."

"That would be amazing, but I doubt if I'll ever leave custody. Even though they don't have anything to hold me for. I'm sure they'll invent something."

"They wouldn't dare trump up charges."

"They would, but actually, I don't care. I'm not here by accident. I've had enough, Teresa. Life on the run is for young men. I might not be in prison, but I may as well be. Every waking moment my mind is spinning with what diversionary tactics I must think of next to stay one jump ahead. I can't cope with it anymore. A warm cell, medical services, and three squares a day sound most appealing. You can visit me whenever you want."

"Is there anything you want me to collect from your home?"

Marquez looked long and hard at his sister, then shook his head.

"Then they would have everything," he said and looked at his watch.

***

Prado called Anna Galvez and asked her to check vehicles in the name of Rodriguez Sanchez Sanchez, and his national fiscal number. Then to call the registration details through to the Granada police and have them check the car park at the Alhambra Palace.

El jefe returned bearing an angry expression.

"Lawyers helpful?" said Prado.

"Harrumph," said el jefe. "They are highly disenchanted with your proposal to take fresh statements from the three alleged victims. Marquez's defense is likely to claim undue bias. They know we have Marquez in custody. You asked them for a statement and surprisingly they gave you exactly what you wanted with no evidence to support their claims."

"That means we have nothing."

"They did suggest that perhaps the former college administrator could make a complaint against him for stealing the advance paid college fees."

"Dorothy? I doubt it," said Prado. "She was on her death bed last time we saw her and there is no physical evidence or accountancy books to back that up."

"What about the college psychologist that Dorothy mentioned, any luck tracking her down?"

"Sadly," said Prado. "Diana Vega passed some ten years ago. The name of the fourth victim went with her."

"Then we'll have to release him," said el jefe.

"Not bloody likely," said Prado. "Look, Sir, he used a false identity to apply for his driving license, purchase, insure, and register the car. Once we've seen the vehicle papers, we'll have plenty to charge him with."

"For such minor offenses, we would normally release him on bail."

"Yes, but given his history of running away, the judge would deny his application on fear of a flight risk."

"Fair enough, but what if he still refuses to tell us the name of the fourth victim?"

"If he doesn't cooperate, we'll transfer him from our cells here to Alhaurin Prison to await trial. I'll let it slip that his victims are also on remand there. Perhaps then, he might cooperate."

El jefe looked at him hard.

"I never heard that," he said. "Keep me posted."

17

A small dapper man approached the hotel Parador reception wheeling two large cases. He had a thin face with a protruding nose and was dressed in green chinos, a dark blue blazer, and an open collar pink shirt with a striped neckerchief.

"How may we help?" said Rama in English.

"I have an appointment with Señor Sanz. My name is Covington, Rupert Covington."

Rama called Sanz's office on the internal phone.

"The painting authenticator has arrived," she said.

"Excellent, I'll be straight out. In the meantime, check him in, please. His room and meals are to be charged to my hospitality account."

Covington scribbled his signature on the registration card, then looked up to see a man in a morning suit hovering near him.

"Welcome, Señor Covington," said Sanz. "Can we help you with your luggage? I'll have a porter take it straight to your room."

"No," said Covington. "This is my analysis equipment; I'll need a room somewhere near the exhibition. We can leave it there and then I would like to have a quick look at the paintings and plan my work."

"Well at least let me give you a hand," said Sanz reaching for one of the cases.

"Thank you, but I can manage," said Covington. "You lead on."

"As you wish."

They left the cases in Sanz's office and squeezed through the crowd in the foyer to the exhibition room entrance.

"I'd assumed the exhibition would be popular," said Covington, eyes drawn immediately to the paintings. "But this is amazing."

Covington barged his way to the front without an excuse me and stood in front of each painting for a few minutes. Then he returned to Sanz waiting by the door.

"At first glance, they look good," said Covington. "Original frames I would say, which is always a strong indicator of a positive outcome. Normally, if the frame is identical then so is the painting because it's harder to age the frame than forge the contents."

Sanz started to relax. Perhaps this would all work out. He led Covington back to his office.

"When are you going to close the doors so I can begin my work?" said Covington.

"We're not," said Sanz. "Some of our visitors have flown here from all over the world to see the paintings. I can't possibly spoil their pleasure at this late stage."

"And I can't possibly concentrate with all those people around me asking what I am doing," said Covington. "I have to work in silence. I'll return when the exhibition closes tonight."

"Regretfully, that will be too late," said Sanz. "As soon as we close, control of the paintings reverts to the

Steinman Foundation. They will be collecting them immediately and before they do, we must know if the paintings are the genuine article. Otherwise, the hotel could be held liable. If you weren't aware, the hotel is a state-owned enterprise. If the paintings prove to be genuine, we don't have a problem, but if not, it might be assumed that the Spanish Government has stolen the originals. I can't be responsible for that. America would be more than furious, and it could invite all kinds of international recriminations."

"I see," said Covington. "In that case, may I suggest that you find a separate room and I will inspect one item at a time. Then we needn't disturb the visitors' pleasure."

"Good thinking," said Sanz.

"Before I start work, the alarms and sensors must be switched off, may I suggest that you beef up security."

"Very well. How long will you need?"

"If the works are genuine, not long," said Covington. "But if forgeries, a lot longer. I'll have to identify how old they are and who might have painted them. But let's not dwell on the negatives. At first glance, they look genuine."

"Rama," said Sanz in English. "I'll go and organize the extra security then turn off the alarms and sensors. My office here is the nearest room to the exhibition. Señor Covington can use my desk. Naturally, he'll want to supervise the dismounting and remounting of each item. Always stay with him, record his progress on your phone, and provide him with whatever he needs. That way we can have no possible misunderstandings later."

"How should the staff respond to visitor questions about the absent paintings?" said Rama.

"Good question," said Covington. "On other occasions, I told them that we were worried about the paintings being affected by dust from the air conditioning. So, we're just checking them under our special lighting and cleaning where necessary."

"In that case, we will simply inform all visitors that one painting may be undergoing a dust inspection," said Sanz. "Then they won't need to inquire what is going on."

"Good thinking," said Covington. "Now, can we bash on?"

Rama cleared the desk while Covington prepared his equipment.

Sanz left to deal with the alarms.

Covington opened the large, heavy aluminum case, which was fitted out with blue velvet-covered polystyrene with cut-outs containing what appeared to be scientific instruments. The other case contained his overnight items alongside a cardboard box. He opened the box to reveal a laptop sitting on top of a slim, flat, UV-A black light. Underneath was a rectangular shaped grey machine that resembled a complicated desktop photocopier but was a spectrometer. Covington turned on his laptop and brought up the detailed specifications of each painting. The descriptions had been taken from old photos and the sales details from the auctions where Anne had purchased them all those years ago.

"This is not like appraising a Van Gogh or Reubens old master," said Covington. "Picasso was a relatively modern painter and most of the materials he used are still around today. Furthermore, we know the precise provenance of each painting and who the previous owners were."

"Will you have to remove the painting from the frame?" said Rama fascinated by Covington's work.

"Oh, yes," said Covington pleased with her enthusiasm. "I can't possibly make an accurate examination through the glazing. Shall we go and fetch the first?"

They went into the exhibition room where Sanz was waiting with a step ladder and three, armed security guards. The crowd watched, now more interested in what he was up to than the paintings. Covington positioned the ladder, climbed up it a couple of steps reached out to the painting of Fernande Olivier, and lifted it off the wall. It was heavy so he lowered it into the willing arms of Sanz and Rama.

"Be careful," said Covington. "This oil on canvas was painted in 1905 and is valued at around nine million US dollars."

The crowd gasped.

Sanz and Rama carried it to the office and set it face-up on the desk.

Covington picked it up and with considerably less reverence turned it over. "Mmm…" he said. "Newish backing paper and no previous auction labels." He removed a scalpel from his aluminum case and delicately cut around the brown paper glued to the rear of the plain timber frame to keep the contents airtight and mold-free.

"Can we find out when the painting was last cleaned?" said Covington.

"Difficult," said Sanz. "The only person who would know is Anne Pennington's husband. I'll call him, but he may have left the house already. Excuse me." He scurried out of the room swiping through the contacts on his phone.

Covington turned the retaining clips and extracted the one-meter by eighty-one-centimeter painting. It was wrapped around a rectangular piece of dense fiberboard with the edges of the canvas fixed with mounting tape to the rear of the fiberboard. He turned it over and sniffed the paint, nodding his approval at the oily smell. He then laid it face-up on the desk, picked out a magnifying glass, and peered at the dark image comparing it with the photo on his laptop. After ten minutes spent examining every single square centimeter, he nodded.

"Looks good," he said. "The craquelure is right for the age; the brushwork and colors are just as expected, and his unique signature is spot on. Now for the canvas."

Sanz returned looking pleased.

"I spoke with Silvano the husband," he said "He confirmed that all seven paintings have been completely restored during the last four years. The frames are the originals, but the glazing has been updated to anti-fade and non-reflective glass. The backing paper is new, mounts and inserts have been replaced with modern high-density fiberboard. Other than saying it was someone in Málaga, he has no idea who did the work and wasn't involved in helping out. Anne had insisted that she arranged it all herself."

"That would account for the glass interior being spotless," said Covington. "Shame that the restorer removed the old auction labels. They are usually an excellent indicator of authenticity. My physical inspection matches my initial appraisal," said Covington. "But I need to take a closer look. In my Lab, I use the latest X-Ray technology but that is too big to travel, so I'm reverting to tried and trusted methods."

Covington lifted out the lamp from its box in his other case, set it up on the desk, connected it to his computer, and with cable and adapter in hand looked around for a plug.

"Here," said Sanz showing him the floor box under the desk.

Covington plugged the lamp and his computer into the mains, turned it on and waited for it to initialize.

"Could we darken the room for this please?" said Covington.

Rama went over to the window and closed the blinds, then turned off the light. Covington held the lamp over the painting and looked at his laptop.

"What are we seeing?" said Rama.

"This is a black light examination," said Covington. "The surface of most paintings is made up of five layers sometimes more. The first layer in this instance is the canvas but could be paper, wood, parchment, or metal. Then the sizing prepares the first layer to receive paint. The third is the paint which might comprise several coats including underpainting, overpainting, and glazes. Fourth is the protective varnish followed by dust, dirt, grime, smoke, and grease that may have built up on top of the varnish.

"The lamp will expose any restoration work or attempts to alter the original work. This is where we see how difficult it is to make a perfect forgery. So many variables that need to be matched identically because modern equipment can so easily spot anything out of the ordinary. Picasso paintings are relatively easy to forge. His style is not complex and most of the materials he used are still readily available. What is not so common knowledge is that he often used ordinary house paint sometimes mixed with coffee grounds to create texture. I know this particular painting was created on top of another work that dissatisfied him. We should be able to see it."

He moved the lamp nearer the painting and looked at his laptop. He frowned and moved it closer still.

"What, the devil?" he said.

18

Prado was sitting in the observation room watching Marquez and his sister when his telephone rang. He looked at the screen. It was Anna Galvez. "Anything?" he said.

"Yes, the Marquez vehicle has been located in the Alhambra car park. The parking ticket is in the glove compartment confirming his arrival at eleven forty-three," said Anna. "It's a three-year-old two-door dark blue Seat Ibiza. Marquez bought it privately in Madrid about eighteen months ago. It's registered in his current name to the same address as the driving license, as is the insurance. It only has fourteen odd thousand kilometers on the clock, so it looks like he doesn't use it much."

"Any clues as to his current address?"

"Yes and no. There are no documents, but the tire edges are covered with red mud and there is a small olive twig stuck in the radiator grill."

"Perhaps he's renting a cottage among an olive plantation but that doesn't help us much. The whole of Andalucía is covered with olive groves."

"I agree," said Anna. "But the red mud will narrow

it down. I've sent a tow truck to bring the vehicle to my lab, but I doubt I'll be able to make any conclusions until tomorrow."

"At least the falsely addressed documents give us an excuse to hold him pending further inquiries. Thanks, Anna. Let me know about the mud as soon as you can."

Prado called the news through to el jefe.

"Better than nothing, I suppose," said el jefe. "By the way, all the cells in the comisaría are temporarily out of action. Something wrong with the toilets. Could take a day or two to fix."

"Really, when did that occur?"

"Whenever you give the word. Understand?"

"Perfectly, Sir. Thank you."

Prado entered the interview room. Teresa and her brother turned and looked at Prado as if he were an unwanted intruder on their brief reunion.

"I'm sorry to disturb," said Prado. "But events are moving on and I now need to formally interview your brother. I'll escort you to reception and arrange for a car to take you home."

Teresa and Marquez hugged. They exchanged lingering glances as Prado led her out of the door and to reception.

"Thank you for your cooperation," said Prado.

"What will you do with him now?" said Teresa looking miserable.

"That depends on him," said Prado.

"Will you keep me informed?"

"As much as we can."

"Did you hear about the car?"

"We did and we have it already."

"I see. Well, at least I saw him. Thank you,

inspector."

Prado returned to the interview room, entered, sat down, and looked at Marquez. He was weeping gently and looked decidedly unsure of himself.

"Would you be prepared to make a statement concerning your involvement in your brother Pablo's death?" said Prado.

Marquez nodded and looked even more worried.

"And how is life among the olive groves?" said Prado.

Marquez paled and looked terrified.

"We've found your car and discovered that you have been driving it with forged papers. That is enough to charge and hold you pending further inquiries. Now I'd like you to tell me your life story. We could start with your incestuous relationship with your underage sister and then move onto your abuse of minors when you were headmaster of the International College in Marbella. That should keep us busy for a day or two but what I need urgently is the name of the fourth victim. You know very well who I mean."

Marquez looked at him. "No comment."

For two hours, Prado grilled Marquez.

It was obvious the man was tiring as Prado wore him down with short sharp bursts of interrogation, but he still refused to cooperate.

"No comment," is all he would say.

At the end of the day, Prado reverted to his bombshell tactic.

"OK, Marquez," he said. "Enough. Regretfully, the cells in the comisaría have developed toilet problems so we'll be transferring you to Alhaurin Prison tonight. You'll be checked by the doctor, fed, and given a remand cell on your own. I'll take you in my car and we can chat on the way."

Marquez was trembling as Prado cuffed him and told him his rights. Prado took him downstairs, released him while he used the restroom, then re-cuffed him and took him out to the carpool. In the car, he cuffed him to the door pull in the front seat then headed out of the city. It was quiet, dark, and blustery. Leaves swirled around and there was a spattering of rain. Traffic was light as Prado headed out of town on the Avenida de Andalucía.

"When Sonia saw you outside Pablo's apartment block, did she say anything else other than ranting?"

"I was more concerned about escaping, inspector," said Marquez. "But I did hear the words torture and long slow death. But all she achieved was to remind me that all four of them are children of dysfunctional criminals. Normal behavior and standards had long been drummed out of them. They will not hesitate to exact the most terrifying revenge upon me. Seeing Sonia forced me to change my identity yet again. And I knew they would redouble their efforts to entice me out into the open."

"You made your bed, Marquez. For one last time, who is the fourth victim?"

"Sorry, but I won't tell you."

"I don't understand why not," said Prado. "We could take him or her out of circulation. It would mean that at least you would be safe from further attack."

"I doubt it," said Marquez. "Their reach is long, and their pockets deep. There is no haven anywhere for me."

"Are you saying that there is someone behind the fourth victim?"

"That is for you to find out, inspector. Should they

find me, silence is my only chance of survival."

"And your silence is their only chance of survival. You heard Sonia. There is only one end for you, and it won't be pleasant. If you cooperate, we could put you into witness protection."

"Inspector, please do not think that you have scored a massive coup by my capture. I knew that I would be either arrested at the exhibition or discovered by my adversaries, yet still, I elected to go there. I'm too old for all this running and hiding and my body is fading fast. Every day it gets harder to exist and I've simply had enough. I'll accept whatever might come to me no matter whether it's tonight or whenever. At least, I'll be warm, fed, can read, or watch TV without one eye ever alert to an escape route."

"Then I can't help you."

"I know."

Thirty minutes later, Prado pulled up at the prison security gate, showed his pass, and drove through. He parked up by the admissions gate, cuffed Marquez to him, and escorted him inside. They did the paperwork and Prado handed his prisoner over to the warden. He'd stopped trembling and looked resolute.

"Wait," said Prado as the warden led Marquez toward the clinic. "You should know that all three of your victims are on remand here. You should be safe in your cell, but you never know what influence they might have among the staff. So, try and sleep well but bear in mind that if you don't cooperate with us tomorrow, you'll be back here every night until you do."

Marquez shrugged.

The warden tugged at his arm and led him through into the prison.

19

"What is it?" said Rama, peering over Covington's shoulder at the laptop screen. "Is there a problem?"

Covington scratched his chin as he puzzled over the image.

"There's no sign of any restoration work, which is good. However, the image I expected to see underneath this painting is there but is fainter than anticipated. It's the correct outline but it should be bolder."

"What does that tell you?"

"The restoration chemicals may have had some effect but not by that much."

"What does it signify?" said Rama.

"Any difference from the provenance is a strong indicator of something wrong. However, it's not that simple. Mistakes can be made and there can be variations between the official description and the actual item. It means I will have to probe deeper."

"How?" said Sanz looking decidedly uncomfortable.

"I need to examine the canvas more closely. Each brand has a distinctive stamp."

"Can we do that here?"

"Of course. Turn the light back on please."

Covington turned to his aluminum case and removed his magnifying glass. He turned the painting over, unpeeled the tape, and removed the canvas from the fiberboard. He laid the canvas face down on the backing paper lying on top of the desk and combed every millimeter of its back. Eventually, he located a faint circular stamp in the bottom right-hand corner. He studied it for several minutes, nodded, and took a photo of it with a special camera from his bottomless case.

"It's the correct stamp from Picasso's preferred canvas supplier and has faded just as it should for its age. The canvas, therefore, seems genuine. Now I'll test the paint."

He extracted the spectrometer from its box and added it to the increasingly cluttered desk. He connected it to the mains and his computer then turned it on and picked up a scalpel.

"Is that what I think it's for?" said Sanz looking pale.

"Don't worry," said Covington picking up the canvas. "I'll be cutting a few tiny slivers from where the canvas wraps around the backing board. It's a usual procedure accepted by all in the trade and I have a steady hand."

Covington cut a miniscule strip of dark color followed by five more shades in different edge locations.

"Can't you test the first one while you cut the others?" said Rama.

"I could," said Covington. "But it takes the machine some fifteen minutes to warm up."

"Then let us take a break," said Sanz. "I'll have refreshments served in the downstairs lounge. The restrooms there will be quieter."

"Good idea," said Covington.

The crowd was still piling into the exhibits as they walked down a grand staircase to the lounge situated outside the restaurant.

"How does the spectrometer work?" said Rama sipping her water as they sat by the picture window looking out over the beautiful hotel gardens and beyond to the Generalife.

"To put it as simply as possible," said Covington nibbling a biscuit. "Paint colors reflect light at varying degrees. By measuring them, we can identify their constituents. If we find a color not around when Picasso painted Fernande then it is a forgery. When we return, I'll insert the samples into the spectrometer and within seconds I can compare them with our records. If the colors match within an acceptable tolerance, it will confirm that the paint is original."

"Despite the inconsistencies on the underpainting?" said Rama.

"Let's wait until after the paint analysis. Excuse me, I'll see you back upstairs shortly."

Rama and Sanz watched Covington head off to the restroom.

"Funny little man," said Sanz.

"I find him fascinating," said Rama. "And he is the key to us getting out of this mess."

"Or deeper in it; depending on his findings."

They cleared the cups back onto the tray, left it by the waiter's serving table, and returned to the office.

Covington entered a few moments later, prepared the first sample, inserted it into the machine, and looked at his computer.

"Not quite perfect," he said after a careful study of the graphs. "But within tolerances."

The remaining samples were also within an acceptable range but still, Covington was reluctant to declare the painting genuine. He walked about the office scratching his chin deep in thought. Covington stopped dead, turned, and looked at them.

"I'm almost ninety-five percent sure that this is an original Picasso," he said. "However, to sustain my reputation, I have to be one hundred percent certain. Due to the urgency of the matter, I'm going to send an email to my lab with a microscopic screenshot of the canvas weave and a photo of the manufacturer's stamp. We have some software there that can precisely compare it with what we know this brand should look like. If they match, I'll be happy to declare this painting genuine and give you a certificate confirming that."

Sanz looked at his watch. "The exhibition closes in four hours. To test the other six paintings during that time will be a close-run thing. Can we make it snappy? The Foundation men are bound to arrive bang on closing time."

"I'll do my best," said Covington. "But good science needs due diligence and I'm not prepared to compromise my standards for any reason."

Sanz left to check on the security. He looked worried.

Rama watched, filming Covington on her phone as he placed the rear corner of the painting under the microscope lens. He held the painting with one hand, altered the lens controls to maximum zoom and focus. It clearly showed the crisscrossing of the canvas weave and the stamp. He took several screenshots and saved them to his hard drive.

"Could you take the painting?" he said. "While I send the email."

Rama put her phone down and complied with his request.

"How long will it take?" she said.

"Not long at all. While we are waiting, we can reassemble this painting and rehang it. Then we'll start on the next one."

"What shall we do to replace the backing paper?"

"We'll reuse the existing and stick it back in place. I have some special tape for that."

"Of course, you do," said Rama.

***

Sanz had returned to his office looking more relaxed than he'd been since the Foundation's bully boys had arrived the day after Anne's death. Even though there had been no confirmation from Covington's lab about the canvas. Matters had now been taken out of his hands.

When the Foundation men had arrived earlier to check on the paintings and wait for the exhibition to close, they had made an enormous fuss as to why one painting was missing from the exhibit. Their phone calls to the Foundation lawyers had elevated the decision-making process to top levels within the Foundation, the directors of the hotel chain, and then up to the Spanish Foreign Office. It was agreed that the Foundation would be sending their official authenticator who would be arriving the following day. Meanwhile, the paintings would remain locked in the exhibition room under shared security starting as soon as Salome's team had cleared out her treasure and artifacts. Salome's team were ready, their security van was outside the hotel entrance. They would begin as soon as Sanz gave the word.

At precisely six p.m. Sanz closed the exhibition. They waited patiently while the last few remaining visitors took a final look at the exhibits and left. Forty-five minutes later, the Las Claras treasure was packed up and the van had departed back to Vélez-Málaga. At precisely seven twenty, an email arrived on Covington's computer.

Rama was standing next to Covington in Sanz's office as he read the message. She looked over his shoulder, but the text was too small for her to see and Covington displayed no emotion to what he was reading.

He turned off the laptop. "Please gather everyone together in front of the paintings for my announcement."

"What were the results?" said Rama.

"Young lady, please assemble everyone as requested."

Rama found Sanz in the office behind reception and told him. Sanz went over to the chief bully boy and they all went through into the exhibit and closed the door. Covington went and stood in front of Fernande Olivier, turned, and faced his small audience.

"Ladies and gentlemen," he said clasping his hands together and rubbing them. "Today I have thoroughly examined these seven paintings of Pablo Picasso's Muses. I have completed my work and am now in a position to publish my findings. However, a complication has arisen which means that I will have to delay my announcement. The owners of the collection, The Steinman Foundation have commissioned their evaluation of these works. So as not to prejudice their proceedings, I will remain silent until they have completed their tasks."

"Surely you can tell us?" said Sanz. "We promise not to say anything."

"Regretfully, that will not be possible. This is standard procedure when two sets of evaluators are examining the same collection. My professional courtesy forbids me from saying any more at this time. If you'll excuse me, I need to pack up my equipment and take a shower."

"Perhaps you'll join us for dinner?" said Sanz.

"Thank you, but I should remain out of sight until the second evaluation has been completed. I'll order room service. Goodnight."

A heated discussion followed concerning the security arrangements for the night. Finally, it was agreed that one member of the Foundation's team would accompany the hotel security team and change over every six hours.

Sanz returned to his office where Covington was carefully packing his equipment.

"Do you know these other authenticators?" said Sanz.

"Of course. It's a small world. And don't worry, they are professional and highly skilled. You can have every faith in their findings."

"What if they are different from yours?"

"Unlikely. Granted there is some level of professional opinion involved, but it is a ridiculously small part of the assessment. This is a scientific process not the toss of a coin. I can assure you that there can be only one result and it will be the same as mine."

"What happens to the paintings if they are forgeries?"

"In Britain, we have a special police force specializing in art fraud. I often collaborate with them in their inquiries. I imagine the Spanish police have a similar team. However, as the paintings now belong to the Foundation, it will be up to them to resolve jurisdiction with the Spanish authorities. Whatever happens, it will no longer be a concern of the hotel."

"That will be a relief. May I send you a complimentary bottle of wine with your room service dinner?"

"Most generous, but I don't drink alcohol."

Covington closed his cases, locked them, and wheeled them over to the door. "Would you mind showing me to my room, please?" he said.

***

The painting authenticator for the Steinman Foundation arrived at the Parador hotel promptly at ten a.m. the next morning. She had been flown down by private jet at the crack of dawn from Paris where she was based, to Granada airport. The hotel limousine had been dispatched to meet her and as she strode toward reception, the driver struggled to keep up wheeling her two heavy suitcases of equipment.

Her appearance was formidable; tall, slender, elegant, and ageless with dark coffee skin, short black pixie hair, and light hazel eyes that oozed authority. She wore a full-length real mink fur coat and knee-high black leather boots.

"Suzanne Blanc," she said in English with a strong French accent. "I'd like to start my work straight away.

My plane is due to depart this afternoon. Can you take me to the paintings immediately and bring my equipment? I'll need a large table, cable extension and two assistants capable of following instructions in English, who aren't afraid to handle expensive paintings.

"Just a moment, madam," said Rama in perfect French and rang the bell. Sanz appeared by the reception desk and ushered Madame Blanc off to the exhibition room with his customary profuse professionalism.

The guards opened the double doors, and they went in.

The four Foundation bullies were sitting in the lounge awaiting her arrival and when seeing her leaped off their respective sofas and ran toward her clamoring for her attention.

Madam Blanc stopped on hearing her name and turned toward them.

"What?" she said.

"We are the Foundation's team responsible for the paintings," said the usual spokesman. "You are to let us know your findings before anyone."

"Young man," said Blanc poking his chest with a beautifully lacquered index fingernail. "My report is for the ears of the Foundation lawyers only. And that does not include you. Now scoot." She fluttered her fingers in dismissal took Sanz's arm and went into the gallery.

The limo driver followed her accompanied by Rama. They would be the assistants. The tall burly guards locked them in and stood in front of the closed doors. One hand resting on their holstered pistols.

Just before midday, the gallery doors were opened to admit Rupert Covington.

Sanz, Rama, and the driver were obliged to wait outside with the guards and bullies who all waited on tenterhooks for the expected announcement.

They waited.

And waited.

Sanz put his ear to the door and just as he did, it opened. Blanc and Covington stood in the doorway and Blanc deferred to Covington.

"Ladies and Gentlemen," said Covington. "After much debate, we are in complete accord with our findings. Regretfully." He paused. "Regretfully, after a telephone conversation with the Foundation lawyers, we have been instructed not to broadcast our conclusions. The paintings may now be taken down, packed up, and shipped to Washington DC where their future will be decided. Thank you for your help. Sanz, you may take us both to the airport."

20

"Seventh of January today," said Amanda in English, slicing up a mixture of fresh fruit into separate bowls and handing them around. "And Sasha, it's your first day in a Spanish school. Are you looking forward to it?"

"I was enjoying the holiday," said Sasha fishing out a green grape with his spoon. "But it is exciting to meet some new faces."

"And what do you think of Spain?" said Salome in Spanish tucking into hers. She always spoke to him in her mother tongue.

"It's different," said Sasha in English. "And I miss Mama, but it's nice having so many people in my family to talk to and play with, and especially being outdoors most of the time. In Russia, I was indoors nearly always and on my own a lot."

"Sure, you'll be OK on the school bus?" said Phillip. "I'll happily drive you."

"Thanks, Papa," said Sasha with a mouthful of mango. "That would be great but so uncool. Not a good start to making friends."

"How old are you?" said Salome.

"You know that I'm seven," said Sasha. "Por que?"

"You sound like ninety," said Amanda. "Such a wise head on young shoulders. Where did you learn that?"

"My cousins," said Sasha. "They've been telling me what it was like on their first day."

"I feel redundant, already," said Phillip.

"Oh, no, Papa," said Sasha finishing his bowl and sipping from his water beaker. "No one can barbecue sausages as you can."

"Well, that's something at least," said Phillip. "Because I'll be useless at helping you with your homework?"

"Homework?" said Salome. "What's that?"

"Ha, ha," said Sasha putting his bowl, spoon, and beaker in the dishwasher. "We don't have homework in the first term."

"OK, the bus will be at the top of the road, in fifteen minutes," said Phillip. "Go brush your teeth, gather your gear and I'll walk you up to the stop."

"Can I take my scooter?"

"OK," said Phillip as Sasha skipped out of the door. "I promise not to ride it back. What are you guys doing today?"

"We're checking the treasure was safely returned and stored after the exhibition," said Salome. "Then seeing how the builders are doing refurbishing Uncle Mario's house. I'm sure that you'll want it to be finished asap so you can have me out of here and return to normal life."

"It will be so boring," said Phillip. "Never a dull moment with you around. Are you meeting with Vicente?"

"Just to discuss the restoration plans for the

convent," said Salome.

"No plans for a romantic lunch?" said Phillip.

"We'll see," said Salome.

Amanda's phone rang. It was Prado.

Sasha returned with his rucksack, dressed in his full uniform.

"This is another classic photo opportunity in your path through life," said Phillip. "Come on, let's take one quickly by the garage door, then off we go."

"Bye, Sasha," said the ladies, pausing their conversation with Prado to give him a big hug. "Have a great day."

Phillip took several poses of Sasha both on and off his scooter, then they joined his three nieces and his sister outside the farm gate. The adults carried the rucksacks while the kids raced ahead on their scooters. It was a chilly morning with a light breeze and a blue sky. The pine trees swayed gently; the birds tweeted happily.

"How do you feel?" said Glenda his sister.

"Being a parent, you mean?" said Phillip. "Or work stuff?"

"Instant father, husband to be, human being?"

"Like a duck out of water, terrified but strangely content."

"Welcome to life's rich and diverse path, bro."

Phillip winced as Sasha narrowly missed a neighbor's car backing out of his drive.

"Watch out," Phillip shouted.

Glenda didn't bat an eyelid.

"You can't wrap them in kid gloves," said Glenda. "Try not to worry too much, you'll be amazed at their resilience and they learn from each disaster. He won't do that again."

"You're accustomed to their antics," said Phillip. "I haven't even earned my rookie badge."

They watched as the children boarded the bus and found a seat each.

Glenda and Phillip waved as the bus departed. The little ones were too busy chatting to notice.

"As from now," said Glenda as they headed back carrying the scooters, they can make their way back and forth to the bus without us. We are surplus to requirements."

"Except when they are hungry," said Phillip.

"Or sick," said Glenda. "And Spring term always kicks off with colds or tummy bugs. It's not all tantrums, cuddles, and giggles. I'll bring you over the appropriate medical supplies, so you're prepared."

"Thanks, sis."

After stashing Sasha's scooter, Phillip went back indoors.

"We're in here," said Amanda.

"I'll just tidy Sasha's room," he said.

"We've done that," said Salome.

Phillip joined them in his study and looked over their shoulders as they looked at the computer screen. Amanda reached out a hand and squeezed his arm.

"Any problems?" she said.

"Didn't even wave," said Phillip.

"Kids love kids but don't worry," said Amanda. "Sasha is bound to make up for it this evening. After his first day, he'll be exhausted and will want lots of hugs. Now, look at this."

"Is that the result of the online appeal for restoration funds?" said Phillip.

"It is," said Salome squeezing his other arm. "And the money is still piling in. Sharing our exhibition with

Anne Pennington proved to be an amazing decision. Her interview has gone viral and we're benefitting from that. The fund has reached the level that together with my investment and the grant from the European Union, we can afford to complete the convent project properly in one bite rather than spread it over several years. My dream of a Flamenco University with affordable accommodation can now go ahead. And it's all down to you two. I don't know how to thank you."

"An invite to the inauguration is more than enough, providing we have the media exclusive," said Phillip.

"Done," said Salome.

"How was Prado?" said Phillip.

Both girls swung around on their chairs and faced him with excited gleams in their eyes.

"They've caught Marquez," said Salome.

"The exhibition flushed him out," said Amanda.

"Awesome," said Phillip. "Has he revealed anything?"

"No," said Amanda. "Nothing."

"Have they found his home?" said Phillip.

"No, but his car tires were covered in red mud. Ana is trying to locate where it comes from."

21

With the assistance of Spain's Society for Soil Science, Ana Galvez had narrowed the red mud on the tires of Marquez's vehicle down to the olive groves to the south of the renaissance town of Úbeda. It's in the province of Jaén, the northernmost region of Andalucía bordering on the autonomous community of Castilla-La Mancha and divided from it by the Despeñaperros mountain range. The soil contained a unique blend of iron and nutrients which along with the vast experience of the growers and oil mills produced some of Spain's finest olive oils.

Ana sent an email to all police stations and accommodation agencies in the area with a photo of Marquez, his car, and driver's license. Recent laws concerning rental properties had prohibited unregistered properties from being let out. But this was a vast, practically uninhabited area with few buildings where the locals knew everybody and each other's business. All Ana had to do was wait.

The location was discovered remarkably quickly.

It was bad news.

Late on the evening of the fifth, gas had exploded

in a remote cottage to the south of Úbeda. The owner, whose farmhouse was less than six hundred meters away, had heard the noise and called the fire service before rushing there with his tractor towing a portable water tank used for irrigation. The pathetic spray hadn't done much but had at least prevented the blaze from taking hold before the fire truck arrived and extinguished the flames. When the building had cooled down, and the Guardia started asking questions, the farmer conceded that the tenant was an elderly man called Rodriguez Sanchez Sanchez, who drove a dark blue Seat Ibiza.

From Málaga, it took Ana and Prado nearly three hours to reach the Guardia barracks in Úbeda including a stop for an early lunch just before Granada. Prado treated himself to the local specialty of fried eggs with Jamon Serrano sprinkled with crispy garlic. Ana had fruit and yogurt.

The traffic was light and on both sides of the road, olive groves stretched as far as the eye could see.

The barracks in Úbeda doubled as a civil guards' academy located in an old stone building on the edge of the historic town. They transferred to a Landrover and were driven by the sartorial and articulate Sargento Gonzalo some twenty kilometers southeast, deep into the olive groves. The final six were along a red mud track.

"It's a hell of a place to live," said Gonzalo. "It's over eight hundred meters above sea level here and winter snow in February can be deadly, let alone blocking you in for days at a time. There's no internet or phone signal and the electricity supply is renowned for regular failures."

"Sounds the perfect place to escape to," said Prado.

"Here it is," said Gonzalo pulling up outside a small single-storey white painted cottage with a terracotta roof. The outer walls were stained badly with black smoke around the window and door frames but otherwise, the building appeared intact.

The cottage had been taped off and a sign taped to the terrace column said, 'Crime Scene, Do Not Enter'. Another announced, 'Dangerous Building'.

"Is it safe to enter?" said Ana.

"Yes," said Gonzalo. "The signs are just to keep the curious away not that there are many of those out here at this time of year, but I recommend a face mask. "The smell of smoke was overpowering when I was here last night."

Gonzalo parked on the hard standing outside the covered front terrace. They climbed out, masked up, slipped on plastic gloves, and squeezed through the semi scorched, half-open front door.

The stone floor was soaking and the sound of dripping water from the oak beams supporting the roof was incessant. The smell of acrid smoke penetrated their masks, but it was breathable. Inside were three rooms and a small bathroom. The front door led directly into a living room which was connected to a kitchenette by a breakfast bar. The bedroom door to the left was ajar and had been badly singed. Prado pushed it open and found the interior, smoke damaged but intact.

"What caused the gas to explode?" said Prado turning back to Gonzalo.

"The propane cylinder was empty," said Gonzalo. "Our forensics team concluded that one of the burners on the hob had been left open, slowly filling the whole place with propane. The remains of a toaster with its workings jammed in the on position was connected to a timer programmed to turn on at midnight. In the toaster was a ball of paper that eventually ignited when the toaster was hot enough. The flame ignited the gas. However, this is a drafty old building and the gas build-up had dissipated marginally, so while this looks bad not all the contents were destroyed."

"Are they here?"

"Those of any use are at our lab. The remainder are still here."

"May we look around?" said Ana.

"Of course," said Gonzalo. "I'll leave you to it. The smoke irritates my asthma."

The living room yielded a melted desktop computer screen, tower, and an inkjet printer. Their twisted black plastic and metal lumps stood on the remains of what was a low wooden shelf adjoining the fireplace. The paper stacked in the printer feed had caught fire and the whole area had burned including transformers and their cables, a large screen TV, a DVD player, and a CD music stack. The kitchen and bathroom contained nothing of interest.

"I would have thought he had a laptop or something to take with him to an Internet café," said Prado. "He booked his exhibition ticket online, but I can't see any sign of one."

"He had one," said Ana holding up a melted transformer and USB cable. "There are three of these. One for the printer, another for the tower, this third must be for a laptop."

"Let's try the bedroom," said Prado.

Ana went to the far side of the bed, checked the bedside drawers then looked underneath.

"He has some fine clothes," said Prado flicking

through the wardrobe. "Armani particularly, but they must be over twenty years old by the state of them."

Prado reclosed the wardrobe doors and on tiptoe stretched his arm and waved it around in the well on top. His hand connected with something solid. He fumbled around, found the handle to a suitcase, and grabbed it. It was heavy but slid easily to the edge of the well. He braced himself, grabbed the handles on each end of the case, and lifted it down. He staggered over to the bed and placed it on the blankets. Small puffs of black dust wafted around then settled. Prado rechecked the wardrobe top but there was nothing.

"It's locked," said Ana fiddling with the case.

"I'll fetch something," said Prado heading off to the kitchen. He returned with a sturdy knife. The case soon yielded to his manipulations and he opened the lid to reveal stacks of DVDs, photo albums, and files. He reached inside.

"Don't touch a thing, Inspector," said Ana closing the lid on his arms. "I can learn so much just from prints and DNA analysis but not with your sticky mitts all over them. You should know better."

Prado withdrew his hands and Ana closed the case.

"Sorry," said Prado. "You're right of course. Did you find anything?"

"Just dirty laundry."

"Then let's go and see what the Úbeda forensics team has for us."

Prado and Ana carried one end of the case each and they went out to rejoin Gonzalo. He was leaning against the Landrover smoking a small cigar.

"Your guys missed this," said Prado.

"Where was it?" said Gonzalo stubbing out the cigar.

"On top of the bedroom wardrobe."

"We better take it to the lab," said Gonzalo, unfazed.

They loaded the case into the back, climbed in, and drove back to Úbeda.

Back in the Cuartel, Gonzalo left them to struggle with the case while he escorted them up to the forensics lab. He smiled warmly as he held the doors open for them, then introduced Dr. Nani Duran, an attractive woman in her late thirties and an old acquaintance of Ana. They placed the case on one worktop and went to see what Nani was analyzing on the other.

He and Ana studied the exhibits laid out tidily and labeled.

"What have you discovered so far?" said Prado.

"The key item is this Picasso sketch," said Nani. "I haven't had time to identify it yet, but it looks like one of his muses. The frame is smoke damaged, but it will be fine after cleaning. Another framed picture is a collage of betting slips from a website called Dabblers, it looks like winnings from gambling on bullfights. There is also a poster of a torero. His cape was sweeping stylishly over the back of a bloodied bull."

"That is Juan Romero," said Prado. "Juan's wife is my wife Inma's elder sister. This poster was drawn from a photo of him appearing at La Goyesca festival in Ronda."

Nani picked up a small bronze figurine of a man in a robe walking with a crop. "This is Saint Christopher," she said.

"What about this?" said Prado picking up a scorched but intact photo frame.

"I haven't touched that yet," said Nani.

"Have you a wipe?" said Prado.

Nani extracted one from a box at the back of the table and gave it to him.

Prado wiped the glass carefully.

The wooden frame was singed, and the glass was smoke damaged. He picked up the wipe and rubbed the glass to reveal a photo of four teenagers.

"That is Crown," said Prado pointing at the left-hand boy. "These two are O'Reilly and Augustin. It follows that this fourth person is probably our missing victim. Prado placed the frame on the table and photographed it with his phone.

"At last, we know what he used to look like," said Prado. "What is that?" He added pointing at a congealed lump.

"It's an old Apple laptop fitted with a DVD player," said Nani. "The casing has melted slightly then solidified.

"Any chance of accessing the hard drive?" he said.

"Not here," said Nani. "What about you Ana?"

Ana picked up the computer and tried to open it, but it proved impossible. She turned it over and found the base reasonably intact. "Maybe, but I can't promise anything," she said. "Have you made sense of anything else?"

"Nothing," said Nani. "But you're familiar with the case. Why not take all this lot with you. You'll stand a better chance of putting them in context."

"That's kind," said Prado. "Thanks, Nani. We'll return them in due course."

"Not necessary," said Nani. "It will only stink out our small archives. Just send me a copy of your report and keep me posted on your progress with the investigation."

22

In Prado's absence, Marquez had been collected from prison and taken back to the comisaría for more questioning. He'd been fingerprinted, photographed, and had a DNA test. El jefe had grilled him on his own, followed by two other detectives but by the end of the afternoon, he'd revealed nothing and was taken back to Alhaurin.

Marquez had been given leave to eat all his meals in his cell. At seven that evening a covered plate was served on a tray with a glass of water. He settled down to his tiny table, lifted the plate cover to reveal an overcooked pork cutlet, green beans, and boiled potatoes drizzled with congealed sauce. There was a yogurt to follow. He tucked in with gusto.

He hadn't had to lift a finger. And he had three of these every day.

Captivity was starting to feel good.

He'd made the right decision to give himself up.

He brushed his teeth, undressed, climbed into bed, and read a few more pages of his book delivered earlier by a trustee from the prison library.

At ten, the lights were turned out. Five minutes

later, he was fast asleep.

It was three o'clock in the morning when a noise woke him. He opened his eyes, but it was pitch black. He couldn't see a thing. At first, it didn't register in his brain fog but then he recognized what the sound was. The computer-controlled lock of his cell had clicked open.

A bright light shone into his eyes and blinded him.

He sat up but was immediately grabbed by gloved hands and a gag stuffed in his mouth.

"Don't move," said a male voice in Spanish.

"Or make any noise," said a female voice.

He didn't react or struggle as he was pushed gently back down into a horizontal position.

Marquez knew who they were and resigned himself to his fate. They couldn't risk being away from their cells for too long or bruising him. Their bribes would have only purchased limited cooperation and the lights and security systems would only be off for a brief period. He suspected that it wouldn't take long or hurt too much.

"I would relish cutting off your balls, you depraved bastard," said the male.

"I'd prefer to spit roast you," said the female. "And twist the spike violently as it's hammered through your disgusting intestines, lungs, and up into your brain."

"We will ask you one question," said the man. "Acknowledge you understand by nodding your head twice."

Marquez nodded, his eyes bulging with fear.

"I will take out the gag," said the woman. "But if you try to shout, it will be rammed back in again immediately. Understand?"

Marquez nodded again.

"The film you sent to Sonia. Where is the original?"

Marquez nodded. The woman removed the gag but held it half in, half out of his mouth.

"Yesterday," gasped Marquez. "Before I left my house, I set a massive firebomb. If I didn't return in time to turn off the timer, it would destroy everything."

"And that was the only copy?" said the woman.

Marquez nodded.

"Where do you live?" said the man. "Our colleague will check it out."

"I rent a cottage in the olive groves south of Úbeda."

"Where is the rest of the money?" said the man.

A look of calm settled on the face of Marquez. He stared at each of them.

"Fuck off,"

The gag was stuffed back into his mouth. Strong hands placed the handle of a table knife into his right hand, gripped it, and guided the blade over to his left wrist.

Marquez resisted with all his strength. But he couldn't prevent the man from sawing the serrated blade through his skin, deep into the wrist joint slashing through his veins, arteries, tendons, and nerves.

Marquez screamed into the gag and tried to turn over, but he was pinned to the bed by the female. His blood spurted onto the bedding and within minutes he felt himself losing consciousness. He stopped struggling and passed out.

23

Prado was dreaming that Málaga Football Club was beating Real Madrid at the Rosaleda stadium when he was dragged from this unlikely fantasy by his ring tone. He stretched out an arm and saw that the duty officer at the comisaría was calling. "This better be good," he said.

"Sorry, Sir, it's Campos. Marquez was found dead in his cell just after six this morning."

"Natural causes?"

"No, he slashed his wrist, Sir, and bled out."

"Has the chief warden been informed?"

"It was he who alerted us, Sir."

"Right, I'll call him."

Prado sat up and draped his legs over the side of the bed while he flicked through his contacts. He found his old friend Calvo's number and pressed dial.

"Hola, Leon. I wasn't sure whether to call you directly."

"No worry, you did the right thing. Tell me what happened."

"The kitchen porter was delivering his breakfast tray and found him. There was a knife in his right hand,

and he'd slit his left wrist deeply. There was blood everywhere."

"Right, please leave him where he is and lock the cell until my forensics officer arrives. I'll be up as soon as I can. Meanwhile, I want Crown, O'Reilly, and Sonia to be held in their cells until forensics have checked their clothing and hands."

"Crown is in the prison hospital," said Calvo.

"Why?"

"Not sure but it could be HIV. They're doing tests."

"I want him checked just the same. He's a devious bastard."

"What about their breakfast?"

"Fuck, their breakfast. Keep them locked up. Is there anything else you can tell me?"

"The security system failed at three am this morning then turned itself back on fourteen minutes later. At the same time, the night guards were suffering from food poisoning so were away from their posts. I've summoned the technician. Hopefully, he can identify what happened."

"Good, see you later."

"Ana," said Prado after calling his forensics colleague. "Where are you?"

"I've just left my apartment. Why?"

"Marquez is dead. It looks like suicide but for the fact that the alarm system was turned off for fourteen minutes around three am, and the night guards were away from their posts suffering from food poisoning. Can you go straight up to the prison?"

"Sure. What about you?"

"I'll be there as fast as I can."

By the time Prado arrived at the prison an hour later, Ana had completed her testing and was tapping out her report on her tablet in the prison visitor canteen.

"Do I need to see the body?" said Prado as he took a seat and sipped his plastic cup of coffee that he'd grabbed when passing a vending machine. He grimaced. It was disgusting but he needed the liquid.

"There's nothing to see but a fat corpse and a bed covered in blood. It looks like suicide," said Ana. "However, you should take a look. You might spot something I missed."

"What did he use to cut himself?"

"A serrated table knife. His bloody fingerprints were on the handle."

"I thought remand prisoners were only allowed plastic utensils."

"They are usually, but Marquez's food was delivered from the visitor canteen. They use metal."

"So, someone screwed up."

"I doubt it."

"A professional disposal job, then. Where were his victims?"

"Crown was in the prison hospital too weak to move without assistance."

"Are you sure his illness is genuine?"

"His body is wasting away. We can safely rule him out."

"Does he still know what's going on?"

"His mind is fine, so more than likely."

"How about O'Reilly and Augustin?"

"They were spotless but looked tired."

"Tell me about the body?" said Prado.

"In my experience, wrist cutters tend to slice both wrists not too deeply, then sit in a bath with a bottle of brandy, where it will usually take some half an hour to bleed out. Marquez had no access to such luxuries. He sawed violently at his left wrist and made an extremely deep cut, probably hoping to bleed out quickly without the blood clotting. He wouldn't have lasted more than ten to fifteen minutes."

"If it was murder, how did they avoid prison security? They have one of the best systems in the country here."

"The system technician hasn't arrived yet so I can't tell you anything about why it failed at precisely three am."

"Were the guards poisoned?"

"Probably, they were both fine when they arrived at work about ten pm."

"How many guards were on the night shift?"

"Three. One on indoor patrol, another monitoring the internal cameras, the other on the front gate watching the external security, which remained active. Both the inside guys were suffering. The one on patrol wasn't so severely affected, but at the time the lights went out, he was in the lavatory. When he felt well enough, he used his torch to get back to the empty security office. Just as he sat down at the console, the system turned itself back on."

"They were hacked," said Prado.

"This was no ordinary hacker," said Ana.

"Probably the fourth victim," said Prado. "It seems that we've been hoodwinked. We've been recording everything the other three say in their cells and restrooms for months but heard nothing out of sorts. Somehow, they found a way to communicate secretly with each other and with the outside. Calvo needs to conduct a thorough search of every single nook and cranny. Their phones must be stashed somewhere and could lead us to their outside contacts."

"What should we do about Marquez?"

"Leave it as suicide. Nobody will be surprised, and it makes the paperwork easier."

Ana closed her tablet. Put on her coat from the back of the chair and headed off to her Lab.

Prado went up to the head warden's office.

Frederico Calvo was old school civil service. A tall, slender man in his mid-fifties, dressed in a grey suit, he'd run the rat-infested hole that was the old prison and taken charge of this modern temple of incarceration when it was completed during the 1990s.

They shook hands, sat down, and faced each other over the warden's desk.

"Nice to see you looking so sprightly," said Calvo. "What did forensics conclude?"

"Suicide," said Prado.

"And you're happy with that?"

"It tidies up a messy situation."

"I haven't read the Marquez file. What were his crimes?"

"Marquez was an abusive headmaster. Crown, O'Reilly, and Augustin were three of his victims. They've been after him for over thirty years."

"Then why not investigate, prove they killed him, and charge them?"

"At what cost?" said Prado. "And what would be the point? They are already behind bars and are unlikely to be leaving for the next forty years. Anyway, there is no evidence to prove it. They made sure of it."

"How do you know for certain it was them?"

"I don't but they had motivation and means. Now he's dead, they can live in peace. In jail but happy that their form of justice has been done."

"You think they deliberately set out to be in prison to await his arrival?"

"It's too much of a coincidence to be anything else."

"Amazing," said Calvo shaking his head. "To deliberately give up your freedom to kill your arch enemy."

"It's not the first time and won't be the last, but I'm not here to debate their twisted minds. What concerns me more is that there was some superb planning, bribing, and bullying involved in setting this up. For that, they must have good communications both internally and externally. Your prison is about as secure as water in a colander."

"We search orifices, persons, and cells regularly for phones," said Calvo. "But without much success."

"They must have them somewhere. Or perhaps someone is hiding them on their behalf. Could you organize the most comprehensive search ever and submit all phones found to my forensics team? They'll check every number dialed to see where that leads us."

"They'll be expecting that," said Calvo. "Everything will be stashed. It's best to leave it for a few days then pounce when they think we've forgotten about it."

"Good idea. Did you learn any more about what happened to the security system?"

"No. I'm still waiting on the technician, but the electrical engineers have been all over the installations. There were no faults at their end, or here."

"We think you were hacked by experts. Hopefully, the technician can confirm that. Any theories on how the two men were poisoned?"

"Their shift starts at ten p.m. The first thing they do is have supper in the staff canteen."

"Are the kitchen workers still there at that hour?"

"No, it's made earlier and kept warm. They help themselves and wash up after."

"So, the food could have been tampered with?"

"It's possible but this is a prison. Nobody can just pop in, do a quick poison, and leave. It had to have been a member of the kitchen staff."

"Are they employees, or outside caterers?"

"Caterers. Their workers chop and change all the time, but each has to apply for a pass. We check their backgrounds and fingerprints rigorously before access is authorized and even then, they are restricted to kitchens and dining areas."

"Then it should be relatively simple to check if any have had a sudden improvement in their finances. You only need to bother with those on the last shift. How many would there be?"

"I'm not sure, but I'll make some inquiries."

"My electronic surveillance expert is finishing another job today. Tomorrow, I want her here to monitor all communications activity in and around the prison area. She'll be able to pinpoint where any calls are being made and devices being stored. While she is here, would you mind if she also checks out your security system? If it was hacked into, she may find some traces of that."

"Certainly, but she'll have to work around our routine."

"I'm sure she won't mind. I'm also suspicious about Crown being in the hospital."

"The doctors say that he is genuinely ill."

"Possible HIV, I understand?"

"They are waiting for more tests."

"Treatment is most effective these days. As soon as

he is on medication, you should see substantial improvements." Calvo nodded. "Meanwhile, may I suggest that you increase security checks on the hospital."

"You suspect an escape attempt?"

"Marquez is dead. They no longer have a reason for being here. This is a clever, well-financed and determined mob. They've already found holes in your security and will continue to look for more. Prison hospitals are always a weak link. Do you have a camera watching its entrance?"

"Regretfully, I have no budget."

"Then I'll ask my surveillance lady to install one on the internal lobby and connect it to your monitoring system."

"Excellent, anything else?"

"Take me to the cell, I want to see the body."

Prado was impressed by the security as doors opened automatically to let them through as they walked to the remand wing. "It's all done by the officer in the control room," said Calvo.

"All fine, until there is no power," said Prado.

"There is a backup generator," said Calvo as they walked into the remand wing. "It should have kicked in automatically within seconds but failed to do so."

"Is that controlled by the system too?"

"Yes."

"Then there is your weakness. Backup power should be separate from the main computer. Once hackers are in your system, they control everything. I recommend that you have it modified as soon as possible."

"I can't see the Government approving the budget," said Calvo.

They paused outside cell number fourteen.

The door slid open and Prado walked in.

Marquez seemed at peace compared with his worried expression at their last interview. I'll have to tell his sister. Thought Prado as he surveyed the scene. After five minutes of intense study, he could see no reason to suspect that his death was anything other than suicide.

He went out and joined a white-faced Calvo in the corridor.

"Sorry," said Calvo. "Blood and I are not the best of bedfellows."

"Me neither," said Prado. "Sadly, I've seen too much of it. Listen, I don't want our trio to notice any change to their daily routine. Make sure your wardens spread the word about Marquez's death. I want all prisoners convinced it was suicide. Hopefully, it will lull them into making a mistake."

They shook hands and Prado left for the comisaría.

24

At supper in the male prison canteen that evening, O'Reilly nodded to a fellow prisoner on the next table. He winked to another on the other side of the canteen. Immediately, another prisoner stole the bread roll from his neighbor's plate. A fight started. The wardens rushed over to break it up.

O'Reilly took out his phone and bending down below the table swiped Sonia's number.

"Where are you?" said O'Reilly.

"My cell door should open any second, then we can head for the women's canteen."

"Did you receive the delivery via the afternoon drinks cart?"

"Our kitchen guy did an amazing job. One can of lemonade filled with petrol, a coke with engine oil, matches, and rubber strips in a packet of biscuits. I'll hang back pretending toilet use while everyone leaves for supper."

"Where will you set the fire? It shouldn't be in your cell."

"I know. There's a real bitch three doors down who

is always trying to provoke me into a fight. She has photos and posters on her wall, which should blaze beautifully. Hers is the top bunk so the flames should also ignite the ceiling paint."

"Can you open her window?"

"No problem."

"Don't forget to jam the door open, the breeze will suck the smoke outwards. Do you have the nurse's uniform?"

"I'm wearing it already under my prison clothing. It's bulky and hot."

"Does Malcolm have his prison overall?"

"He should be wearing it underneath his pajamas by now."

"OK. I'll see you by the women's entrance as soon as the fire truck parks up, and the hosing starts, I'll text if there's any change. It will be too noisy to talk."

"There's the cell door now," said Sonia. "I'll be lighting up in around three minutes. Good luck."

"You, too." O'Reilly swiped end call, pocketed his phone, sat up, and tucked into his tray of food.

Seven minutes later, the fire alarm sounded. It wasn't the usual test that took place on Monday mornings, but nobody was sure if it was an extra practice, the real thing, or where it was. One warden went off to inquire, while the remainder swung into their well-rehearsed procedures. The emergency exits were opened up which led to the exercise yards. Complaining prisoners were directed to their respective marshaling posts in the exercise enclosures.

"False alarm," shouted some as they ran out into the chilly night air.

"I'm taking my supper with me," said others.

Many spilled their food on the floor in the rush to

get out.

The floodlights were illuminated, and armed guards took their positions in the solitary observation tower that overlooked the prison grounds. Within seconds, thick black smoke was billowing from a window in the ladies' wing. It overwhelmed their marshaling area, so the women were admitted into the adjacent male enclosure. The hospital was part of the ladies' wing so that was also evacuated. Malcolm Crown and one other patient were wheeled out to join the other prisoners. Their nurse hovering between them. A prisoner pushing each bed.

The official capacity for the prison is eight hundred and thirty-seven but it had been planned to accommodate the native population. The substantial quantity of unforeseen criminals among the millions of tourists and foreign residents had completely screwed up the anticipated numbers. Nearly two thousand prisoners of mixed nationalities were packed into the inadequate yard. Cussing in a variety of languages flew back and forth. Squeals of laughter could be heard tempered by cries of anguish as someone tripped and fell under the crush of bodies. With that and the screeching alarm, communication was impossible.

Seconds later, a mentally disturbed prisoner serving life for the killing of three young girls couldn't resist the temptations of women walking by right in front of him, he attacked. He was immediately set on by several other women and some of the male prisoners dived in to separate them.

The under-resourced wardens all stopped what they were doing and barged their way through the crowd waving their batons screaming at them all to stop.

More male prisoners jumped on the wardens.

The nurse was bundled away from her bedridden charges. Another nurse replaced her.

Chaos ensued.

A police helicopter arrived flicking its spotlight back and forth over the pandemonium commanding over its loudspeaker that every prisoner should stand and remain still. Meanwhile, the smoke worsened.

Many of the prisoners carried on having fun despite having no jackets. Many stood still and shivered.

A single fire engine arrived at the external main gate which opened slowly to admit it into the staff area. It stopped outside the inner gate which led to the male exercise yard. There was only one route to the women's wing and that was via the men's enclosure.

The prisoners turned to see the inner main gates open. With sirens blasting and lights flashing, two wardens escorted it into the crowd clearing a path through the mass of bodies with their batons.

"Come on," screamed a Spanish voice. "The gates are open, let's get out of here." Hundreds swarmed around the truck heading for the metal gates but armed guards pointing their weapons blocked any escape. The prisoners resigned themselves to their fate, turned, and watched the slow progress of the truck as it crawled into the ladies' yard and parked outside the furiously smoking window.

Four uniformed fire officers jumped out, unraveled their hoses, connected them to the hydrants, and aimed their powerful jets of water into the window where the smoke was originating. It only took a few seconds to extinguish whatever was causing the blaze.

Two fire officers donned breathing equipment and entered the ladies' wing. One went to turn off the sprinklers and reset the alarm at the main panel. The other to check the scene of the fire and to make sure there were no secondary flare-ups.

The wardens blocked the doorway to prevent the prisoners from entering until the firemen gave the all-clear. Hundreds of prisoners streamed toward the wardens demanding to be let into the female entrance even though the majority were male.

One prisoner supported another as he limped toward the truck. A nurse sat him down on the fire engine cab doorstep so that the vehicle was between them and the women's wing entrance. Sonia and O'Reilly heaved Crown into the back of the cab, laid him on the floor, covered him with a blanket then struggled into fireman's uniforms left for them on the seat. They added the bulky yellow helmets and goggles, strapped up their chin guards, and climbed out to help their colleagues recoil the hoses. The still swirling smoke blurring their activities.

The fire alarm stopped.

The smoke continued to swirl but dispersed as the light breeze cleared it away. An eerie silence prevailed momentarily quickly replaced by a low murmuring as the prisoners asked of each other and the wardens when they could return to the warmth of their cells.

Three minutes later, the two firemen emerged from the ladies' wing, spoke briefly with the wardens, and headed for the truck. There was a massive cheer when the wardens waved the prisoners back in through their respective entrances.

Some of the men tried to edge inside with the women but the wardens were ready for them. A lighthearted tap on the arm with a baton soon deterred them. The men were directed back to their canteen, the women to theirs where they would be counted. Long queues to each restroom soon formed. It would take ages to seat everyone so the count could begin.

When everyone was inside, the outer doors were locked, and the wardens began an inspection of the ladies' wing. Everything was soaked from the sprinklers and the smell of rubbery smoke was so overpowering, nobody would be sleeping there that night. Calvo was summoned from his home nearby. His approval was needed to convert the canteen into a temporary dormitory for the ladies.

Outside, the firemen packed away their equipment, climbed into the cab, removed their helmets and goggles, hung them on the hooks behind and above the seat, then departed.

Just as the fire truck was leaving the outer main gate, a large white SUV arrived. An arm stretched out the window and flagged them down.

The driver opened the truck window. "My name is Calvo," said the driver of the SUV. "I'm the chief warden. What was the problem?"

"It was nothing to worry about, governor," said their driver in perfect Spanish, through the open window. "The ladies took objection to some bedding. It didn't take much to extinguish everything, and the sprinklers prevented any spread, but you have a scorched mess and severe smoke damage to have fun with. Sorry, but you have one cell less in the ladies' wing."

"Did you check for secondaries and reset the alarm?"

"Of course," said their driver laughing. "Your staff were most insistent that we did?"

"You guys from, Alhaurin station?"

"Going back there, now," said the driver.

"Not seen your face before?"

"Newly arrived from Estepona."

"OK. Thanks for your prompt assistance. Hopefully, we won't be seeing you again soon."

"We hope so too, but you have a spirited lot up there. They'll be up to mischief before long."

"Won't they?" said the Calvo grinning. "As long as they don't escape. The last thing Málaga needs is two thousand prisoners on the loose."

"Might spice things up a bit," said their driver.

"Especially if they mix with the soccer fans," said Calvo closing his window and driving into the prison.

"Shit," said Sonia. "That was close."

Crown mumbled.

"What?" said Sonia bending over removing the blanket.

"Are we out?" he croaked.

"Yes," said Sonia stroking his forehead.

Crown sighed and slumped back.

"Everybody's phones turned off?" said the driver.

"We did that before you arrived," said O'Reilly. "How long before the anesthetic wears off the real firemen?"

"About thirty minutes," said the driver checking the clock in front of him. "We'll be far away by then."

"Won't the firemen be able to describe you?" said Sonia.

"They didn't know what hit them," said the driver. "All six of them were in the recreation room, sleeping, or playing on their phones. We squirted nitrous oxide into the air conditioning until they were unconscious then injected them with Propofol."

"Did you bring everything with you?" said O'Reilly.

"Have a little faith," said the driver turning left onto

the main road. "Nothing was left behind, and nothing can go wrong."

"Perhaps the escape alarm has sounded already," said Sonia.

"Impossible," said O'Reilly. "The fastest ever was twenty minutes. With the chaos we arranged, they won't have had time to count everyone."

"Then we're clear," said the driver.

Three minutes later, they turned onto a country track that took them straight through the middle of abandoned scrubland. Within seconds, they stopped outside a ruined barn. Untended pine trees and rambling oleander bushes lined the edge of the rutted access area in front of it. Hanging above the massive rusty metal barn doors was an illegible sign, half hanging from the wall. It squeaked as the breeze moved it back and forth. From the outside, they could see nothing unusual in the headlights except crumbling stone walls and that half the corrugated iron roof was missing. Three of the firemen climbed out to wrestle open the entrance, each door requiring all three of them to lift and push. When the space was wide enough to accommodate the large truck, the driver squeezed it through into a spacious recently swept interior that had been emptied of junk and weeds. They parked by two white Mercedes Viana vans with tinted windows and a Taxi sign on each roof. A small plain white Renault was parked on the far side of the taxis.

The driver turned off the engine but left the sidelights on, so they had some vision. They scrambled out and quickly hugged each other.

A blond woman with similar looks to Sonia scrambled out of one of the taxi's and stood to the rear of the vehicle saying nothing. Sonia went over and looked at her. They were the same height and build, their hair was practically identical, but the eyes and faces were different. She was dressed in a thick sailor's jacket, T-shirt, jeans, and sports shoes. Sonia nodded her approval, climbed back into the firetruck, and helped Crown out.

"Good to see you all again," said the driver in unaccented English. His face was older but there was no mistaking his blue eyes and distinctive black hair, but his features were disguised by an impressive full beard and large, black-framed spectacles.

He was the fourth victim, Paul Bosque.

"We need to change quickly and be on our way," said Paul removing the glasses and peeling off the beard.

Sonia helped Crown out of the fire engine and then undressed him. In his boxer shorts, he looked weak and pathetic leaning against the truck door, struggling for breath.

"Place your helmets, uniforms, and prison gear in the open suitcases in the trunk of the left-hand taxi," said Paul adding the beard and glasses and his fireman's jacket to one of the four cases. "Then put your phones in the metal bucket on the floor. There's a pile of clothing for each of you laid out on the back seats. Our four Moroccan helpers will take one taxi to Algeciras, abandon it there, and return to Tangiers on the same private yacht they arrived on two days ago. They'll drop the cases overboard mid channel. We will take the remaining taxi."

"How long did it take to set this barn up?" said O'Reilly struggling out of his pants.

"We did it all last night," said Paul undoing his fireman's belt.

"I assume the van was stolen and the taxis have been borrowed from friends," said Sonia removing her jacket.

"You're right about the van but they're not real taxis," said Paul leering at Sonia's semi-naked form. Sonia ignored him.

"We stole all three from separate car parks in the city yesterday using the latest electronic key cloning technology. As the owners departed and their key cards closed the doors, we recorded it then used the signal to open it when they had left the car park. We had to try several before we had ones with the parking tickets left inside. The signs, number plates, Public Service stickers, and taxi licenses are copies matching actual cabs."

The Moroccans changed into similar clothing to the blond woman. Sonia dressed in blue jeans, red and white stripe football shirt, and a thick black jacket then helped Crown. The four of them were soon similarly attired.

"We look like football supporters," said Sonia.

"Precisely," said Paul as they slipped on a variety of light waterproof jackets and baseball hats from Almeria Football Club. "All we need now is a rattle."

"Did you disarm the GPS trackers?" said O'Reilly.

"On all four vehicles," said Paul.

"Then all that remains is to destroy the phones and we can go."

Paul took a gas can out of the taxi trunk, poured some into the bucket, and placed it on the stone floor away from anything combustible. He set light to the fuel and they all watched from a safe distance until the black smoke and flames had down. Paul checked the bucket. There was nothing recognizable, just a black glutinous mass of mainly plastic. Paul replaced the cap on the fuel can and placed it back in the trunk of their cab.

They all shook hands with the Moroccans. Climbed in their respective vehicles and reversed out onto the hard standing in front of the barn, the Moroccan men jumped and closed the barn door. They departed first and where the track met the country lane, turned right in the direction of the motorway.

Paul followed them but at the lane turned left.

All four remained silent as they wound their way around the hairpin bends toward the mountains.

They were out of prison.

But they still had a long way to go before their final destination.

25

The first port of call for Calvo's inspection of the fire damage was the hospital. Within ten minutes of his arrival, he had declared it usable and the nurse was able to return. She'd been forcibly separated from her patients during the chaos outside but saw no reason why they wouldn't be returned.

Within minutes, one of the patients had been delivered.

"The guy with Crown is on his way," said the prisoner who had been pushing him.

She checked him over, administered his medication and he settled down to sleep.

"How is Crown?" said the nurse.

"Fast asleep last time I saw him," said the prisoner on his way out the door. "And there is a huge queue waiting to see you. You need to prepare for an invasion of guys suffering from the smoke."

"Immediately the foyer door opened, and men piled in coughing and spluttering. She rushed around fitting the worst with oxygen masks, dispensing inhalers, and cough medication forgoing her usual diligence of writing down their names and prison numbers. Eventually, every bed and floor space were full of someone recuperating. She vaguely registered that Crown had been returned and seemed fast asleep although all she could see of him was a mop of dark hair.

The nurse had been forced to miss her usual break. She was hungry, thirsty, and desperate to use the restroom. She double-checked the worst patients and satisfied that no lives were in immediate danger slipped out. After a visit to the staff facilities, she sat at the tables by the vending machines with a sandwich and a cup of coffee.

When she returned to the hospital, it was empty. Oxygen masks and inhalers were scattered around the floor. Miraculous recoveries all round she thought or was something else afoot. She called security. They informed her that the prisoners had requested to be escorted back to their cells except for the one guy in the bed. She rushed out of her office and opened the curtains to check the first patient. He was still fast asleep but when she looked behind Crown's curtains, the bed was empty.

She called security again.

"Crown has gone," she said her voice trembling.

"So, the sick is walking now," said the guard.

"I'm not joking, you fool," said the nurse. "Crown is a seriously ill patient, who can hardly move. He was asleep in his bed not fifteen minutes ago and now he is gone. You have to inform Calvo."

Calvo sat in his office jotting down the totals as calls came in from each wing confirming the headcount. He'd just ended one call when there was a knock on his door and the security officer burst in.

"Don't bother me," said Calvo. "I'll lose count."

"It's Crown, Sir," said the officer. "He's disappeared from the hospital."

Calvo looked at the officer long and hard then dialed the women's canteen. "This is Calvo," he said when a female warden answered. "I want you to find Sonia Augustin and bring her to the phone immediately."

"It might take a while, Sir, it's chaos here," said the warden.

"I'll wait," said Calvo looking up at the security officer. "Go and check O'Reilly's cell, quick as you can." The officer scurried off leaving the door open.

"Sorry, boss," said the female warden into his ear some minutes later. "No sign of her anywhere and the count is one person is missing."

He hung up and the phone rang again.

It was the security officer.

"O'Reilly is not in his cell and the count is one short, Sir," he said.

Calvo hung up and paced around his office swearing to himself. Now he knew what the fire was all about and if his suspicions were correct, he'd talked to their helper as they drove away in the fire truck.

Calvo phoned Prado.

"I'm missing your three favorite prisoners," said Calvo when Prado answered.

"Shit," said Prado. "How?"

"A fire in the women's wing, probably set by Sonia Augustin set the motion in play," said Calvo. "I'm sure they were driven away in the fire truck. It was extremely well organized."

"Any camera footage?"

"No, the smoke blurred everything."

"The driver sounded like the guy in charge," said Prado. "Can you describe him?"

"Difficult, it was dark, he had a full beard and glasses."

"Age?"

"Forty, maybe more."

"I'm going to send you a photo?" said Prado thumbing through his gallery for the photo of the four teenagers. He tapped it and shared it with Calvo. "One of them could be of a younger version of the driver. Let me know what you think."

"OK."

"Did the fire truck seem genuine?"

"It was a truck from Alhaurin station. They looked the part, extinguished the fire, and reset the alarm just as pros would have done."

"You didn't check their IDs, or at least count how many were in the truck?"

"Leon, the prison was in danger of burning down. What do you prefer? We delay the fire engine by precious seconds while we check papers of what appeared to be bona fide fire officers or let two thousand prisoners, some extremely dangerous, loose on the streets of Málaga."

"Point taken."

"Photo received but I can't see any resemblance to the driver."

"Sorry, I'll have to put you on hold, there's an urgent call coming through."

Prado switched over to the incoming. It was the comisaría desk sergeant.

"We've just had a call from Alhaurin Fire station. All the staff is recovering from being gassed and someone has stolen their only fire engine. They would quite like it back."

"I don't think we should make that public information," said Prado. "They already think we're useless. Misplacing an emergency vehicle of that size would only confirm it. Inform all patrols and check traffic footage, it shouldn't take them long to track down something that large."

"Will do, Sir."

"Do they have CCTV at the fire station?"

"They do but it had been turned off," said the sergeant.

Prado switched back to Calvo.

"The officers at the Alhaurin fire station were gassed," said Prado. "They're recovering but missing their uniforms and truck. Did the driver sound foreign?"

"Spoke perfect Spanish. I had no suspicions he was anything else. Shit, I even joked with him. He was as cool as a cucumber."

"Had you seen him on previous callouts?"

"No, in fact, I commented that he was new. He said he had recently been transferred from Estepona."

"Was his accent Andaluz or Madrid?"

"Well educated, I would say. More newsreader than a fireman."

"What about the others?"

"There was a male officer in the front passenger seat and another in the nearside rear seat. It was too dark to see further inside and none of the others said anything."

"Great thanks, now excuse me, I have an emergency vehicle to recover and a manhunt to organize."

26

Prado went down to the command room and watched the small night shift scanning traffic cameras. An hour had passed since the truck had driven away from the prison. There had not been one single sighting.

"Are they fucking magicians?" said Prado. "Where the hell has it gone?"

"Perhaps they've stashed it near the prison and switched vehicles," said a young female officer turning to Prado with an expectant expression on her face.

Prado looked hard at her. She trembled, wishing that she hadn't said anything. But Prado was just thinking about her words.

"You're right," he said. "Well done, good suggestion. Then the cameras won't help us. We'll need a large-scale map of the area surrounding Alhaurin. To hide a truck of that size and an escape vehicle or two needs a large building rarely used."

"I'll fetch one from archives," said the girl jumping up, her enthusiasm returned.

"Don't bother," said Prado sitting down at a terminal. "Online will be more up to date." He opened up a digital map service, tapped in Alhaurin Prison, and switched to satellite view.

The three young officers stopped what they were doing and stood behind him as he zoomed in.

"Where's the nearest traffic camera?" said Prado.

"Only one on the A-404 Coín Road," said the girl pointing at the screen. "It's at this roundabout."

Prado sped through the traffic recordings for the last hour.

"Nothing," said Prado shaking his head. "They had to hide the fire engine as fast as possible, say no more than three to four minutes driving time. That's around two kilometers from the prison. Send all available patrols to the area and have them search every building, or ruin, large enough to hide a fire truck plus one or two escape vehicles. Call me when you find it."

Prado went back up to his floor, knocked on the boss's door and walked in.

El jefe was on the phone.

Prado had never seen the man with such a meek and humble expression. El jefe signaled Prado to sit and keep quiet as he listened to the speaker.

All he said was, "Yes, Sir. Of course, Sir." Then eventually replaced the phone and glared at Prado.

"That was the minister of prisons," said el jefe. "And before that the home office minister. Prior to that, the chief of police.

"I expect that they are all worried about their necks," said Prado not giving a damn.

"You're probably right, Leon," said el jefe. "But wounded politicians need scapegoats. We have precisely twenty-four hours to find the prisoners and return them to their cells. Otherwise, we will be taking their places. What progress?"

"There have been no sightings of the fire truck, Sir,"

said Prado. "It's likely they switched vehicles within minutes of departing the prison. Our patrols are limited. There's a football match between Málaga and Almeria tonight at the Rosaleda Stadium. Those officers available are searching every possible building within two kilometers of the prison large enough to accommodate a fire truck, but that will take a while. Meanwhile, all we can do is wait."

"We can't afford to sit on our fat butts while we eliminate this possibility," said el jefe. "We need to set up roadblocks and now."

"I disagree, Sir. The only time for roadblocks is within minutes of an escape. It's now an hour later, they could be a hundred kilometers in any direction of the compass. We would need to call out the army and all the Civil Guard for it to be effective, which would just raise questions among the public and cause unnecessary disruption and fear. Let alone the chaos when the football finishes."

El jefe glared at Prado, then nodded and sighed.

"Then we'll have to rely on intelligent policing. Can we at least check all vehicles seen leaving the area and track their destinations as far as we can?"

"Good idea, Sir," said Prado, accustomed to el jefe telling him to do what was already in progress. He tolerated it and let him claim the kudos because occasionally, he came up with a little gem.

"Any ideas on what type of vehicle they might be using?" said el jefe.

"Not yet. Thankfully, the evening traffic on the road to Coín will be light until the football ends. We're checking all the vehicles and so far, none cross-check with the stolen vehicle list."

"What if the thefts haven't been reported yet?"

"We'll contact all the owners captured on camera and have them confirm their movements at the time. Could you arrange border and transportation checks?"

"Of course, but before you rush off, let's think this through carefully," said el jefe. "This was a brilliantly executed operation that must have taken substantial planning. Men would need to be recruited and trained. They knew the proper fire drill. Where did they purchase the gas cylinder, hoses, and anesthetic? Where were the burner phones bought to communicate with the prisoners? They didn't walk to the fire station, so how did they travel there? Have they left another vehicle in the area? Was there another driver? Their escape transport had to be in place well beforehand, did they steal, hire, or buy it? They'll have filled the gas tank before hiding it, check gas station CCTV."

"I'll need more resources for that, Sir."

"Leave the football match to the hands of the stadium marshals and instruct all shifts and reserve officers to report immediately. No excuses for not attending. Remember, we only have twenty-four hours to find them. All of us are obligated to sweat buckets for every single minute. Keep me informed."

Prado returned to the command room and calmly issued his instructions.

He regarded the staff hanging on to every word then rush back to their respective tasks. There had been significant moments on previous cases but nothing as big as this. He couldn't fail to notice their renewed enthusiasm.

He watched them proudly.

27

Prado headed out of the comisaría. He took a seat at his regular café in Plaza de la Merced, nodded to the camarero, and waited for them to deliver his morning coffee and mollete. He had been up all night, yet adrenalin pulsed through his tired body and his mind was as sharp as the razor that would normally, at this early hour, be scraping his face. He reflected on the night's activities and the progress being made.

Over thirty detectives and seventy officers were out in patrol cars swarming over every likely looking building within two kilometers of the prison. In the control room, they ticked off each item as it was searched. Borders, trains, bus stations, and motorway toll booths were being closely monitored. At Málaga airport, passenger manifests of scheduled and private departures within an hour of the escape were being poured over and images of every departing passenger were being scrutinized.

The first plane of the morning had taken off at six a.m. That and every subsequent scheduled and private departure was boarded, and passports rechecked before take-off. All flight plans for private planes and helicopters for the day were appraised in advance. At every port and marina, all ferries, and private boats about to sail were searched. Lists of all sailings within half an hour of the escape were being compiled.

Particular attention was paid to anyone in a wheelchair causing many anxious and stressful moments when rigorous examinations of their occupants went ahead without explanation.

Photos of three of the four were circulated to every ticket office, taxi, car hire establishments, all forms of accommodation, motorway service cafes, and gas stations.

Eduardo was working up an aged photo of the fourth boy. It would be broadcast on every TV station throughout Spain as soon as it was ready.

Every footage of road traffic had been analyzed twice by separate teams.

All stolen vehicle reports were being followed up immediately.

As Prado took his first sip of coffee, he racked his brain for anything they hadn't covered. The fire station had revealed no clues, gas equipment, or discarded syringes used to deliver the anesthetic and no unaccounted-for vehicle had been parked in the vicinity.

CCTV footage from gas stations had found nothing so they had widened the search parameters to those within thirty kilometers of the prison.

Just before lunch, an alert female officer in a patrol car spotted tire tracks and some footprints outside what should have been a ruined barn. The recent rain had softened the mud on the normally dry and rutted hard standing in front of the building. She peeped through a small hole in the rusty door and saw something big, bright, and red with what resembled a ladder on top. She tried moving the door, but it wouldn't budge so summoned her partner. Together, they couldn't move it and were worried about tainting what could be a crime scene. They both agreed. It had to be the fire engine. They returned to the car, called it in, and waited for all hell to let loose.

Prado was in the control room when the message came. He had to see it and decided to drive out there by himself and meet the forensics team on site.

***

Ana Galvez was bending over the footprints peering at them through her magnifying glass when Prado approached the still closed barn door.

"Conclusions?" said Prado joining her.

"I count three men," said Ana. "All wearing the same pattern trainers opening and closing both doors several times. There is one large set of tire tracks, probably the fire truck, going in. There are two sets of medium tracks going in once and leaving once. There is one small track going in and out several times."

"Are we ready to go inside?" said Prado.

"Yes, I've photographed everything from a variety of angles and measured the depths of treads. I should take plaster casts, but I imagine that you don't want to wait any longer to go inside."

"Is there another entrance?"

"No."

"Is there another way to open the doors without disturbing this lot?"

"No, brute force is the only way."

Prado summoned up the two officers that had found the barn and together they heaved both doors fully open.

They stood on the threshold and looked about.

"Initial thoughts?" said Prado.

"Two vehicles were parked in the space between the truck and the van," said Ana.

"And by the width of the axles, they were larger than the van," said Prado.

"I can't see any footprints," said Ana.

"You would have thought that an old barn would be full of junk, and the floor overgrown with weeds and fallen bits of roof," said Prado.

"It seems to have been cleared, then swept thoroughly," said Ana.

"Perhaps they left the cleaning equipment on the other side of the truck," said Prado.

"I'll go look, you stay here," said Ana.

Ana entered the barn, checked out the interiors of both vehicles then disappeared behind the fire truck into the depths of the building. She returned shaking her head.

"They've taken everything," she said. "Even the uniforms and helmets. I'll check for DNA and prints but I doubt we'll find anything."

"Can you identify the vehicles that were here by their axle widths?" said Prado.

"When I add tire dimensions, I can certainly narrow down the options but from the length of the vehicles my instincts are pointing to identical large people carriers with a sizeable trunk."

"Taxis," said Prado swiping his phone with the control room number. "Have to be."

Prado paced up and down on the track as he waited

for the traffic footage to be revisited from just after the escape.

"There's one white Mercedes Viana," said the control room officer a few minutes later. "It headed west down the slip road at fourteen minutes after the escape. We're tracking it's route from camera to camera now."

"Tell everyone to drop what they are doing and concentrate on this," said Prado. "Do you have the registration number?"

"Yes, and there are officers on their way to the taxi admin center in El Palo as we speak," said the control person.

"Compare the number with the stolen vehicle list," said Prado.

"I'll call you back, Sir."

"Quick as you can," said Prado heading back to Ana and telling her the news. "Check the departing tire tracks of the people carriers on the entrance mud. They were probably the same model. Then we should go to where the track joins the main road. We might be able to establish if both vehicles went in the same direction."

Ana examined the tracks and photographed them.

They climbed into the forensics van. Ana drove them the three hundred meters to the main road and parked. They both prowled around looking at the ground. A huge modern tractor and empty trailer approached along the main road and tried to turn into the track. Prado held up his ID card and waved the middle-aged driver down. The tractor stopped and turned off his noisy engine. The driver removed his headphones and clambered out looking exasperated.

"Is this your land?" said Prado as he approached.

"No, but I'm the tenant farmer," said the man buttoning his jacket against the chilly wind. "Why can't I go down the track? I need to pick up fodder for the pigs."

"Police crime scene," said Prado pointing at the barn. "Would that belong to your farm?"

"It does but we haven't used it for years."

"How often do you check inside?"

"Once a year perhaps."

"When was the last time?"

"Five months past."

"When did you last drive down this track?"

"About a week ago."

"Did you notice anything unusual about the building?"

The man shook his head.

Another car stopped behind the tractor and tooted its horn.

"Wait until we're done, please," Prado said and returned to Ana.

The car behind the tractor continued blaring its horn. The farmer went and informed the driver what was going on. Its driver got out and stood by the farmer watching Prado and Ana. The two chatted.

"What do you think?" said Prado.

"The track has dried out so I can't see much but look at the left-hand verge here, you can just make out a tread mark in the softer mud. It matches the rear tire of the second people carrier to leave."

"Are you saying at least one van turned left here?"

"Just the one."

"So, the other turned right," said Prado as his phone rang. It was the control room.

"We've just had a call from the officers at the taxi

company. The registration plates of the taxi we are tracking were copies of an actual one," said the control room officer. "Also, we have a video of the white taxi passing through three motorway toll booths between ten fifty and eleven twenty last night. The details are too dark to identify the occupants, but wait, Inspector, there's a new message from the Guardia Civil in Algeciras. They've found the vehicle."

28

"Amanda and Salome were brilliant at the exhibition in Granada," said Prado when Phillip answered his phone.

"Your bait worked well," said Phillip, sitting in his study editing a video.

"Yes, but Marquez revealed nothing, and was murdered early yesterday morning in his cell."

"The other three killed him?"

"There's no evidence to prove that so we're putting it down as suicide but yes, we're assuming he was murdered by at least two of his victims. But now we have a more pressing problem. Last night, the three of them were sprung from jail. The whole of Málaga police force, border controls, and the Guardia Civil have dropped everything to hunt for them."

"They escaped?" said Phillip. "How?"

"Sonia set a fire in the ladies' wing and they drove out dressed as fire officers in the fire truck. We think the fourth victim was the driver."

"Sounds incredibly well organized," said Phillip.

"And needed incredible nerves, I'm almost

admiring them. Oh, and by the way, we found a photo in Marquez's cottage of four teenagers. I'll send you a copy. You'll recognize three of them, but I think the other one is the person we are looking for."

"OK. Where are you now?"

"Driving to Algeciras. The Guardia located one of the taxi's abandoned in the marina parking lot, but that's not why I'm calling. I need you to help me with two things. Will you have time? Only you've been avoiding me since before Christmas."

"Sorry, something came up."

"Amanda indicated there was a problem. May I ask, what?"

"My ex-wife turned up to tell me that she is extremely sick and is dying. She's gone off to a hospice somewhere to see out her last month or two. However, she brought something with her that was both shocking and delightful."

"Your ex-mother-in-law?"

"Hardly, anyway she was quite sweet. No, my son."

"That must have been a surprise. Are you sure he's yours?"

"He's a mini version of me."

"That's both a tragic and happy story," said Prado. "Do you want me to trace Valentina?"

"Thanks, but no," said Phillip. "We'll abide by her wishes and my son is settling in well to his new circumstances."

"What's his name?"

"Sasha, he's seven."

"How do you and Amanda feel? Instant parenthood can't be easy on either of you."

"We're both thrilled and relishing every moment but it's certainly challenging. A whole new mindset and approach to our well-established routine have been needed but now Sasha has started school, we're managing to delve back into business as usual. What two things can I help you with?"

"The escape is going to need my undivided attention for the next few days so the investigation into the fourth victim will have to be put on hold. Yet identifying him may well help us solve the escape."

"You think he was involved?"

"Possibly. All we know is that the fire truck driver spoke perfect Spanish, had a full beard, and wore large, black-framed spectacles. He may well have been the fourth victim. Eduardo is working up an artist's impression of him as he might look today, with and without a beard. We'll be broadcasting it as soon as it's ready, probably tonight. Take a look and keep his face in mind. Then ponder over the second taxi. It headed up into the mountains from the barn where they switched vehicles. Try and work out where it could have been headed? Don't forget that there was a football match between Málaga and Almeria last night. The roads in the city and those heading north, and east were jammed with returning fans between ten-thirty and midnight. Exactly, the diversion they needed."

"You think that was deliberate?"

"It can't be a coincidence. Listen, Phillip, I don't care if you send me on a wild goose chase, but we're more likely to catch them by using our brains rather than chasing shadows. I'm hoping your survival experience might narrow down the possibilities. Where would you go in the same circumstances?"

"Can you send me the GPS coordinates of the barn?"

"Sure. The other thing is more delicate. Marquez

was living in a rented cottage in the olive groves south of Úbeda. He'd set a firebomb on a timer to go off after his departure, but the explosion was only partially effective. I'd like you to appraise the files and DVDs we found there along with a damaged hard drive we've managed to salvage. We have the guys at the lab looking but it needs someone familiar with Crown's, O'Reilly's, and Augustin's histories to make sense of the stuff on it. There are also photo albums and a dozen or so DVDs. I've only glanced at one movie which was frankly just sick. I'm assuming the remainder are similar, but they might contain some new faces that could help us. Would you mind me shipping them to your house given that you now have a child there?"

"Yes, send them, I'll keep them secure in my strongbox and only work on them when I'm alone."

"Thanks, Phillip. I'm just arriving at the marina. I'll let you know my findings on the way back. Marquez's stuff should be with you in a couple of hours."

A few minutes later, Phillip received two emails. Prado had sent the photo of the four teenagers; Ana had sent him the barn coordinates and copies of her case notes. Phillip pulled up a map of the barn on his largest monitor and studied the plethora of winding roads and tracks leading to it. He went to satellite view and road by road, track by track eliminated those that went nowhere, or were unsuitable for such a large people carrier. As he crossed them off, his mind drifted back to his military days. What was the advice to lay a false trail? These were the sort of useful tips he was never supposed to forget. The instructor's words slowly reformed. There are two possible scenarios: I have help, or I'm on my own. They had used extra firemen for the escape, he thought, so were not averse to buying assistance. I'll bounce around some ideas assuming they did.

One of the taxis is probably a decoy, but which one? Algeciras marina suggests they had a boat. If so, that gave them easy access to Africa, Canary Islands, Azores, or anywhere in the Mediterranean and were probably long gone. However, would they have risked such a journey with a sick man on board? Crown is still waiting for test results. To travel without a doctor or at least a diagnosis of his disease would be foolhardy.

Or would they ditch Crown?

This had all started with his father back in the mid-1980s. A crooked property developer who built a college in Marbella for the children of fellow criminals. When all that fell apart, Crown senior moved his family back to the UK where he had pioneered internet systems and servers for Spanish hotel bookings. His elder twin children, who were also at the college, had taken over the business on his passing and now ran what appeared to be a legitimate server business from their cottage outside Bournemouth, England. However, they had been touring the world last time Phillip had inquired and were not responding to emails.

Crown or his siblings were therefore probably the bosses of this enterprise meaning they controlled the money. O'Reilly, Augustin, and the fourth victim may be old friends, but they were likely helpers, not decision-makers. They would need to keep Crown alive to access their share and Crown needed them to help him move around.

It was therefore of mutual benefit for the gang to stick together and aim for a haven where Crown could be treated. For that, they would need a tame doctor.

That implied an isolated property to maintain privacy but reasonably close to quality facilities and travel connections.

It's dark, they have nine to ten hours until daylight, but the roads are quiet after midnight. After that, any vehicle would be conspicuous.

The escape was at ten p.m. They would have needed ten to fifteen minutes to dump the fire truck, change, and leave in the taxi. They wouldn't speed or drive dangerously meaning they had around ninety minutes to reach their base before the bewitching hour. Say a maximum of one hundred and sixty kilometers on main roads, or much less on country roads, say ninety kilometers.

He printed out the map and drew two circles around the abandoned fire truck. If his reasoning was correct, somewhere in that space had to be their base. He racked his brains, challenging his assumptions. These were intelligent people. They wouldn't make rash decisions or take uncalculated risks. He looked at the map. Within his estimated range was Granada City and its airport to the east. To the south were Málaga City, it's airport and Marbella, to the north Córdoba, and to the west a slow mountain road to Ronda.

Forget Ronda, thought Phillip. Too small to hide, few roads in and out, short on advanced medical services, and no airports. Córdoba is well beyond the midnight deadline and its small airport has limited destinations. Málaga city would have been jammed solid with the aftermath of the football, but Marbella was a distinct possibility. They know the area and there are loads of foreign doctors there. Otherwise, they could have headed east toward Granada hidden among the football fans heading back to Almeria.

He typed up an email to Prado explaining his logic and sent it off.

For a second, he hoped that he wasn't wasting their time but then cleared his mind and returned to the video editing. He had to finish it then prepare a snack for Sasha coming home from school. The dear boy was forever hungry.

29

Phillip was shutting down his computer in preparation for Sasha's imminent arrival back from school when the doorbell rang. He opened up to see a young, uniformed officer leaning over his gate. Phillip recalled seeing him occasionally on his visits to the comisaría.

"It's heavy," said the officer. "Could you help me carry the box to where you want it?"

Phillip opened the gate and together they heaved a brown cardboard container out of the trunk of an unmarked car and into Phillip's study. He opened up his secure storage cupboard and they inserted it into the bottom shelf. Phillip had to push the door hard to shut it. He then twisted the numbers on the combination lock. He escorted the officer to the door just as Sasha ran in through the gate.

The officer said Hola to Sasha, then left.

"Why were the police here?" said Sasha, a puzzled expression on his face.

"Just a chat. I'm helping them find some criminals."

"Oh. Is my snack ready?"

"No, want to help me make it?"

"I'll change out of uniform first. What am I eating?"

"Avocado toast to your liking?"

"Yummy."

"Don't forget to wash your hands."

"Do I ever?"

"I'll be inspecting."

"OK."

Sasha, in jeans and polo shirt, joined Phillip in the kitchen, presented his squeaky-clean hands, stuck out his tongue, and went to the fridge to pour himself a beaker of water. Phillip sliced the avocado onto the warm wholemeal bread then drizzled olive oil and sea salt over the top. They sat down together at the island. Phillip extracted the tea bag from his mug of boiling water, threw it in the trash, and took a sip as they chatted about the school day. He adored Sasha's enthusiasm for learning. He was enjoying the experience and making friends fast. The toast disappeared rapidly.

"These criminals," said Sasha licking his lips. "What have they done?"

"Bad things, but not for your ears."

"Tell me what you can and how are you helping the police?"

"They have escaped from prison and I'm helping find them."

"Have you met these criminals?"

"Yes, I help translate sometimes."

"I'd like to try that when I'm older."

"Good. You should always try and have fun with whatever work you are doing. Are you going to your cousins today, or are they coming here?"

"I'm going there. Can you help me with my jacket?"

Sasha slipped off the stool and stood waiting by the coat rack. "Arms please," said Phillip. Sasha held up his arms and Phillip slipped the jacket on him and zipped up the front. "OK?" Sasha nodded. "Back for supper at seven, please. Chicken fillets with Papas pobre."

"Goody. Will the ladies be back?"

"Maybe."

Phillip patted his head and watched him go, glowing inside.

When Sasha disappeared between the gate that joined the two properties, Phillip returned to his study, opened the secure storage, and ripped open the taped box. Inside were neatly arranged files, photo albums, DVDs, and a blackened hard drive. He removed the files and photo albums, placed them on his desk, and relocked the storage.

He sat down in his chair, piled the files before him, picked up the first album, and turned the pages. It was all family stuff. The next was the same, documenting Marquez's life until he was a teenager. The next was college, followed by his early teaching career. It all looked so normal, somehow, he expected a monster to be different. The last album was the Marbella International College, from open parkland to finished buildings and sports facilities. It looked impressive. He picked up the top file and opened it.

It contained the printed yearbooks for the College for the years 1983 and 1984. He flicked through. There were lists of names and photos of all teachers, pupils, and college governors. A syllabus, sports activities, college trips, exam results, and university entrants. Phillip scanned the photos of the pupils. He spotted the fourth victim standing behind Crown. His name was Paul Bosque.

"That can't be," he said out loud.

He looked at the photo of the college governors for

the same year.

The chairman was Pablo Bosque. The late husband of the Duquesa de Aragon, former Chairman of the Royal Taurino Society, and majority shareholder of the massive Bosque Hotel Group. He'd featured heavily in their inquiry into Patrick O'Reilly during the summer. What was he doing all those years previously as chairman of a college in Marbella owned by a British criminal? Could he and the fourth victim, Paul Bosque be related? Their resemblance was uncanny.

He called Prado.

"You are not going to believe this," said Phillip when Prado answered.

"Does this mean you're making progress," said Prado speeding back toward Málaga.

"This is red hot. There are a couple of yearbooks here with photos and names from all, staff, governors, and pupils of Marbella International College. There are no images of John Crown senior but Leon, there is one of the fourth victim."

"Fantastic, what's his name?"

"Bosque, Paul Bosque."

"Bosque?" said Prado as he maneuvered the narrow Málaga streets leading to the comisaría. "Could he be related to Pablo Bosque?"

"More than likely because from 1983 until 1984, Pablo Bosque was chairman of the college governors."

"So, Crown senior and Bosque senior knew each other," said Prado. "I'll contact the Duquesa. Perhaps she can throw some light on it? I wonder what other little gems are buried in that box."

"As soon as Sasha is asleep, I'll reconvene. Did you read my report?"

"Sorry, no. I'm driving."

"Anything useful at the marina?"

"Three men and a woman arrived in the taxi at twelve forty-five last night. The camera captured some poor-quality video of them rolling four large suitcases from the cab to a small yacht, which sailed within minutes of them boarding."

"Was she Sonia?"

"No."

"How can you be so positive?"

"The yacht arrived three days ago from Tangiers in Morocco. All four of the crew presented Moroccan passports and explained the reason for their visit as shopping in Málaga. They had the correct travel visas and the yacht's papers were in order, so they were granted access. Last night, as it was so late, there was no staff manning the marina, so they departed without any customs checks."

"Did they take photocopies of their passports?"

"Of course. That's how I know it wasn't Sonia. What was interesting is what the three men had as their profession, fireman."

"Moroccan firemen are paid a pittance. I expect they were tempted by the extra cash. Any chance of cooperation with the Moroccan police to find them. They may have overheard something useful?"

"Unlikely, but the request has gone off already. So, what conclusions did you come to?"

"With Crown being so ill, it's unlikely they would risk a long boat trip or even a car journey. I suspect they took him straight to a safe house at least until they have a diagnosis and his treatment kicks in. They may have used the football traffic as cover to head for Granada or they went to old haunts in Marbella. I prefer Granada. If the second taxi is abandoned in

Sevilla or somewhere in the opposite direction, it might confirm that."

"I can't disagree with your thinking," said Prado. "But where should we begin searching for them? Both Granada and Marbella are huge."

"You said that Crown is suspected of having HIV?"

"Right."

"There is one group of medications that can keep him alive and they are called antiretroviral therapy, or ART for short. Simply, warn all chemists in the areas to inform you of any new customers."

"That's brilliant but what if they buy it on the dark web?"

"Highly unlikely. These are complex and expensive drugs with manufacture and distribution tightly controlled by the makers. Patients wouldn't risk buying dodgy ART drugs over the web. They'd want the genuine pure item. It's not like having a headache or a heroin addiction. With this disease, their lives are at stake."

"This is the best news I've had all day. Thank you."

"It's just a theory."

"How about a little flutter on where the taxi is abandoned?"

"It was my idea, so I choose first."

"Go on."

"I'll stick with Sevilla. You?"

"I'll go for Marbella, safety among all the crooks there."

"And what will be my prize?"

"In the unlikely event that you are right, how about a bottle of Arzuaga?"

"My favorite Ribera del Duero, perfect."

"Don't count your chickens."

30

Phillip sat ruminating in his study, staring at the slideshow screensaver on his computer. He made a mental note to scan some of the photos of Sasha that were in the envelope from Valentina and add them to his collection. He heard the gate slide open and Amanda's car stop in the driveway.

He listened to her heels clicking on the stone floor as she came in to see him.

"How was your day?" said Amanda giving him a big kiss. "What are all those papers, where is Sasha, and I'm famished?"

"Always with the questions."

"But that's what you love about me."

Phillip hugged her and laughed. "Sasha is at his cousin's," he said stretching and yawning. "He'll be back shortly and will need feeding. Other than that, it's been quiet day, well apart from Marquez dying, and his victims escaping from prison."

"Dead, escaped, but how?"

"Officially, Marquez committed suicide, but Prado thinks he was killed by O'Reilly and Augustin. At three am yesterday morning, the security system was hacked, and the night guards suffered from food poisoning. For quarter of an hour, Sonia and Patrick had free run of the place. Needless to say, when Ana checked them later, they were squeaky clean. Last night, Sonia set a fire in the women's wing. The fire engine was not manned by the genuine crew but by the fourth victim and some helpers. They put the fire out and drove away with the three of them in the fire truck dressed as firemen."

"Didn't you tell me Crown was in the hospital?"

"Yes, but somehow, they took him too."

"What are all these papers?"

"Prado is too busy hunting the escapees to look at them, so he sent them over for us to take a look at. In the security cabinet are also a bunch of DVDs. He found them in the cottage of Marquez."

"Then aren't they likely to be….?"

"You probably ought not to see them, but they might not all be sick stuff. There could be crucial evidence among them that links all this together, or at least a clue pointing us in the right direction."

"Then, I'll want to see them."

"Don't say I didn't warn you. You want to start the supper while I finish up here?"

"Fine."

"Where is Salome?"

"Buying a bed and then having dinner with Vicente."

"Does this mean what I think it does?"

"Yes, her uncle Mario's house is now more or less ready for her to occupy. We've been furniture shopping most of the day, but I left her to do the bed with Vicente."

"Understandable, he'd have a vested interest in its bounce ability."

"Ha, ha."

"When will she be moving in?" said Phillip.

"If they can have the bed delivered, she's going to try it out tonight and see how it goes. She'll let me know if she's coming back here."

"Does this mean we're back to normal?"

"Don't you mean the new normal, what with Sasha's arrival?"

"I guess, so. You OK?"

"I adore him and being his new mother."

"It shows, and I think it's reciprocated."

"That's what I feel. Will you be able to have him on Saturday?"

"I'm happy to have him every day, why?"

"Salome and I are going to be measured for my wedding dress and her matron of honor outfit."

"Fantastic. Where, in Málaga?"

"No, Vélez-Málaga. Vicente introduced us to this amazing shop just around the corner from Las Claras Convent."

"I suppose I ought to think about rings, hotels, and honeymoons?"

"Booking the day might also be helpful, darling."

"That too."

"I'll make a start on the supper. Chicken and Papas, right?"

"That's what his lordship is expecting."

The kitchen door slammed shut. They both looked lovingly at each other. The walking stomach was back.

***

After reading Sasha his story, settling him down for the night, and leaving Amanda soaking in the bath, Phillip returned to his study, picked up the next file, and flicked through it. It was reasonably thick and contained papers associated with the formation of the college and management company, the acquisition of the land, the construction of the buildings, and the sale to Greentrees, the golf course developer.

It contained no surprises. The papers confirmed what they already knew.

The following file though held new information concerning Greentrees. Attached to the escritura, the deed describing the formation of Greentrees, was a shareholder agreement in the form of a side letter. It was between Marquez, his brother Pablo, three other directors and nominees on behalf of John Crown. The nominees were the Sanchez brothers, lawyers based in Málaga who acted for the Crowns on most of their legal matters in Spain. They had been arrested when Malcolm Crown's voyeur website and recording studio had been discovered full of abducted girls and illegal migrants. However, the lawyers had pulled some strings, been released on bail, and absconded, never to be seen again. The letter described Crown as a ninety percent shareholder in Greentrees.

So, Crown had sold the college to himself, thought Phillip but where did Greentrees obtain the money?

The final paper contained damning evidence. A bank statement from Greentrees. The opening deposit had been received from the Bosque Hotel Group.

Phillip phoned Prado.

"I'm in my office," said Prado before Phillip could speak. "The taxi was found at the railway station in Antequera. I've sent Ana this time."

"No winner of the wine then," said Phillip.

"I'll treat you to a bottle of Arzuaga anyway because your hypothesis was along the right lines," said Prado. "No idea what this says about their base though. Did you consider Antequera?"

"The wine is much appreciated, and I did think of Antequera but deemed it unlikely," said Phillip. "There are few options around the town for a discreet property. It's an area of agriculture and olive groves on a vast flat plain interspersed with small villages and towns where everyone knows each other and their business. Any stranger comings and goings would be visible to the locals and gossiped about."

"Then why dump the taxi there?"

"To do exactly what they have achieved, confuse us."

"Now we'll have to inform even more chemists to look out for new HIV treatment clients. But before I do that, I'll call the prison," said Prado. "We need confirmation of Crown's diagnosis and what his recommended treatment is. Then we'll warn every chemist in the land. Did you have a reason for calling?"

"I've found another file about the golf course developer, Greentrees. It confirms that John Crown and Pablo Bosque did have a business relationship."

"How?"

"The deposit made to open the Greentrees bank account was made by the Bosque Hotel Group."

"Great news. Any thoughts on what brought them together?"

"Again, it's just my silly reasoning."

"Phillip," said Prado. "If I didn't appreciate your thinking, I wouldn't ask. You've set us on the right track so often since we started to work together, I've come to rely on it. So come on, please. Tell me."

"If you insist. Let's go back right to the beginning. What was driving John Crown? What were his dreams and motivations? How did he decide to build a school for the children of criminals? Why did he sell it after a few years even though it was performing well as a legitimate business?"

"Go on."

"It was the beginnings of the Costa del Golf. The Junta de Andalucía had just announced a new policy to attract winter tourists to the Costa del Sol. Golf course developments were suddenly everyone's priority including Crown. He could build luxury properties, a hotel around the course and make a fortune compared with what the school income was bringing in. Then he could afford to send his kids to the best boarding schools anywhere. The college grounds were perfect for such a project. He'd have needed more adjacent land to qualify for planning permission and for that he needed an investor. And there he was right in front of his nose."

"Pablo Bosque," said Prado. "Chairman of the college governors. Owned an expanding hotel chain."

"Precisely," said Phillip.

"But how did Bosque come to send his son to a school for the children of criminals? He was an intelligent man and must have known who Crown was and he still accepted the position of governor."

"I have no idea but maybe at the outset of his career maybe Bosque sailed a little too close to the wind."

"In those days you could," said Prado. "Money laundering through property development was rife."

"And opening an offshore bank account in Gibraltar was easier than falling off a log."

"And international arrest warrants were almost unheard of. All of which added up to ideal conditions for Marquez to steal the lot and make his escape," said Prado. "You couldn't do it today. Have you seen the films yet?"

"No, I'll wait until Sasha is asleep. I wouldn't want him to inadvertently see what Marquez was up to."

"Understand but quick as you can please. The guys at the lab are dragging their heels. All we have is a bank statement linking Bosque's company with Crown's. If we could find a film of the two of them together, it would confirm a closer personal relationship."

"But what would that prove?" said Phillip.

Prado paused.

"Leon? You still there?"

"Sorry, just thinking about your question," said Prado. "Listen, all this is leading us somewhere. At the moment, I only have vague hints as to where, but I don't wish to prejudice your searches by telling you. You may end up fitting the evidence to the hypothesis. See what you can find, then we'll talk again."

"I'll work on it all night, but I can't say I'm looking forward to all that depravity."

"After a while, you become desensitized to it, and Phillip, I advise you not to let Amanda and Salome help. Their reactions will detract you from focusing on what we need. Fast forward through the bad stuff. Concentrate on images of Crown and Bosque and maybe others together. Marquez kept the films for a reason, and I believe that it wasn't just to fuel his masturbation fantasies."

31

Prado twisted his chair around and gazed out his office window. The darkening sky matched his somber mood.

The phone rang. It was the Duquesa.

"Your call was a pleasant surprise, Inspector," she said in beautiful Spanish. "I trust you are keeping well?"

"Fine, thank you, ma'am. Yourself?"

"Couldn't be better but you can't be interested in my health. Was my chauffeur driving too quickly?"

"No ma'am, it's more delicate than that."

"Oh dear, sounds ominous."

"It concerns your late husband."

"Go on."

"Am I right in saying that you had no children?"

"Correct."

"Was Bosque your only husband?"

"I was married only once. Can you get to the point, Inspector?"

"Sorry, but this is important? Did you know anything about your husband's business affairs or his contacts?"

"He was in hotels and earned lots of money. That's all I needed to know. After he died, I sold the lot to one of his old friends."

"May I inquire who?"

"Severiano Pizarro."

"The engineering magnate who also served on the committee of the Royal Taurino Society?"

"That's him."

"Thank you. Were you his first wife?"

"I am Catholic, so one would never have been allowed to marry a divorced person. Although Pablo did have a son with an English lady before we met. He told me that the mother had died when the boy was still in nappies and was brought up by an aunt in Marbella. I never met the boy or knew his name, but my husband did his duty by him. He visited occasionally, paid for his education, and living costs but never discussed these matters with me. I made it clear to him that I wasn't interested. Is that all?"

"No, ma'am," said Prado. "Do you have any of your late husband's papers stored anywhere?"

"Good Lord, no. I gave you his laptop and handed everything else to his lawyer. A nice man. He came here regularly for dinner."

"Do you have his contact details?"

"Not to hand. His name is Sanchez, Cristobal Sanchez. He's based in Madrid. I'm sure directory inquiries will have his number. Goodbye, Inspector, oh, and keep me informed."

"Yes, ma'am," said Prado swiping end call.

"Another bloody Sanchez," mumbled Prado.

But then he smiled. The jigsaw pieces were falling into place.

32

"I need to talk to someone about the missing man's picture on tonight's national news," said a croaky female voice in well-formed but badly accented Spanish.

"Do you mean the one of Paul Bosque?" said the desk sergeant at the comisaría.

"I do, he's my nephew," said the woman. "My sister was his mother."

"Are you happy talking in Spanish or would you prefer an interpreter?" said the sergeant.

"Spanish is fine," said the woman.

"Hello," said Prado answering his internal phone.

"There's a lady on the line who saw the broadcast about Paul Bosque," said the sergeant. "Claims to be his aunt."

"Put her through," said Prado.

"This is Detective Inspector Prado," he said. "I'm handling this case. I understand that you recognized the missing man on our broadcast this evening."

"I did, yes. My name is Virginia Newman," said the croaky voice. "I'm English but I've lived in Marbella since 1968. Paul Bosque is, or was, my nephew. As far as I'm concerned, he's been missing since he walked out of my house when he was eighteen in 1990. That was nearly thirty years ago, and I haven't seen him since. I don't know if he's alive or dead."

"We have no record of him as a missing person. Did you report it back then?"

"No, I had no reason to. He had money and said he was going off to find his way in the world. Has someone reported him missing?"

"No, but we urgently need to interview him about a number of matters."

"What's he supposed to have done?"

"I'm afraid I can't tell you that, Señora," said Prado. "It's police business. All I will say is that it's an extremely serious matter."

"So, he is alive?"

"We have no proof of that," said Prado. "But we have good reason to believe that he might be. What image did you recognize, the one with the beard or without?"

"The one without the beard was vaguely similar but I wouldn't have recognized him without the name."

"Really? What can you tell me about him?"

"His mother, my sister Anita, died when he was still in nappies, so I adopted him officially."

"Did his father support that?"

"You do know whom we're talking about here?" said Virginia.

"Pablo Bosque, who later married the Duquesa de Aragon."

"That's right."

"Did you know him?"

"Oh, yes."

"Where did you meet?"

"In 1971, in Marbella. He was looking for promotion girls to work in his hotel in Marbella. I was never sure what our exact job description should have been, but my sister and I were there to make sure that his English-speaking investors had a nice time. Do you understand what I mean by that, Inspector?"

"I'm a policeman, not a priest," said Prado. "Of course, I know what you're implying. Did you live in the hotel?"

"Pablo had a penthouse on the top floor which we shared with him. He was away most of the time but when he was there, we, well... I'm sure you understand. Unfortunately, Anita became pregnant. Pablo offered to send her back to the UK for an abortion, but she declined. She was so desperate to marry Pablo and presumed the sight of a cute baby might persuade him. However, he was never going to wed an English slut and told her so repeatedly. She became more and more depressed with his rejection and eventually killed herself with an overdose. Pablo told me to take the child, or he'd put him up for adoption. I was more than delighted to take responsibility for Paul but really, I had no choice. Pablo made it crystal clear that he hadn't approved of the pregnancy and had accused Anita of trying to trap him, which she was. However, he happily bought me a small apartment in Marbella, provided generously for me and Paul, and made sure he was well educated but only until eighteen. After that, it was up to both of us to make our way."

"Tell me about Paul's education?"

"I thought you might ask me that."

"Why?"

"It's how it all began."

"Meaning?"

"Paul attended the state school near my apartment, but he was having problems there. He was a gifted child but wasn't pushed hard enough. He was depressed and his behavior suffered. Then I met John Crown."

"How?"

"He arrived around 1980. I met him at a party with his wife Gillian almost the day after they landed. They partied hard and were out of their minds on booze and coke. Within weeks, John had enough of excesses and settled into a more normal routine, but Gillian had become a hopeless drunk. John asked me to help with the kids, so I was at his villa almost every day. Paul joined us after school and became great friends with his youngest son Malcolm. John and I became lovers."

"That's exceedingly frank of you."

"I wanted to marry him, but no matter how hard I pushed, he wouldn't leave Gillian."

"Who was Crown, where did he stem from?"

"He was an east Londoner with a garage in Hackney where he chopped stolen cars and provided get-away vehicles for local villains. He was a technical genius and could make anything mechanical out of anything. However, he found his niche when computers started making headway in the late seventies. He taught himself how they worked and programmed them to do all kinds of stuff, much of it illegal. He made good money quickly, was often under suspicion but never caught by the old bill. One day, he took the family on a package holiday to Marbella where he fell in love with it and the weather. He decided that he'd had enough of cold gray skies and was one of the first of his crooked cronies to set up here."

"To retire?"

"Initially, yes but then as more of his fellow crooks arrived, he helped them buy property, acquire vehicles and maids, etc. then managed their illicit earnings. I met most of them."

"He spoke Spanish?"

"He learned quickly. I helped him."

"He came with a lot of money?"

"Yes, but after the initial madness had calmed down, he was careful with it and was well paid by his cronies for helping them. But as his kids settled into the state school, he realized, as I had with Paul, that they were too advanced for what was being offered. He looked around for a private school, but they were either too posh or German. So, decided to build a bilingual college that followed the British curriculum."

"Did he use his own money?"

"Initially yes, but to start with he didn't need much. He took an option on some land and concentrated on the planning permission. At first, the Town Hall was reticent to grant a foreigner the necessary permits. John realized he needed a local Spaniard as a member of the project team and teaching staff. His bank introduced him to a local teacher called Rodriguez Marquez. But Marquez wasn't the innocent fellow the bank thought he was. Marquez set out to exploit this rich foreigner as much as he could. To achieve that he insisted on becoming Crown's business partner, administrator of the school management company and headmaster of the school on an extremely well-paid contract. Reluctantly, John agreed. It cost him a lot more then he'd planned, but at last, he had his outline planning permission and could complete the land purchase and begin building. At that point, John started looking for investors. A few of his cronies stumped up a bit but what he ideally needed was a wealthy Spaniard to lend him and his project credibility among the local business community. I introduced him to Pablo Bosque."

"How did that go?"

"They hit it off instantly. They were both ambitious driven men going in similar directions. John admired Pablo's wealth and connections. Pablo was impressed with John's understanding of computers and their role in business."

"Did Bosque invest in the school?"

"Yes, but unofficially. He and Crown had an interest free loan agreement. If the school were sold, Bosque would be repaid and share in the profits. So, the college was built, and Marquez arranged for the mayor of Marbella to open it at the end of 1982."

"Bosque was chairman of the college governors. How did that come about?"

"In exchange for a free education for Paul, plus he knew that his involvement would enhance the profile of the school and attract more students and it added to his overall Mr. respectable image. By now, he was engaged to the Duquesa and moving in exalted circles in Madrid. Yet, every time he came to Marbella to visit Paul, he would drop his guard and have fun. We would er, well you know."

"You slept with him despite being Crown's mistress?"

"They liked to share me," said Virginia laughing. "I was uncomplicated and gave them anything they wanted."

"At the same time?"

"Often. They were both kinky buggers, but this was the eighties. The swinging sixties were tame compared with what we did, especially in Marbella."

"It's even worse now," said Prado. "Or better, depending on your preferences."

"Quite funny for a copper," said Virginia, chuckling.

"I have my moments. Listen, how did the idea come about to turn the school into a golf course?"

"I need to put that in context. Back then, Marbella was a dump packed with crooks, drug addicts, and a high crime rate. Consequently, tourism, its only source of tax revenue had slumped, and Pablo's hotels were suffering. Spain had recently applied to join the European Union and to ensure its acceptance was slowly implementing its rules and regulations. One of those being a change to its extradition laws. Spain would shortly no longer be a bolt hole for any crook including the hundred or so Brits languishing on the Costa del Sol. While their revenue was welcome, their presence was rapidly becoming less desirable. As they started leaving in droves, the town council used the opportunity for a redesign of its image. They harkened back to the glorious days of the 1960s when royalty and film stars flocked there.

"To achieve that, they resolved that luxury hotels and villas surrounding designer golf courses were needed. For John that was a gift from above. As the criminals departed and took their brats with them, the college was losing students faster than new ones were arriving. John knew instinctively that the college grounds were perfect for golf development. However, he needed more adjacent land for it to be big enough, and for that, he needed an investor."

"Enter Pablo Bosque," said Prado. "Friend, chairman of the college governors, owned an expanding hotel chain and their sons were bosom buddies."

"Precisely," said Virginia.

"Then Marquez ran off with the proceeds from the sale of the college to Greentrees including advance payments of college fees."

"Correct, inspector, and shortly after that, Crown went back to England."

"Did he explain why?"

"No."

"Did you stay in touch?"

"I tried but he didn't reply."

"What about Pablo?"

"After John went, Pablo offered me administrative work in his hotel where I stayed until I retired nearly two years ago. I had a contract, a company pension, plus this apartment."

"Did your relationship continue?"

"After he and the Duquesa married, I never saw him again."

"Did you know that Marquez abused Paul and three other children including Malcolm Crown?"

There was silence for a moment then Prado heard Virginia sniff. "Are you OK?" he said.

"No, I didn't know that Paul had been abused, but it explains a lot."

"How?"

"As he matured, he became depressed and withdrawn. I had a hell of a job getting him to college in the mornings, but I put it down to being a teenager."

"Why wouldn't Paul tell you that he was being abused?"

"That's a tough one Inspector but would you tell your mother?"

"Probably not, I'd be too ashamed, but I don't think Paul or Malcolm could be blamed for not informing anyone. I suspect that Marquez had a hold over them."

"Such as what?"

"Something to do with their parents, perhaps."

Virginia paused.

"You still there?" said Prado.

"I'm thinking," said Virginia.

"What about?"

"Whether I should tell you."

"Do you want to see your nephew again?"

"More than anything but I'm worried that I might be in trouble."

"It's too long ago to worry about that," said Prado. "And I promise there won't be any recriminations, there are larger fish to fry here."

"Marquez and his sister ran a swingers club. John Crown and Pablo Bosque took me there with other English girls. I wouldn't be surprised if Marquez recorded what was going on."

"And that is how he controlled Crown and Bosque?"

"Exactly," said Virginia.

"And Marquez used that power to become school administrator and to being a minor shareholder in the golf course."

"John and Pablo hated him for it. Yet they refused to fire the creep."

"Or dared not to," said Prado.

"Is Marquez still alive?"

"No, he committed suicide in prison."

"That makes me happy. Has his death triggered anything about John and Pablo?"

"Not that I know of, but he only died recently."

"How did you find him after all these years?"

"He knew we were chasing him and getting close, so he handed himself in. He was aging badly, not in the best of health, and had enough of looking over his shoulder all the time."

"I wonder if his victims know of his death?"

"They do indeed. We're working on the premise that Malcolm, two others, and Paul clubbed together and have been searching for Marquez ever since he disappeared. They nearly had him two years ago, when he visited his brother, Pablo. It reinvigorated them to find him. Sadly, they resorted to criminal activities to flush him out which I uncovered. I had three of them in Alhaurin jail."

"Had?"

"They escaped on the evening after Marquez died."

"So, he was murdered?"

"The evidence strongly points to suicide but yes, he could have been killed."

"Your TV broadcast didn't mention anything about an escape."

"We're keeping it quiet for the moment, hoping to lull them into a false sense of security."

"Isn't Alhaurin meant to be a high-security jail?"

"It is, but they had outside help."

"Now I understand. You believe it was Paul who led the expedition to get them out."

"I can't think who else had the motivation to take such a risk."

"Who were the other two?"

"Patrick O'Reilly and Sonia Augustin."

"That hardly surprises me, the four of them were always together."

"Can you tell me anything about O'Reilly or

Augustin that might help me track them down?"

"O'Reilly's father was a property developer. He was wrapped up with Bosque in several apartment block schemes around Marbella. I heard he died a while back. Sonia Augustin used to stay with the O'Reilly's during the week. Her father Max picked her up and brought her back from Vélez-Málaga each weekend. Sometimes he stayed for the weekend and joined in the swinger club activities."

"Did Max have any business relationship with Crown?"

"Max supplied sculptures to some of Bosque's hotel lobbies and to the golf course when it eventually went ahead. Every few years he turned up to clean them. Then he stopped and Sonia came instead."

"When was that?"

"Just before I retired."

"Did she explain why?"

"No, and I didn't ask."

"Mmm... Is there anything else you can tell me that might help me find Paul?"

"Such as?"

"Did he have any passions, or did he excel at anything?"

"Most of his schoolwork was crap, inspector. Except for photography, information technology, languages, and skiing. He was extremely talented at all four."

"Do you have any idea where he went after leaving you?"

"Sorry, no. He just wanted to wander and see where his journey took him."

"Did he leave anything behind?"

"I did keep his room exactly as he left it for ten years

or so, just in case he came back. However, after not a single contact I dealt myself a dose of reality and converted it into a study for me. His old computer is still here though but I don't know if it works."

"Would you mind if our experts played with it? He may have left some clues."

"Not at all."

"Anything we could test his DNA with?"

"I have some locks of his baby hair. Will a few of those do?"

"Perfect, may I send my forensics officer to your apartment early tomorrow morning? We'll return everything of course."

"Please do."

"Thank you, Señora Newman, you've been most helpful. Other than Dorothy, the school secretary, you're the only person I've met that has any information about the college and what was going on in Marbella at the time. Can you tell me your address and number, I may need to plague you with more questions?" Prado tapped her contact details into his cellphone. "Thanks, again," he said.

"My pleasure. How is Dorothy?"

"On her deathbed I'm afraid. She's in the hospice in Benalmadena. She's blind but still has most of her faculties. I'm sure she'd appreciate a visit."

"I'll go tomorrow lunchtime," said Virginia. "Will you keep me posted about Paul. I'd love to see him again. He is my only living relative."

"If we find him, you shall be the first to know."

Prado ended the call, typed up a summary for the file, and sent a copy to Phillip.

33

Phillip hung up from Prado telling him all about Virginia Newman. He browsed the final Marquez file with these new revelations in mind. The content had set his pulse racing. Was the man deliberately trying to lead him somewhere?

There was a list of all the student's parents with their identity documents, professional qualifications, jobs, and contact details. About halfway down was a name that made him sit up and look more closely.

"That can't be right," said to himself fumbling for the 1984 class yearbook.

Standing in front of the Crown twins was Daniel Hidalgo. He was the son of David Hidalgo; whose profession was a doctor of pathology for the Guardia Civil in Marbella. Daniel Hidalgo was the current senior national police pathologist. The similarity between the boy and the man Phillip had worked with on several occasions was remarkable.

He compared the Greentrees director's names against the parent's list.

There were three matches: Angel Barrio, lawyer,

and father of Susana Barrio, Juan Salvini, engineer, and father of Jose Salvini, and finally, Manuel Carrera, accountant, and father of Natalia Carrera.

He checked the class photo again and spotted the three children. They were next to each other on the front row directly in front of Marquez.

Then he saw the name John Crown. Profession property developer, children George, Georgina, and Malcolm.

"What does all this mean?" he said looking up at the ceiling.

He needed to watch the DVDs. He went to check on Sasha who was fast asleep.

Amanda was just getting out of the bath and slipping into her housecoat.

"How's it going?" she said.

"I've made some progress."

"You've seen the DVDs?"

"Not even started but I've finished going through the albums and files."

"Show me what you've found," said Amanda hugging him.

They went through to the study and sat down at the workstation. Phillip flicked through what he'd found.

"I've discovered the identity of the fourth victim," said Phillip showing her the yearbook and pointing to the boy.

"Paul Bosque? That has to be more than a coincidence."

"Pablo Bosque was the boy's father. He had an affair with an English girl before he married the Duquesa. Paul was the result. The boy grew up with his aunt in Marbella but when he was eighteen, he said goodbye and went to make his way in the world. His aunt has never heard from him since. I've also proved that Pablo Bosque and John Crown were business partners since before the college was built. Pablo was even the Chairman of the college governors."

"So, this is all linked together," said Amanda."

"By the main players, yes but I still don't understand how Marquez fits in."

"Perhaps the DVDs will clarify matters?"

"Then let's start with the first one."

"Lock the door," said Phillip going over to the storage cupboard and taking out the DVDs. "Nobody should see this, especially Sasha."

Amanda flicked the bolt while Phillip placed the discs on the table and piled them in date order. Oldest on the bottom, latest on the top.

"Fifteen," said Amanda touching each with her finger.

Phillip picked up the top one and read the title.

"1982, Swingers," he said inserting it into the player.

"Did they have DVDs in the eighties," said Amanda. "I vaguely remember my parents had a huge library of video cassettes."

"DVDs arrived in 1997," said Phillip. "Marquez must have converted the original videos into digital so whatever is on these DVDs, he felt was worth keeping. Ready?"

Amanda gulped, took his hand, and nodded.

Phillip pressed play.

An orgy flashed onto the screen. Mountains of naked flesh writhing on sofas and carpets. The grunting and wailing noises were dreadful.

"Turn the sound down," said Amanda.

Thankfully, the cameraman was more interested in people's faces. Pablo Bosque featured heavily, Phillip recognized some of the parents faces from the college John Crown, Angel Barrio, Juan Salvini and Manuel Carrera. There were also others. Phillip vaguely recognized one of them. "We've seen him somewhere," he said.

"At the Ronda bullring," said Amanda. "It's Severiano Pizarro."

"Of course," said Phillip.

When the faces started repeating, he ejected the disc, picked up the next one.

"1984," he said. "Dark Room." He inserted it. It started automatically.

The screen flickered and settled onto a well-lit room lined with shelves filled with various cameras, flash equipment and boxes of spare bulbs, film canisters, developing papers, bottles of chemicals, and rectangular ceramic trays. At the far end, to one side, was a sink with washing lines suspended from sidewall-to-sidewall with pegs for drying prints suspended over it. Four tables had been pushed to the far end under the lines. In the foreground, lying on the floor were two mattresses each covered with a black sheet. The light was turned off and a dark red glow permeated around the setting. They heard what sounded like the click of a door closing.

"Take off your clothes, put on the blindfolds and then stand on the mattresses," a gruff male voice said in Spanish.

"Not bloody likely," said a female voice. Probably Sonia thought Phillip.

"Then I will have no choice but to summon your parents and show them these pictures."

"What pictures?" said a young male voice. There was a sound of papers rustling. "These," said the gruff male.

"But we were just messing around," said a young male voice.

"You were in detention," said the gruff male. "It's meant to be a punishment for your terrible behavior in class, not an opportunity for intimate examinations."

"Then why did you make us wear our swimwear and lock us in this room?"

"I wanted to see what you did when bored. Most of you get up to something. This time I decided to film you."

"Pervert," said another young male.

"I agree," said the gruff voice. "But that doesn't change anything. Now are you going to disrobe, or shall I go to my telephone?"

There was some indecipherable murmuring.

"As far as we are concerned, you can go fuck yourself," said a young male voice with an Irish accent. "If you touch us, we'll beat you to a pulp. There are four of us against only you."

"That's extremely brave, O'Reilly," said the gruff male that had to be Marquez. "Only to be expected from you but what will your father think? What will all your parents think?"

"We don't care," said O'Reilly.

"Then I have no choice," said Marquez. "Why do you think they sent you to this school?"

"Probably because it's cheap," said Sonia. "And to get us out of their hair."

"You could be right," said Marquez. "But actually, no other school would accept you."

"Why not?" said a young male. "Our money is good as anyone else's."

"That's easily said," said Marquez. "But sadly, for

you, it's not true. Where do you think the money comes from to pay for your massive villas, luxury apartments, and top-end cars?"

"Our parents work hard," said Sonia.

"I'm not decrying their efforts," said Marquez. "But haven't you ever wondered what they do to earn those obscene amounts of cash. Didn't you know that most of your parent's earnings are obtained illegally? If the police or tax authorities knew what I know about them, they would all be locked up and you would be thrown out on the street, or into a children's home. Is that what you want?"

"You're lying," said Sonia sobbing.

"I could be," said Marquez. "But are you prepared to take that risk?"

"Our parents will kill you," said O'Reilly.

"They would like to, but should I die suddenly, all the evidence will be sent to the police and newspapers," said Marquez. "Believe me, I've thought of everything. There is no way out of this. Now take off your clothes or start thinking about life in a children's home without money, love, or your fancy toys."

An eerie silence followed as they pondered their circumstances.

"Bastard," said O'Reilly.

A pair of shoes clumped one-by-one onto the parquet floor. More shoes clumped, followed by the rustling of clothing and zips being undone.

"That's better," said Marquez. "Sonia, blindfold the others with the masks and make sure you fasten them properly. Then lead them one-by-one to the mattresses. After that, I will take care of you."

Amanda and Phillip gasped as the naked Sonia led

the three boys to stand facing the camera. Marquez appeared leading her by the hand to stand at the end.

Marquez then stood before them regarding each for several seconds. He then fondled each of them intimately one by one for several minutes then walked off the mattress.

Marquez returned accompanied by two unrecognizable men.

No one said a word.

They each took it in turns to touch the youngsters who despite the awfulness of their situation couldn't help but respond to the experienced manipulations. The men swopped over from time-to-time. After half an hour, the men left. Not a sound had been made. The youngsters wouldn't have known who was abusing them.

The film stopped.

Amanda and Phillip looked at each other.

"Can you bear another?" said Phillip.

Amanda nodded.

For several hours they worked their way through the discs, which grew progressively worse. The children now showed symptoms of deep distress as they were forcibly penetrated by different still unknown men, but they made no sound. Phillip saved screenshots of each adult and masked child. They were dark but legible.

On the tenth disc, there were four different children. This time, they were filmed entering the darkroom. Phillip compared their faces with the class photo and identified them as Daniel Hidalgo and the three children of the Greentrees directors. They could only have been ten or eleven and wept as they undressed, were masked, and then mishandled.

The eleventh disc was the most shocking.

Two of the men were Pablo Bosque and John Crown. They even abused their own sons.

"Enough," said Amanda. "We get the point; the police can do the rest."

"You go to bed my love, I'll fast forward through the rest, and email the screenshots to Prado. Then, as you say, the rest is up to him."

"I can't go to bed without you," said Amanda. "I'll have nightmares."

"Then a couple of large brandies should help calm us both. Bring them here and snuggle up to me while I finish up."

The penultimate disc was different. It showed parents chatting with each other at the college gate. Pablo Bosque was in many of the shots shaking hands and talking with different men in a friendly manner. Most of the other men had also starred in the abuse films at one stage or another.

The final disc was much newer than the others and dated just over two years previously. Not long after Marquez had been nearly confronted by Sonia outside his brother's apartment. It was a cameo of each child being abused by four men. The only one they recognized was Pablo Bosque.

"It seems too fantastic," said Phillip finishing his brandy. "But could the other two men be Max Augustin, and O'Reilly's father?"

"That is so sick. What did Marquez hope to achieve with all these discs and why that cameo one?"

"Two years ago, just after Sonia nearly caught Marquez at his brother's apartment, I think Marquez sent it to one or all of the victims."

"What on earth for?" said Amanda.

"When Sonia saw Marquez, he panicked. He knew how incensed they were and what they would do to him if they found out where he was."

"So, to distract them from chasing him, he let them know who their abusers were."

"Exactly," said Phillip. "The disc must have enraged them beyond our comprehension."

"So, the victims could have taken revenge on their parents?"

"Possibly, that will be for Prado to follow up on."

"Perhaps there is more on the hard drive," said Amanda.

"Possibly but it will have to wait until tomorrow. I'll send these screenshots off to Prado, then we can go to bed."

"I hope I can sleep," said Amanda. "But my mind is spinning with the horrendous damage Marquez has done to ruin so many people's lives."

"I wonder what was driving him?" said Phillip as he locked away the DVDs.

34

Sasha had just left for school when the phone rang. Phillip was still in his housecoat drinking tea in the kitchen. It was Prado. "I see from the time you sent the email that you were up late," he said.

"There was a lot of footage," said Phillip. "What did you make of the screenshots?"

"It's becoming clearer but there are still loose ends," said Prado. "I'm off to forensics with your images and documents. I want Ana to double-check everything, match identities to the unknown men, and check the current status of Daniel Hidalgo and the other three children. Once I have something more tangible, I'll confront Daniel Hidalgo. See what he has to say."

"The images I sent you don't convey the torture and horror they suffered," said Phillip. "They made me feel so sorry for all of the victims. I can completely understand their thirst for retribution."

"Me too," said Prado. "And a sympathetic judge will take that into consideration, but we can't be seen to condone vigilante justice or allowing people to escape from a high-security prison, otherwise everyone will be doing it."

"What were the conclusions on the abandoned taxi in Antequera?"

"It was dumped there just before midnight, two hours after the escape, it confirms they switched vehicles for a second time. There were no prints, but Crown had drooled on the rear seats, so we have a DNA match. On the station CCTV, we have only one person walking away quickly from the vehicle in a ski hat and a thick jacket but once he turned the corner there were no further sightings."

"Perhaps they stayed overnight and were picked up the next morning?"

"We're checking all the accommodations but as yet nothing. What it does mean though is that we have no idea where they've gone. The likelihood of a quick recapture is receding fast and I'm expecting a bomb to go off among my superiors at any minute. If I'm not here next time you call, you'll find me on my farm in Ronda setting up a goat's cheese factory."

"Inma will be delighted," said Phillip.

"In many ways, so will I but I would like to see this wrapped up before I go. We've been working nonstop on it since last May. Have to run. Ana is in her office now."

"Keep me posted."

"Don't forget the hard drive. I think there might be more to this than just the abuse. It might hold more surprises."

"Such as?"

"Again, see what you can find, then we'll discuss it."

Phillip finished his coffee, loaded the dishwasher, set it running, and went into his study. He paused to admire his collection of old Apple and Sinclair computers before unlocking the storage cupboard. "I really must move on from all this junk," he mumbled out loud. "Some photos of the family and our forthcoming nuptials would be far more pleasurable. Shit, I better call the registry office in Gibraltar to book a date."

He picked up the Marquez hard drive and inspected it from all angles. The plastic surrounds on the connector sockets were brittle and partly damaged. The aluminum casing was warped slightly from the heat. It was from an Apple MacBook Air, 2012.

Now Phillip thanked the lucky stars that his museum collection was still adorning the office shelves. He took down his old Apple MacBook Air. It was a year older than the hard drive, but they should be identical. He switched over the drives, plugged it in, and turned it on. The drive screeched as it was powered up and the discs tried to spin. It took a few minutes, but the password window eventually appeared. He set his password cracker running then went to shower and shave.

He was about to dress when a finger beckoned from under the covers.

"Pay attention to me," a muffled voice said, He laughed and slipped in next to Amanda.

When he sat down at the hard drive sometime later, the crack was waiting for him. He typed it in and inspected the names on the mix of file types.

One was entitled, diary of abuse. Marquez had photographed the pages from a lined notebook and assembled them into a PDF file. It described who attended the darkroom, photos of them committing abuse, dates, and how much they paid. They were all there. Crown, Bosque, Augustin, O'Reilly, the other three directors of Greentrees, the Sanchez brothers, and Pizarro.

"At last," mumbled Phillip. "We know what they look like and who they are." He sent the screenshots off to Prado.

The folder entitled Banking was protected by another password. Once again Phillip set his software running and adjourned to the kitchen.

"Booked the registry office?" said Amanda sipping her filter coffee at the island stool.

"Next on my to-do list, darling," said Phillip pouring himself a glass of water and giving her a quick kiss before a shower. Fully dressed, he headed back to the study and was distracted by the password ready for the Banking folder. He opened it, scanned the several files, and found a login link.

It connected him with an account in the name of Gilbert Brown at a Danish Bank on Main Street in Gibraltar. It had been left permanently accessible, so he went straight to the current account details. The balance was seven thousand odd UK pounds with the last transaction being a cash withdrawal of five hundred Euros from a Marbella ATM that morning. The previous withdrawal had been from a Úbeda ATM on the early morning of fifth January. Phillip examined the account information. It had been opened in 1985, the day after Marquez absconded with the cash from the sale of the school, with an initial deposit of the equivalent of twenty thousand British Pounds in Pesetas in cash. It had been paid in by a Gilbert Brown who identified himself with a Gibraltar passport. A copy of the document was attached to the account showing that Marquez's upper lip was still adorned by his bushy mustache. The cheeky bugger must have been planning this for years because the passport was already over a year old at the time the account was opened. How the hell had he qualified for Gibraltar citizenship? Perhaps he had property there or paid someone to sponsor him and used their address?

Almost a year later, nearly seven million UK Pounds were transferred in from a bank in Andorra. The balance had been slowly eroded since then with a steady amount of around two hundred thousand pounds being withdrawn annually through ATMs in Andorra, Toulouse France, and several locations in Spain including regular visits to Marbella and Madrid.

There were still ninety thousand pounds in a deposit account earning practically zero interest and some ten thousand shares in Apple Inc. purchased back in 1997 just after they had been rescued from near bankruptcy by Bill Gates. Back then, the stock was valued at just over twelve dollars a share. Phillip checked the current Apple stock price and whistled. Nearly eighty dollars a share and growing. If there has been a withdrawal since his death, Marquez must have passed all these assets on to his sister Teresa. Perhaps there's a letter? He thought.

Phillip scanned the rest of the Banking folder and found a Word Document dated fourth January. The day before Marquez was arrested. He must have posted it on his way to the Picasso exhibition. It described fully what Teresa needed to do to transfer his accounts and the Gibraltar apartment into her name. Attached to the letter were copies of the documents she would need to affect the transfer and the last Will of Gilbert Brown leaving everything to her. A signed blank transfer of Apple shares to her name and instructions to the bank signed by Brown. Teresa was now a wealthy woman.

Phillip sent all the bank files off to Prado with his observations at the same time wondering what the police could do to recover assets stolen in Spain. Especially, that they were now based in a British Protectorate that rigorously defended private banking.

Another file was a film of Pablo Bosque and the men he now knew as the seniors Crown, O'Reilly, and Augustin talking across a board room table. In the background, pinned to a corkboard on the wall was a large sketch of a golf course with villas lining the fairways. Phillip turned up the volume.

Crown leaned toward Bosque and said in Spanish, "The outline planning permission has been granted and the detailed plans are ready. As you can see on the sketch, your hotel has the best location on the highest point of the terrain. The views of the course will be fantastic. Now we need the cash to complete the acquisition of the college."

"Good," said Bosque. "Has the slice of National Parkland been given back? I don't want to be associated with any illegal developments."

They all laughed.

"The land we, er… borrowed from the state for the college sports pavilion has been excluded," said Crown. "The building has gone, and the fence returned to its original position. The plot is now squeaky clean."

"Very well, I'll transfer the funds today to Greentrees. Then you can pay that into the college account and repay the loan and my share of the profits."

"No problem, where do you want me to send it?"

"I'll take it in cash and personally deliver it to the Gibraltar Bank. How is the hotel booking system coming along?"

"Fine but slowly."

"Will it be Internet-compatible?"

"That's our intention. However, it will be ten years or so before we can take direct bookings from the public. The first phase is only for travel agents."

"When do you think we can start taking a percentage of each booking and putting it offshore?"

"As soon as server and banking technology has improved enough, we can operate everything from Gibraltar, collect all payments there and only send the bare minimum to the actual hotels."

"Wait, are you saying that Gibraltar has space and know-how to set up servers?"

"No. I will build the servers here in Spain to start with until we are confident about their smooth running. I'll start looking for land as soon as the golf course development is all sold. After that, we can move them to whichever country has the most advanced systems and lowest cost offerings."

"Where is that likely to be?"

"Philippines, India, Korea, or Taiwan. India particularly is investing heavily in educating their workforce in computer programming."

"Great foresight of them, seems incredible that The West isn't doing the same."

"The West seems more focused on what you can do with the technology, not how it works."

"Such as how to avoid paying tax. I wonder if Governments are aware of the revenues they will lose when people like us have moved our businesses offshore. Everyone I know will likely be changing their operating structures along similar lines."

"Once we are up and running, maybe we could help

them? You already have the contacts."

"That's brilliant, John," said Bosque. "I'll start sounding people out."

The film faded to black.

Phillip copied the film, reduced the resolution to a smaller file size, and sent it off to Prado. He penned a brief note with the email.

'Was this what you were hoping for?'

35

Daniel Hidalgo was sweating as he chewed away at his fingernails like a rat on a corpse. Prado and el jefe watched him through the one-way mirror as he waited for them in the comisaría interview room.

"Are you certain about this?" said el jefe. "Only it would be a shame to lose such a talented officer."

"The evidence is stacked against him, Sir," said Prado. "If he cooperates, perhaps we can let him off with a warning and keep it quiet. After all, we only need to know where the others are hiding."

"I'm tempted," said el jefe. "Let's find out what he has to say."

They switched off the camera and recording devices, Prado picked up the file containing printouts sent by Phillip and they went next door.

Hidalgo looked up as they entered. His hands trembled. Prado and el jefe sat down opposite.

"Daniel," said el jefe. "You know why we are here?"

Daniel nodded once as his eyes flicked nervously between the two senior officers.

"I'll be direct," said el jefe. "Did you attend the

Marbella International College between 1983 to when it was sold in 1985?"

"Yes," said Daniel, his shoulders slumping.

"Why did your parents send you there?" said Prado.

"They were friends and business associates of the headmaster, Marquez."

"Do you know what this is?" said Prado presenting Daniel with a copy of the abuse diary. Daniel glanced down at it and turned deathly white.

"Is that what I think it is?" he said.

"It is," said Prado, nodding. "The diary of abuse kept by Marquez. It includes names, photos, dates, and payments for every single incident. We just need you to confirm the identities of the men involved."

Prado opened the file and placed a photo of Marquez in front of Daniel.

Daniel glanced at it, stood, rushed to the corner of the room, and vomited into the wastebasket. El jefe went out to fetch a glass of water. He returned to find Daniel sitting back down wiping his mouth with his hand.

"Sorry," he said.

"Understandable," said Prado.

El jefe placed the water in front of Daniel, who took a sip and held the plastic cup in his hand.

"Are you alright to continue?" said el jefe.

"Yes," said Daniel looking at Marquez. "That is Marquez."

Prado placed the next photo on top of Marquez.

"Bosque," said Daniel.

Prado followed more quickly now as color returned to Daniel's cheeks.

"Crown," said Daniel, "My father David, Augustin, O'Reilly, Barrio, Salvini, Carrera, the Sanchez brothers and Bosque's best buddy Severiano Pizarro."

"Incredible," said Prado. "Are the Sanchez brothers related to Marquez?"

"They're cousins," said Daniel. "There is another brother based in Madrid but as far as we know, he was never involved in the abuse."

"How do you know for sure?" said el jefe. "You were always blindfolded."

"Until the DVD arrived, we didn't," said Daniel. "Even then we didn't recognize some of them. Malcolm Crown paid for a private detective to identify them all and find out where they were living."

"Was the detective successful?" said Prado.

Daniel nodded.

"Before we discuss the abusers, answer me one thing," said el jefe. "One thing that has consistently puzzled me, is how did a pathetic and impoverished teacher like Marquez manage to attract these powerful, wealthy men into his pedophile ring?"

"We've been asking the same question for over thirty years," said Daniel looking relieved. "We've been around the houses with all the options so many times we're dizzy. In the end, we agreed that they felt that there was safety in numbers. They all had evidence on each other which balanced out any single one ratting out the others. However, we believe that what Bosque, Crown, and Pizarro failed to consider, is that most of the group were best mates of Marquez. They didn't realize that Marquez had set up the abuse ring to deliberately defraud them of their money until he'd disappeared with their millions. It hit them hard."

"I can imagine," said Prado. "How did they know that Bosque and the others favored sex with minors?"

"Did you know that Marquez had an incestuous

relationship with his sister Teresa?" said Daniel.

"Yes, she told us," said Prado.

"But I bet she didn't mention that she and her brother were founder members of a swingers club in Marbella. It expanded rapidly among local businessmen, including my father. Crown joined in bringing various foreign girls, mainly English. Then Bosque made an occasional appearance followed by Pizarro and others. One of the games was sharing your fantasy. What none of the participants knew is that Marquez recorded everything they said. That was when he overheard Bosque declaring his secret desires for young flesh."

"How do you know all this?" said Prado.

"Paul Bosque told us."

"How did he know?"

"His mother and aunt were two of the English girls in the swinger's club. Before Paul left his Aunt on his eighteenth birthday to find his way in the world, she told him something about his father's preferences."

"Does that mean Paul Bosque has known his father was one of the abusers for all these years?" said Prado.

"He suspected but didn't know for sure until we tracked him down two years ago and showed him the DVD. All his aunt had said, was that Bosque had often asked if his son could join in their lovemaking, but the aunt had categorically refused."

Prado exchanged glances with el jefe. It confirmed the earlier conversation with the aunt.

"Where was Paul for all those years?" said el jefe.

"To start with," said Daniel. "He worked as a chalet assistant in Switzerland during the ski season, where he learned French and German and made enough money to pay for his computer studies in Geneva. After graduation, he worked for IBM until starting his consultancy. He sold it several years ago and now just does select assignments. He's a genius."

"Was it him that hacked into the prison security system?" said Prado.

"I don't know," said Daniel. "But he is more than capable."

"Now let's talk about your role," said Prado. "You conspired with Sonia and the others to kill the abusers and flush out Marquez."

"I took no part in the flushing out."

"I believe you, but do you admit killing your father?"

"He deserved it."

"Did you tell your mother, what had happened?" said el jefe.

"No, she was devastated at his death. I couldn't hurt her further. We haven't seen much of each other since."

"Would it help her to know what transpired?" said Prado.

"No, she worshipped him. She wouldn't believe it."

"How might she react when you appear in court?" said Prado.

"It will finish her."

"I'm sorry," said Prado. "If your father hadn't been greedy, this would never have happened."

"Thanks for your concern, Inspector but it is, how it is."

"Your father's death certificate describes his cause of death by misadventure. Is that the case?" said el jefe.

"My father was a known heavy drinker, I added maximum strength ethanol to his whiskey. His liver couldn't handle the extra alcohol by volume. He passed out in his chair and drowned in his vomit. The medic with the ambulance saw the empty bottle and presumed death by an illicit overdose of alcohol but as I anticipated he didn't think to test the drink."

"Did Malcolm Crown set the fire at his parents' server center near Ronda?" said Prado.

"Yes," said Daniel. "But there was no need for my services. The local pathologist in Ronda didn't have a clue. It was designed to look like an accident. He just reported what he saw."

"What about Max Augustin?" said Prado.

"Sonia locked him into the crypt, just like he had Salome's parents. His body is bricked up behind one of the tunnel walls, so there is no certificate. He'd always been a wanderer and often disappeared without reason. Everyone assumed he'd done it again."

"What about his wife?" said el jefe.

"She's in a mental institution in Madrid. When she discovered his preferences and what he'd done to Sonia, she flipped her lid."

"O'Reilly's father?" said el jefe.

"Calcium Gluconate. It's injected to counteract the effects of excess potassium in the body but produces heart arrhythmias. O'Reilly's father was suffering from angina so it was logical he would die of a heart attack at some time. His doctor never noticed the needle mark under his arm and issued the death certificate."

"But you provided the drug?" said el jefe.

Daniel nodded.

"And Pablo Bosque?" said Prado.

"That was of natural causes, just as I reported."

"Will you tell us about the other cases?" said el jefe. "It will signify your cooperation."

Daniel nodded.

"For now," said Prado. "I'm only interested in finding Crown and the other three. They don't know it yet, but they could be in extreme danger."

"Marquez is dead, how can they be?" said Daniel.

"What you don't know," said Prado, "is that Marquez had other evidence against Bosque and his wealthy business friends. They will be concerned that Marquez may have informed your friends to try and save himself. These are powerful men who will take whatever steps necessary to prevent that information from falling into our hands. They are probably hunting down your friends as we speak. Your friends should be better off in our hands, at least until we have apprehended their adversaries or clarified the situation. Do you understand?"

Daniel nodded.

"Do you know where they are?" said el jefe.

"Sorry, no, but I have a phone number. You could trace that."

"Is it in your contacts?" said Prado.

"Yes, under Sonia."

"Thanks," said el jefe. "You will remain here until we have found them. After that, we will consider releasing you on bail. Eventually, you will have to go to trial. It's just a question of what charges we bring against you. I can't promise anything, but we will do our best to keep them to a minimum."

"Thank you and I'm so sorry. I should never have let Crown draw me into this."

"Nonsense," said el jefe. "Given similar circumstances, we would probably have done the same."

36

The Sierra Nevada National Park is Spain's second-largest. It stretches from the Alpujarras mountains to El Marquesado and the Lecrín Valley, covering a total area of 85,883 hectares. Mulhacen is its highest peak at 3,479 meters above sea level. Fifteen hundred meters lower in a north-westerly direction lies the Disneyesque village of Pradollano. The southernmost ski resort in Europe. With its backdrop of snowy peaks covered with ski runs, cable cars, and skiers in bright colors sliding hither and thither, it competes strongly with anywhere in Switzerland or Austria. The season starts in December and lasts until May with over one hundred and nineteen runs covering over ten kilometers.

Sonia's phone was traced to a large, isolated property located on the northwestern edge of the park away from the main road heading up from Granada to the village.

Throughout the morning, unnoticed by the skiers relaxing in the many cafes and bars, unmarked vehicles had delivered a dozen plainclothes officers from

Granada comisaría in dribs and drabs to one of the larger hotels on the outskirts of the village. Some were dressed as hikers, others as tourists. They lounged around drinking coffee and chatting waiting for Prado and his team.

Just after ten, Prado and Ana arrived with Phillip.

They weaved their way through the bodies and stood with their backs to the picture window.

Outside, dark gray clouds hid the uppermost peaks. Flurries of light snow wafted around in the light breeze adding to the heavy overnight falls. The light was murky with reduced visibility.

Prado glared at everyone and the chatter faded as they waited expectantly to be briefed on the mission. Prado removed his red bobble hat and bright blue ski jacket and draped them over the back of a nearby chair.

"Good morning everyone," he said. "Thank you for being so patient and I hope that you don't object too strongly to taking orders from us Málaga campesinos, peasants." Prado paused until the laughter had faded then pointed to his colleagues.

"This is Dr. Ana Galvez, our forensics officer, and our English translator, Phillip Armitage. We had to wake up the proprietor of the only shop in Málaga offering ski clothing at four o'clock this morning. As you can see, he only had the one color but at least they fit."

He paused while they chuckled politely.

"Both my colleagues have detailed knowledge of the culprits and their plethora of crimes. They will want to examine any computers or papers we might find.

"Despite my inadequate attempt at frivolity, this is a ruthless group of individuals who have committed several murders between them. If they do use weapons against us, please shoot to kill. They will do the same, I can assure you.

"Ideally, we would wait until tomorrow and hit them before dawn while they are sleeping but we anticipate they won't remain there for long. It has been confirmed that one of them is suffering from HIV but as soon as medication has been sourced, they will want to leave the country as quickly as possible.

"They are located at a huge property some four kilometers down from the village. It's owned by an obscure offshore company in Gibraltar, so we have no idea who the actual owners are. Our drone has surveyed the area and will continue to provide us with live images before and during our raid. Thanks to the fresh snow overnight, we can see that nobody has departed the property and there are footprints between the two buildings. So, someone is there.

"I've been reliably informed that all I have to do is swipe this App on my phone and the drone pictures will appear on the TV screen here. Please gather around so we can all familiarize ourselves with the terrain. Hopefully, we can then avoid wandering around like a herd of goats searching for fodder. Prado made a drama of swiping his screen. Everyone came closer and looked expectantly at the TV, but the screen remained blank.

Prado kept prodding but no images appeared. Phillip walked calmly up to the TV and turned it on. After a few moments, a bright, clear picture appeared. Everyone applauded. Prado grinned.

The property consisted of a long, narrow, meandering plot of land cut into a natural gently sloping ledge on the steep mountainside. It was located near the end of a cul de sac with nothing beyond it, except dense pine and fir forest. However, where the road ended, a narrow walkway had been cut through the trees to a viewing point some six hundred meters further in. The plot was some two hectares in size and covered thickly with a mix of walnut, almond, pine, and fir trees. A green, solid metal gate provided access to a driveway about half a kilometer long that curved its way through the trees to a parking area in front of two buildings. Some distance to the left of the gable end of the larger building was a wide level rectangular space with a windsock fluttering in the gentle breeze.

"Is that a helicopter pad, Sir?" said a female officer.

"I believe so," said Prado.

The main brick-built building resembled something straight out of the Swiss Alps. It consisted of four floors under a triangular roof with wide overhanging eaves. Fake timber shutters were mounted to the sides of each window on the lower two floors. The top two floors had dormer windows set among the gray slate tiles. The blinds on the ground floor were all raised. Lights were on in most of the rooms which overlooked a terrace and parking area. The main entrance was in the middle of the two half-height windows. It was a large oak door framed with fir trees in decorative pots on either side. Ornate lamps were mounted on the wall to each side of the door.

The second, much smaller building was situated on the other side of the parking. It was a two-floor cuckoo clock style log cabin. Smoke wafted out the chimneys of each building. Two sets of footprints led directly from the front door of the cabin, across the parking area, threading through the vehicles, to the rear entrance of the main building. Three large powerful snow-covered saloon cars and a small white van stood in the parking area.

"There is a two-meter-high wire fence that surrounds the plot," said Prado. "It's electrified and fitted with sensors supposedly to keep the deer and foxes out according to the planning application. There is no way to approach the house without the occupants receiving ample warning, so we have to be devious, hence our request for your, if I may say so extremely elegant mountain attire.

"In three minutes, a small tour bus will arrive and take us down to the property under the pretext of visiting the viewing point. It will suffer a puncture just outside the gate. To make sure we are in the correct position, the driver will remotely trigger a spike device fitted to the inner rim of the front left wheel. The bus will lurch to the left and stop dead so be prepared, hang on tight.

"Now, some of the culprits know what Phillip and I look like. So, we will stay on the bus. You guys will all climb out chatting and waving your arms about complaining of the cold then gather around the punctured wheel feigning a heated discussion about what to do. The driver and one of you will then change the wheel. Once it is done, you will cheer, take your hats off, and throw them in the air as if we were newly graduated students. There is a reason for this fiesta like approach.

"Two rotating cameras are covering the gate. One is about a meter above head height. I want the tallest of you to cover it with your hat at the same time the others are catching theirs. Who will be that person?"

"That would be me, Sir," said a tall burly man in a bright pink pullover covered with cute dog faces. "They call me larguirucho; lanky."

"Looking at your pullover, I would have thought hotdog more appropriate," said Prado, waiting for the laughter to stop. "Meanwhile, camera one is yours. The second camera is trickier. It's on top of an extended gate post to the left of the entrance. Do we have someone athletic enough to shimmy up on the side away from the camera lens and cover it with a hat at the appropriate moment to fit with our theatrical production?"

"That would be me, Sir," said a pretty female officer with short dark hair in a striking Christmas pullover."

"No fancy name?" said Prado.

"Sergeant will do, Sir."

"Thank you, sergeant," said Prado nodding. "OK. As soon as Lanky and the sergeant have blinded the cameras, we will then extract three-step ladders from the bus luggage hold and climb over the gate. I will go first, the rest of you follow. Phillip and Ana will be last. They are unarmed. The driver will remain with the bus.

"We will sprint up the drive as fast as we can, which in my case will not be that impressive. We suspect that everyone will be in the main house," said Prado swiping his phone again. "These are the four culprits we are after." Prado described their names and crimes as each mug shot appeared on the screen before continuing. "There could also be a doctor and other staff. I want one of you to check the cuckoo clock and five of you to check the grounds for any other installations under the trees and the perimeter fence for other entrances. When done, watch the back of the main house. The remainder will enter through the front door after me. We won't bother to knock. Please have weapons drawn and ready to fire. It's likely that these people would prefer to die rather than be arrested. Any questions?"

Prado surveyed the room as the officers looked at each other.

"Do you know who will go with whom?" said Prado.

"Yes, Sir," said Lanky. "We'll stay with our usual partners. How will we communicate?" said Lanky.

"Good question. There will be no talking, so we'll set up a WhatsApp group on the bus and text. Anything else?" Shakes of heads all around. "Then let's take a bathroom break and go play tourists."

The visibility improved marginally as the bus descended and turned off the main road into the cul de sac, but the light snow continued relentlessly. As the gaudily painted vehicle approached the property, the driver shouted, "Hang on everyone," and pressed the remote. There was a muffled bang as the spike burst the tire, the front left wheel dug into the packed snow and the bus slid to a stop over a distance of two meters.

The play unfolded as scripted until it was time to break into the impressive front entrance of the main building. Just as the battering ram was about to be swung, the door opened.

"No point in ruining a perfectly good door, inspector," said George Crown in Spanish, his sister Georgina standing behind him. Both were breathing heavily. The resemblance between the two and Malcolm was uncanny. All three were short and skinny, with slender hands, blue-gray eyes, and greasy dark hair. "Come in out of the cold please, we've been expecting you. There are hot drinks available for your team in the kitchen. Everyone is waiting there. Please put those weapons away, someone might be shot, and I abhor violence."

Prado instructed two officers to search Malcolm Crown's elder twin siblings, but they were unarmed. Prado waited with Phillip and Ana while the other officers filed in.

The officer checking the cuckoo clock cabin arrived shaking his head. "Nobody, Sir."

"Follow the others," said Prado. "But stay alert. We're not sure what's going on here."

"This isn't what we expected," said Prado turning to Phillip and Ana. "Any comments?"

"No idea," said Ana.

"I reckon George is bluffing," said Phillip. "To give him time to think and maybe create a diversion until their lawyers arrive."

"What makes you think that?" said Prado.

"The twins are living here," said Phillip.

"How do you know that?" said Ana.

"The pictures," said Phillip. "Remember at their Cortijo Infierno farm near Ronda, there were marks on the wall where two pictures used to hang. Their lawyer let slip that they were scenes of snowy mountains. Then we saw the actual pictures at their cottage when we visited them near Bournemouth, England. They were hanging in the hallway."

"And?" said Prado.

"Look at the wall just inside the door. There are the same pictures. They are of these Sierra Nevada mountains. The one on the right is the Mulhacen Peak. It implies that they hang these pictures wherever they are living at the time. And that means there must be communication equipment installed and a backup infrastructure in place including lawyers."

"Then we should search right away," said Prado. "Follow me."

They went into the hallway where George was standing waving an arm amiably toward the kitchen. They followed his direction and joined everyone in the enormous cozy room. The culprits were sitting around a huge rectangular oak table, each with a mug of tea. A uniformed maid passed among the intruders serving drinks from a tray. Another maid brought more chairs so everyone could sit.

A range stood at the far end, with cooking pots hanging over it and a huge fridge next to it. Along the inner wall were display cabinets, two sinks, cupboards, and worksurfaces.

Malcolm Crown was looking slightly better. The other three seemed nervous. There was one other dark-haired woman in her early-forties standing by Crown. "Dr. Susana Barrio," she said when Prado raised his eyebrows at her.

Prado regarded Paul Bosque.

Bosque stared back at him. For forty-seven years old, he was a fit, good looking man. His black hair swept straight back from his forehead His blue eyes were cold, almost dead.

"Your Aunt Virginia sends her regards, Señor Bosque," said Prado. "She is looking forward to renewing her acquaintance."

Bosque remain expressionless but he looked down at the table, not so sure of himself.

"Inspector," said George, "we owe you an…."

"Sorry to interrupt, Señor Crown but we have a search warrant for these buildings, and much as we would enjoy your kind hospitality, we have a job to do. You will all remain here under guard while the rest of us carry out our duties. Right," said Prado pointing at the four officers nearest the door. "You look after this lot while we search. Nobody is to leave until I give the word. The rest of you split up, one to each floor. Don't let any locked doors slow you down. As soon as you locate the communications room, come, and fetch me. I'll be searching the dining room on ground floor and there is bound to be a basement."

"I can't let you do that, inspector," said George looking decidedly unnerved. "Not until our lawyers arrive. They won't be long. I insist that you wait."

Prado exchanged nods with Phillip.

"If you try and prevent or delay us from our tasks," said Prado. "I will have no other choice but to restrain you." Crown started edging toward the kitchen door. "Secure him please him, sergeant," said Prado to the female officer nearest to him.

Crown made to run toward the door, but the sergeant tripped him, turned him on his front, and cuffed his hands behind his back. The look on Crown's face as she forced him onto a chair was a mixture of rage and embarrassment. The police were not responding as anticipated. This was not what he was accustomed to.

The officers replaced their still steaming drinks on the table, filed out of the kitchen, and began searching the beautifully decorated house.

Phillip found the basement door in the hallway, but it contained only an impressive stock of wine, racks of ski equipment, empty suitcases, and in a separate room at the far end, the heating system. Seven minutes later, just as Prado was opening another drawer of cutlery in the dining room opposite the kitchen, he heard a shout.

"Found it, Sir. Top floor," said a female voice from one of the upper landings.

Phillip, Prado, and Ana rushed up three flights of

stairs and into an attic room with black painted beams supporting the apex ceiling. Dormer windows looked out over front and back. To the rear, was a spacious garden with a frozen fountain in the middle of a snow-covered lawn bordered by nut trees. The lawn was dotted by lines of footprints from various sized birds.

Prado had never seen so many screens and equipment in one place. Yet only three office chairs stood in front of them. The three separate desktop computers were turned off.

Phillip sighed with relief. They were the latest Apple machines. He and Ana checked the cables and quickly established which was the main control. Phillip sat in the comfortable swivel chair in front of it, inserted his pen drive in an available USB port, turned on the machine, and ran his password cracker. Prado and Ana hovered over his shoulder. Prado drummed his fingers on the back of the chair.

Three minutes later, he was in.

He clicked on the activity log.

The screen turned black.

"Fuck," said Phillip.

"What?" said Prado.

"I've just set off an automatic shutdown."

"What does that mean?" said Ana.

"It's wiped everything from the hard disk."

"What about the other machines?" said Ana.

"They're all linked," said Phillip. "As soon as we turn them on, the same thing will happen."

"Shit," said Prado.

37

"Before we start panicking," said Prado. "Let's think this through. Ana, have you come across this problem previously?"

"Yes," said Ana.

"Tell us what you learned," said Phillip.

"It was at the offices of the Sanchez brothers in Málaga. They had an almost identical set up to this. Once the master computer was initiated and the automatic shutdown was initialized, it sent instructions to any computer connected to it by cable or wireless network. As soon as those machines were turned on, they wiped everything."

"Now we are faced with the same problem," said Prado.

"I know something we could try," said Phillip. "Let's disconnect the cables from the other machines, turn off the Wi-Fi, physically remove the hard drives and access them from another machine. Ana, did you bring your laptop?"

"Of course," said Ana opening her bag and extracting a well-worn Apple MacBook Pro. She placed it on the desk and set it up while Phillip disconnected the other two desktops and extracted the hard drives.

Phillip connected the first drive to the laptop. When it registered, Ana clicked on it.

Her screen flashed and turned black.

The same thing happened with the second drive.

"What does this mean?" said Prado.

"Any evidence that may have been on these drives has vanished into the ethernet," said Phillip.

"Surely, they have backups," said Ana.

"Probably on the Mumbai servers," said Phillip.

"They can have as many backups as they like," said Prado. "But they are useless unless they can remember how to access them. An operation like this must have many URL's, files, and accounts. They would have made a list to keep in a safe but easily accessible place. There must be a notebook or pen drive somewhere?"

"Notebooks are for old farts," said Phillip. "And pen drives are notoriously fickle. They must have them stashed online somewhere."

"Don't forget they are also experts on the dark web," said Ana. "They could have hidden them there."

"I don't agree," said Prado. "The twins are experienced IT experts in their early fifties. They are mature enough to know the frailty of human memory and that electronic storage can be hacked, or devices break down. They will have heard of the Californian Bitcoin investor who forgot his password. He has eleven attempts to remember it and he's used up nine of them. If the final two don't work, that's two hundred and eighty million dollars up in smoke. The Crowns have far more at stake and a lot more to remember. Believe me. They will have a non tech failsafe solution. And unless aliens have taken over, there is still only one totally secure method to do that. They would have written them down in a book."

"You could be right," said Ana. "But the book could still be elsewhere. They just update it from time to time."

"It's a matter of trust," said Prado. "Who do they know that could be relied on with such sensitive information?"

"One of their clients?" said Phillip.

"Would you?" said Prado.

"Personally, I'd want it with me at all times," said Phillip.

"Me too," said Ana.

"Then it's somewhere here," said Prado.

"So far, we've not found a safe?" said Ana.

"Let's think before we go rushing around looking behind paintings," said Prado. "There was no way that they knew we were coming. The earliest they must have realized that something was going down was when we blinded the cameras. It means that they had only a few minutes to activate the system defenses, turn everything off and be at the front door when we arrived. The twins were out of breath when they let us in, so they had only just managed to complete their tasks. It hardly gave them time to update the notebook and hide it somewhere."

"There were only two sets of footprints coming in and nothing going out," said Ana. "It has to be in the house."

"But where?" said Prado going over to the window that overlooked the back garden and gazing out at the flurries of falling snow.

"What would we be looking for?" said Ana.

"A secret hiding place," said Phillip. "That is easily

accessible between this room and the front door. A sliding panel, or disguised door perhaps?"

"Check the windows on each floor that overlook the garden," said Prado. "If one has been opened recently there will be melted snow on the windowsill or carpet."

"You think they threw it outside?" said Ana. "It would need a waterproof bag."

"There are deep drifts of soft snow up against the back of the house," said Prado peering at the carpet under his feet, then going over to the only other window and wiping the sill. "Any container would settle underneath the surface and quickly be covered by the still falling snow. Before we tear this place apart, we should check."

"There are no signs of water in this room," said Prado. "Let's go look at the other floors."

They trooped downstairs and into the first room that faced the lawn on the floor below. It was a bedroom. Ana checked the bathroom, while Phillip and Prado tried the windows.

Seconds later, Ana came back into the bedroom. They looked at each other, shook heads and filed into the next bedroom.

"Nothing here," said Phillip from his window.

"Same," said Prado.

"Look at this," said Ana.

They joined her in the spacious bathroom and found her leaning out of the open window. She stepped back and indicated for Prado to take a peek.

"That has to be it," said Prado turning back inside the room. "In the drift below, I can just see an indentation. Let's go and see what it is."

Ana closed the window and pointed to several water

drops on the marble floor. "I could hardly see them," she said. "And now there are more from when I opened the window. They fell in exactly the same place from the top of the window frame."

But Prado was already heading downstairs buttoning his coat.

They chased after him and went via the kitchen to the back door. All the prisoners looked at them expectantly as they walked by saying nothing.

George exchanged anxious glances with Georgina.

Prado led the way through the deep snow to the drift immediately below the bathroom window.

He cleared the space around the indentation.

And revealed a clear but sealed plastic container normally used for food storage.

He picked it up in his gloved hands.

Inside was a blue hardback notebook and pen drive.

They grinned at each other and went back into the kitchen.

George and Georgina visibly paled when they saw what Prado was carrying.

Their shoulders slumped.

37

Silvano Furlan read through the letter again. After his first attempt, he was inclined to rip it up and dispose of it, but something nagged at him to at least give it some thought. He placed the letter in his pocket, struggled into his heavy coat, and went for a walk.

It was a grey morning, but the temperature was mild for January as he headed out of his sister's apartment building out onto Via Salicotto and headed uphill in the direction of Piazza del Campo. The square, popular for its festivals and events, was practically empty. He walked around its perimeter, head down, hands in pockets, as his mind battled with the letter and a handwritten note folded inside it.

The main letter was from his late wife's lawyer, in Granada, probate was complete, and her assets were ready for distribution. The list of assets was short but substantial. Most of its value was in her row house near Capitol Hill in Washington DC. There were a few shares, but they had lost most of their original value plus the remnants of cash left in her bank account. All he had to do was sign the enclosed letter of acceptance, append his bank account details, buy a stamp, and post it off. But he was instinctively reticent.

Accepting ownership of the house would mean a legal battle with her brother. He had a long-term rental agreement and had claimed that she promised to leave him the house. It was originally left to the brother, but after they married, Anne had changed her will in favor of Silvano. After Silvano's instructions to Anne's lawyer to put the DC property on the market, the brother had threatened to challenge the revised will on the basis that she was suffering from Alzheimer's and didn't know what she was doing. Furthermore, since her death, he had stopped paying the rent. So potentially, the property could turn into a liability.

By accepting the will, it meant that he would be forced to resolve this conflict which could go either way. The property was worth well over a million dollars, but a long legal battle could bite into that. But it wasn't the potential reward of the money. He had more than enough for a simple life with his sister. He didn't want any hassle at this time of life. Life was too short to be battling against greedy, adversarial assholes.

He was highly tempted to rip up the letter and forget about it.

He reread the handwritten note from the lawyer. 'I have a sealed envelope from Anne addressed to you. My instructions were to give it to you personally in my office after we have been to the notary appointment where you accept your inheritance.'

A sealed envelope?

What could that be?

The battle in his head between curiosity and commonsense raged back and forth.

There was only one way to resolve it.

For that, he would have to fly to Granada.

"All that way and for what?" he mumbled to himself attracting some quizzical glances from occasional passersby.

He sat down at a terrace table of a café and ordered a cappuccino.

As he wiped the foamy milk from his upper lip, he made up his mind. He would go. The draw of the envelope contents was too strong to ignore. What if it were a final farewell from his beloved Anne. That would be worth the journey.

He finished his coffee and headed back to the cozy apartment where he turned on his laptop and started making his travel and hotel arrangements.

39

Prado was seated at the dining room table flicking through the notebook. He passed it over to Ana and Phillip sitting opposite. "There are several pages of lists," said Prado. "But it's gobbledygook to me. What do you make of it?"

Phillip turned the pages while he and Ana absorbed what was indeed written nonsense.

"Probably a code of some sort," said Phillip.

"We'll never crack this here," said Ana. "We'll have to wait until we can use the full resources of my Lab."

Prado's phone buzzed. He checked the screen. It was a text from the drone man. 'Helicopter approaching,' it said.

'Is the drone still up?' Prado tapped into his phone. 'I have a black screen.'

'Changing the battery, Sir,' was texted back. 'Ready in one minute. Where would you like it?'

'Over the main road junction into the cul de sac. Warn me if you see any vehicles heading up here. Is your van out of sight?'

'No, but I can see a track leading into the trees. I'll

pop it in there, then set the drone loose.'

They all heard the unmistakable distant whirring of a helicopter.

'Chopper approaching,' texted Prado to the group. 'Driver, are you with the bus?'

'Yes,' came the reply.

'Leave it in front of the gates, remove hats from cameras, ladders from gates and hide them back in bus. Then lock the bus and take cover in trees opposite. Prepare weapon but stay out of sight until we know what they intend. Those of you searching the grounds split up but stay under tree cover. Three cover the gate, two monitor the helipad. Wait for my word. Those of you searching the house report to the downstairs hall, weapons ready.'

"Phillip," said Prado. "There are at least seven people to be flown out. What size of machine would they need for that?"

"Plus, the pilot and at least a couple of helpers. I would say a minimum of a ten-seater which is huge. The only place it could land would be on the helipad."

In the kitchen, George Crown heard the helicopter.

The culprits exchanged glances. Their expressions of hope were obvious to the watching officers. All four drew their pistols and made them ready.

"Please lay down your weapons," said George. "They are completely unnecessary. It's only our transport. We're trying to leave the country, not start a war."

"Are they armed?" said Prado entering. He went over to the giant window and closed the venetian blinds, then took his weapon out of his shoulder holster.

George said nothing.

Prado walked over to Georgina, pointed his pistol against her temple and cocked the trigger.

"The lives of my officers are at stake here," shouted Prado. "Tell me now. Are they armed?"

George nodded. Georgina burst into tears.

The doctor moved to comfort her.

"Stay where you are," said Prado going over to the kitchen window and peeking out through one of the slats.

'A van just turned off the main road, Sir,' texted the drone operator. 'Moving fast.'

'Keep it in view,' tapped Prado.

The thump, thump, thump from the helicopter grew louder.

Phillip turned off the light, went over to the dining room window and peeked out from behind one of the drapes.

He couldn't see much detail in the murky light, just an occasional hint of green paint.

The helicopter slowed to a hover some thirty meters above the landing area, it's belly, a creamy white. Even with the double glazing, the noise was overwhelming as it sunk lower and lower toward the landing spot. The snow surrounding the helipad slowly spiraled into the air, surrounding the machine so it resembled a ghostly apparition. When the twirling mass settled on the ground, the engine was turned off and the blades slowly stopped spinning. The revolving snow settled back down on top of it covering its identification markings. Phillip eased himself out of sight as the door burst open and he caught a glimpse of two men in black body armor and helmets, automatic weapons at the ready, stumble over the snow toward the front door.

"What are they expecting?" said Prado jabbing his gun into Georgina's ribs and whispering into her ear.

"For someone to open the door," she said.

Prado dragged Georgina into the hallway.

George tried to stand and follow her.

The other culprits stood.

The officers pointed their weapons indicating that they should sit.

In the hallway, the four officers who had been searching the house aimed their weapons at the front door.

Prado indicated they should hide out of sight in the dining room.

He moved Georgina to the door let her go and pressed himself into the corner pointing his weapon at her.

He nodded.

She opened the door.

"Are you all ready," said a male voice in Spanish.

"Not quite," she said. "Come into the warm while you wait, we won't be long."

The two men lowered their weapons and entered.

Prado and his four colleagues stepped forward pistols pointing at the men's heads.

"Drop your guns," said Prado. "Then go into the dining room."

The two men slowly placed their machine guns on the floor and warily edged toward the dining where they were handcuffed then searched.

They each carried a pistol, a knife and a one of them had a radio.

"How many in the chopper?" said Prado.

"Pilot and copilot," said the man.

"Are they armed?" said Prado.

"No," said the man.

"Sit down on the floor," said Prado. "One move and you will be shot."

Prado texted the two men watching the helipad. 'Approach and apprehend unarmed crew. Bring them in here.'

'Confirmed,' came the reply.

'Van approaching gate,' texted the bus driver. 'He's stopped. Now he's on the phone. Now he's turning around. He's gone.'

'When gate opens bring bus to main house,' texted Prado going into the kitchen with Georgina and seating her down next to George again.

The two pilots were shown in, cuffed and were sat down next to the gunmen.

Prado went into the kitchen. "You," he said to one of the maids standing by the back door. "Can you open the front gate from here?"

She nodded and opened a panel in the wall by the door revealing a small monitor with buttons on the side. She pressed one and Prado could see movement on the small screen as the gate slid open.

Ana and Phillip joined Prado in the kitchen.

Minutes later, the bus stopped by the parked cars.

"Take them all out to the bus," said Prado. "And lock them in while we finish up here."

George Crown was apoplectic. His complexion bright red, his eyes bulging.

"Bastards," he shouted repeatedly as two of Prado's men dragged him over the snow.

"What's he saying?" said Prado.

"I'm not sure if he's cursing us for spoiling his plans or his rescuers for failing at their task," said Phillip.

Georgina tried to calm him as he was manhandled

up the bus steps and cuffed to a seat. The others followed and sat down. In contrast to George, they were quiet, reflecting on what might have been.

The maids sat in the back seat and chatted with each other as if they were excited about the journey.

"Can I have a word, Inspector?" said Phillip after the driver had locked the bus door.

"Sure."

"We should still look for a safe," said Phillip. "It might contain pointers to breaking the code. And we need all the computer equipment upstairs taken to Ana's office. There's an off chance that we can still access the hard drives."

"You're right," said Prado. "I'll have a word with Ana to send her team over and collect all the forensics from the building and the equipment. I need to move the prisoners to the comisaría in Málaga as soon as possible. The van driver made a phone call. It might not signify anything, but I can't risk that. You can stay here or come with me."

"I'll stay," said Phillip. "There has to be more to discover. Hopefully, something to help us crack the codes."

40

Later that afternoon, the bus delivered the maids and culprits to the comisaría in Málaga where they were split into three groups. The helicopter pilots and two armed mercenaries were extremely cooperative. They had been hired by Severiano Pizarro to transport everyone at the house to Granada airport from where they would catch a plane to Casablanca. They were released without charge.

The two maids had no idea what type of business was being transacted from the house but confirmed that there were regular helicopter visits from distinguished men and women. One of whom was identified as Severiano Pizarro.

The others were left to stew in separate cells.

Phillip discovered a built in safe in George's wardrobe. One of Ana's team opened it and found two pistols and a huge wad of notes in various currencies. There were also several passports both genuine and false, but the key item was a book on codes.

They returned to Ana's Lab early that evening in the forensics van with the computer equipment, mobile phones, fingerprints and DNA samples.

Between them Ana and Phillip were able to translate the nonsense in the notebook to something useable. What they discovered when clicking on all the files located at the URL's was mind shattering.

It clarified exactly what the Crown's had been up to and was more than enough evidence for extremely long jail sentences. They also gained access to the backup servers in Mumbai. Bank accounts, client details, trading history and so much more.

They printed out the key documents and summoned Prado.

He arrived five minutes later, read them through, smiled and nodded.

"Just what I thought," he said. "We should confront the twins with this immediately.

He and Phillip reported to el jefe.

They discussed their tactics and adjourned to the observation room.

George and Georgina Crown were already sitting on one side of the table. They were holding hands but looked confident.

"Is there something we don't know?" said el jefe.

"I'm expecting interference from high places at any moment," said Prado.

"Bring it on," said el jefe.

Phillip and Prado went through to the interview room. El jefe listened in.

Prado placed the documents on the table.

The pair looked them, an aura of doubt creeping into their body language.

He looked at the both of them.

"We cracked the code in your little blue book," said Prado. "And have analyzed all the data that the URLs, logins and passwords led us to. We've seen all your bank accounts and those of your clients and are now in a position to bring charges against you as follows."

"I demand that we wait for our lawyer to arrive?" said George.

"You may demand what you like," said Prado but at this stage, we are only informing you of the charges that we will be bringing against you and inviting you to comment. We can discuss them with your lawyer as and when he is here."

Prado paused, opened the file and moved the top paper nearer to him.

"This document confirms that you, as majority shareholders, and directors of CVS Holdings Ltd were the financers and masterminds behind your brother Malcolm Crown's perverse website, Patrick O'Reilly's illegal gambling, and Sonia Augustin's auctions for stolen artifacts. All the bank account details are here, including those offshore in the Turks and Caicos Islands. I would remind you that the murders of two bullfighters and your parents were a consequence of this conspiracy."

Prado turned that paper over and reached for the next.

"This document confirms that you have been providing tax evasion services to thirteen of Spain's largest companies for over fifteen years. I'll summarize how that worked using the well-known Spanish clothing retailer as an example. It's a Spanish company registered in Madrid. They have stores in most major cities throughout the world. For items sold in its physical stores, they combine their global sales, submit accounts in Spain and pay tax in Spain as they should. However, their fastest growing market is online trading."

Prado paused again.

Now the pair looked completely shattered.

"For that," said Prado. "They have a separate accounting structure in place where they contract out the administration and money collecting to CVS Holdings registered in Luxemburg."

"To put it simply. If a customer buys a pair of pants from one of their online stores, payment is made to CVS in Luxemburg. CVS then pay the retailer, minus a collection fee. The retailer also has a company registered in Luxemburg. However, this fee is larger than it should be. CVS pay some of that to the retailer's account in Luxemburg to cover costs, but the lion's share is transferred into the CVS Holdings offshore account in Turks and Caicos. From there, most of it is transferred to the retailer's account in the same island bank. It means that the retailer declares practically no profit on its online trading in Luxemburg, pays little to no tax there, and accumulates a nice tidy sum offshore for the directors to play with as they wish.

"And that is completely illegal. What I'd like to do now is link all this activity to Marquez, your brother's abuser at school.

"We found a video on Marquez's laptop confirming he knew you were cooking up a tax evasion scheme thirty years ago. Your father was in cahoots with Pablo Bosque and through him to Severiano Pizarro. We also know that Marquez and his sister ran a swingers' club in Marbella where your father and his buddies were members. Marquez knew that they were men of low moral fiber and wouldn't be able to resist the promise of some young flesh. Marquez recorded them abusing their children and others and kept a diary of all the abuse activities. We have the diary and those films.

They are what Marquez used to become headmaster of the school and involved in the golf course project."

Prado paused and checked them out.

They were both weeping quietly.

"That is why they never reported Marquez for stealing the golf course proceeds and that is why you have been so desperate to find him and exact your revenge. You may have succeeded in that. But we are not considering any charges for his death. However, for all the other crimes, you must pay.

"When your lawyer turns up, we will present him with this evidence and leave you to discuss it."

Phillip and Prado withdrew to the observation room.

The twins just held each other and sobbed.

Their world had ended.

"With the statement we obtained from Daniel Hidalgo," said el jefe. "Confirming the murders of their parents, we should have enough to lock the twins and the rest of them up for years to come. A satisfactory outcome don't you think?"

"From a legal standpoint, I agree," said Phillip. "However, I can't help but feel a little sorry for them. In part, they were driven to this by the behavior of their parents and friends. It's no excuse for their crimes but at least you can sympathize with their motivations and it's a terrible shame about all that money, though."

"Sorry?" said Prado.

"Over the years, the twins and each of their clients have accrued huge sums of cash stashed offshore; the exact balances are in the files. Have a think about how to make them repatriate everything. I'm sure the Bank of Spain would be grateful for even a percentage of it."

"Mmm…" said Prado rubbing his earlobe.

"Actually, I've been thinking about that for a while. Maybe there's a way?"

"Such as?" said el jefe.

"I have a proposal," said Prado. "But I'd rather wait until their lawyer arrives. I'll explain then."

41

The Crown twins looked up as Prado and Phillip entered.

"Your lawyer is on the way up," said Prado.

"What have you done with the maids?" said Georgina wiping her eyes. "They had no involvement in or knowledge of our affairs."

"They've been released without charge," said Prado. "But please don't imagine for a moment that you will ever find time to enjoy your ill-gotten gains."

"I might have something to say about that," said a tall, distinguished man in his fifties shown into the room by a uniformed officer. "I'm Emilio Ramos, Inspector, their lawyer. I'd like a few moments alone with my clients and for this, I demand that you leave us and turn off your cameras and recording devices. I'll summon you when ready."

Prado regarded all three carefully, nodded, and left the room with Phillip.

Phillip and Prado joined el jefe in the observation room, turned everything off, and watched the heated discussion through the one-way mirror.

At one stage, Ramos approached the mirror almost

kissing it as he explained something to the twins. Shortly after, Ramos waved at them to rejoin them.

Prado turned everything back on, they went back into the interview room leaving el jefe to listen in.

The twins looked much happier.

Phillip and Prado sat down opposite the three of them.

"I've advised my clients not to answer any of your questions," said Ramos looking at his watch. "And, in about three minutes your bosses will be receiving a call from a Government minister instructing that all charges be dropped, and my clients released."

"Does that include their brother Malcolm and the others?" said Prado unfazed.

"It does," said Ramos looking puzzled by Prado's reaction.

"And do those charges being dropped include those of conspiracy to murder Marquez?" said Prado.

"No," said Ramos. "By your own records, Marquez committed suicide."

Prado stood and switched on the TV screen. He nodded to el jefe who set the video running.

It showed Sonia and Patrick O'Reilly meeting by the open door to the remand wing for male prisoners. The clock read one minute after three am on the eighth of January. They then ran down the corridor and entered the cell of Marquez. Ten minutes later, it recorded them running out again, hugging and separating. Both had blood on their hands and orange jumpsuits.

"Where did you obtain this?" said Ramos.

The twins looked decidedly uncomfortable.

"Our technicians recovered this from your cloud database located on a server owned by your company CVS Holdings in Mumbai, India."

"Idiots," said Ramos glaring at the twins.

They were both preoccupied with the tabletop.

"This is enough evidence for us to reopen the investigation into the death of Marquez," said Prado. "May I suggest that you call your minister friend and update him."

Ramos rushed out of the room.

He returned a few minutes later looking decidedly embarrassed.

"What now, Inspector?" he said.

"I have a proposal," said Prado. "It will save face, and justice will be seen to be done."

"Go on," said Ramos. The twins looked at Prado, a gleam of hope in their eyes.

"I want to pool all your client's crimes into one conspiracy and manslaughter pot for which they are all equally responsible. Everyone will plead guilty and receive the same punishment. In return, they will have to agree to relinquish ownership of all the funds in the CVS offshore accounts which are to be transferred to the Bank of Spain. I should say that we have changed all the logins and passwords so the funds are useless to them anyway, but their cooperation will be looked on favorably."

"Is that all?" said Ramos.

"Hardly," said Prado. "For fifteen years, their clients, all major Spanish companies, have evaded paying the correct tax on their online trading. Currently, the sales volumes on this category of business have overtaken those from their physical premises. This represents a huge amount of revenue obtained fraudulently at the expense of Spanish taxpayers. But if we lock up the major shareholders and directors responsible for these monstrous crimes, their companies will suffer tremendously, and thousands of jobs are likely to be lost. Our Primeminister wishes to avoid this disaster."

"How does this impact my clients?" said Ramos.

"It's simple," said Prado. "They will persuade their clients to repatriate their online trade and voluntarily pay the unpaid taxes, plus interest, and a fine. If their clients agree, they won't be taken to court, and the deal will be kept under wraps."

"Have your bosses approved this?" said Ramos.

"Right up to the Primeminister," said Prado.

"What punishment did you have in mind for my clients?" said Ramos.

"That will be up to the judge," said Prado. "But I will recommend to the prosecutor to ask for a maximum of three years each in an open prison. With good behavior, they can be out in half that."

"What if some of the clients don't cooperate?" said Ramos.

"It has to be all or nothing," said Prado.

"I can think of at least three that will refuse," said Georgina Crown. "So, we're wasting our time discussing this."

"Wait," said Prado. "Think beyond the money and concentrate on the principle. Most of these businesses rely on the public favoring their products and services. If they agree to this deal, their cooperation will be kept under wraps. However, if they don't, then it will be announced on the news. What do you think the public will make of that?"

"That they are inconsiderate of fellow taxpayers and are morally impoverished," said Georgina. "Followed rapidly by mass customer boycotts and bankruptcy."

"Exactly," said Prado.

"It's blackmail," said George Crown.

"I call it peer pressure," said Prado. "And if it works, it means that all of you will soon be free to get back to work and rebuild your lives."

"How do you envisage us persuading everyone while we're stuck in here?" said George.

"I'm going to put you into a conference room and let you discuss the idea. Should you agree, then I'll equip you with telephones and contact numbers so you can persuade your clients to come on board. Once everyone has made their bank transfers, including you, then we can go straight to court, after which you can begin serving your sentences immediately."

"What about Dr. Susana Barrio?" said Georgina. "She wasn't involved in most of this."

"No, but she did kill her father," said Prado. "On the other hand, Patrick O'Reilly murdered two people in cold blood and his father. My point is that you all conspired together, so you share the consequences equally, or would you prefer to spend the remainder of your lives behind bars?"

They all nodded to each other.

"Good," said Ramos. "But don't forget. At this stage, we are only discussing the possibility. We'll let you know our decision in the morning."

42

"How did it go with Prado?" said Amanda, as Phillip took off his leather jacket, hung it on the hook behind the door, and plonked himself on a kitchen stool.

"Fine," said Phillip yawning.

"Poor thing, you look exhausted. Take a seat on the terrace and I'll bring us both some wine."

"Good, thanks, some grape juice should fix my brain fog. How is my boy?"

"Fast asleep. We went for a run together after school. As usual, he was determined to beat me. Ye gods, that boy can shift, he almost won but it tired him out. After supper, he went straight to bed and off to sleep without a story. Now tell me about the case."

Amanda poured the wine, sat next to him, and leaned on his shoulder. He put his arm around her shoulder and related the day's events.

"It sounds like an innovative deal," said Amanda. "And good for the economy. Do you think they and their clients will accept it?"

"Why wouldn't they?" said Phillip. "When the alternative is twenty or more years behind bars."

"And," said Amanda. "It's fast, effective, fair and will save state funds on lengthy trials and imprisonment. It will also encourage other companies to repatriate their fiscal base back to the mother country and deter those that might be in the process of setting up such a scheme. Everyone benefits, especially the taxpayer. Perhaps it's time to adopt such a fresh approach to justice."

"Let the punishment fit the crime you mean?"

"Exactly. The focus has to change from punishment to converting culprits into responsible citizens. We can't afford to keep building more and more prisons. Anyway, good luck tomorrow."

"Thanks, darling. How was your day?"

"Oh, you know, washing, housework, child management. The usual stuff."

"I should be back by early tomorrow afternoon. Then it will be my turn."

"I'm not complaining, darling. It has to be done but I can't pretend that I enjoy the ironing bit."

"Perhaps we should look for some help?"

"Now that would be amazing, darling," said Amanda shifting over to sit on his lap. She wriggled provocatively and kissed him.

"It will reduce my stress levels," she said pausing for some air. "And you know how that affects me."

She kissed him.

"Are you up to this?" she said.

"I'm always pleased to see you.

43

The next morning dawned a gloomy, cold day with a bitter breeze. Prado and Phillip met at what was now their regular café in Plaza de la Merced. This time they sat indoors where a blaze raged in the open fireplace. However, the new waiter wasn't familiar with their usual order. "Any idea?" said Phillip after the waiter had left.

"I'm feeling confident," said Prado.

They finished their coffee and headed off to the comisaría.

The Crown twins and their lawyer Ramos were waiting for them in the interview room.

"Have you come to a decision?" said Prado.

"My clients are happy to accept your proposal," said Ramos.

"Good," said Prado taking a folded paper out of his jacket pocket. "Then I'll escort you back to the conference room, set you up with the phones, and bring the others. These are the new logins for your own accounts and a list of telephone numbers of your clients. We extracted it from your database at the house." Prado handed the list to George.

Georgina grabbed it from her brother and quickly scanned the thirteen Company names.

"The numbers next to the names," said Prado. "Are the amounts to be transferred to the Bank of Spain by two pm today. The account number is at the bottom of the list. Payment terms will not be accepted. If all monies are received before the deadline expires, you will be taken to Málaga court, plead guilty as charged, and be sentenced."

"And if they are not?" said Ramos.

"Then the deal is off, there will be no refunds, and each of you will be charged individually for your crimes. Just to give you a flavor of what that means for you two. The first charge will be conspiring to at least four counts of murder, being your parents and the bullfighters. Other charges will include human trafficking, sexual slavery, illegal gambling, stealing religious artifacts from many of Spain's finest cathedrals, and tax evasion. I estimate that as twenty-seven years behind bars. That will apply to all of you except Dr. Barrio. There will also be an announcement on the news summarizing your crimes and the services you provided to these businesses."

Prado looked at his watch. He stared the Crown twins in the eye. They glared back.

"Then let's make a start," said George.

Fifteen minutes later, they were all ensconced in the conference room. George and Georgina did the phoning. The others listened hard.

Prado and Phillip went up to the top floor and sat down across from each other at Prado's desk.

"And now?" said Phillip.

"We wait," said Prado.

After five minutes, both were nodding off in their

respective chairs.

An hour later, el jefe burst through the door grinning like a Cheshire cat.

"The first payment has just arrived," he said. "And it's from Pizarro. That means all the rest are bound to follow. At long last, we are within striking distance of wrapping up this exhausting case."

The remaining payments dribbled through painstakingly slowly. With thirty minutes until the deadline, Prado went into the conference room to find everyone depressed and doing nothing.

"Do you have time to sit here and look miserable?" said Prado.

"Like I informed you," said Georgina. "Three refuse to pay. We've tried every argument, but they won't budge."

"What type of businesses are they?" said Prado.

"Wine exporter, international engineering, and shipping," said George.

"Get them on the line now," said Prado. "I'll speak to all three of them at once. Put them on speakerphone."

It took a few minutes.

The twins nodded and clicked Prado onto the speakerphone.

"Ladies and gentlemen," said Prado. "Thank you for your time. I understand that you have declined to pay the monies requested as a voluntary settlement for evading tax. I'm sure that you have been informed of the consequences the Crowns and associates will suffer as a result of your actions. I am equally sure that you don't care too much about that. You also don't seem worried about the potential effect on your business as a result of public backlash against your lack of patriotism and moral standards. Let me enlighten you. First you will all be jailed for at least four years and be banned from serving as directors for life. If that isn't a strong enough argument, consider this. I note that all three of you rely on exports as your main source of revenue, which is why you feel that any actions taken against you by the Spanish public will have little effect on your profits. That may be the case. However, you do rely on the infrastructure of this country and its taxpayers to carry out your business. As you know approvals for infrastructure plans in Spain need the support of local and national authorities. Annual accounts need an agreement with the tax authorities. Business licenses need constant renewals, vehicles need testing, and insurance premiums are calculated on your track record of efficiency and safety. All I wanted to say, is that if you make the payments within the next half an hour, all these activities will continue to happen smoothly. If they don't, I will personally ensure that your businesses are disrupted daily to the extent that your ability to operate throughout this country will be completely throttled. You have half an hour to stop me. Goodbye."

Prado took a seat next to George Crown who nodded with respect.

The others around the table mumbled amongst themselves.

"Thank you," said Sonia. "There was no need for you to do that."

"I know," said Prado. "And it might not work but I had to try."

"Why?" said Malcolm.

"Because if we continue to let big business evade their responsibilities to the society they exploit to make their money, they will only take more liberties with ordinary people. Where will it end? This is my humble attempt to redress the balance. If big business behaved impeccably, they wouldn't need people like you, and with all due respect, you're just as bad as they are. Even worse, you are foreign opportunists depriving Spanish people of what they are entitled to. For that, you must go to prison."

For ten minutes nobody said a word.

Nobody looked at each other, preferring the intricate whorls of grain in the oak table.

Then el jefe barged into the room accompanied by two officers.

"Lady and gentlemen," he said, his face expressionless. "The final three payments have arrived. Now let's go to court. The minibus is waiting downstairs. These officers will escort you there."

Prado and Phillip watched the minibus pull out of the comisaría with the prisoners on board.

It was immediately replaced by an unmarked car with el jefe in the front seat next to the driver. Prado and Phillip took the back seats. Nobody said a word as they traveled the six odd kilometers to the modern courts located at Málaga's justice department at Cuidad de la Justicia on Calle Decano Agustín Moreno on the northern side of the city.

They were dropped outside the main entrance and made their way to the criminal court.

In the timber paneled courtroom, the defendants were taking their seats behind the defense table. Ramos was with them. Prado, Phillip, and el jefe sat behind the prosecutor. They stood as the judge entered through a door behind his elevated platform. He was a balding man in his sixties dressed in the traditional black robe and white ruff. The clerk announced the case and the judge sat down. The flags of Andalucía and Spain were hanging on the timber paneled wall behind him.

The prosecutor, an elegantly dressed mature woman with short grey hair summarized the manslaughter conspiracy case against each defendant. One by one, they pleaded guilty. The judge retired to consider the verdict. He returned ten minutes later and sentenced each to three years imprisonment. But the judge wasn't going to let them be taken down without a few words.

"I'm treading extremely close to the line here," he said, his booming voice echoing around the court through the PA system. "I'm in danger of commenting on matters political, something my position forbids me from doing. But as this case is being heard behind closed doors, and there is no chance of appeal, I should be able to get away with it. Underneath these robes lies a man with opinions and today, for the first time I am damn well going to make them known. I want to make these points so that your well-connected defendants can pass them on to their clients who will transfer them to theirs and further. This is a most unusual case that I and my learned colleagues initially found unsettling. On the surface, it could appear that in return for large sums of money being paid to the state, lesser charges have been brought and lighter sentences have been passed. We were all of the opinion that this might open the doors for a two-tier justice system where wealthy defendants could simply purchase their way out of trouble. Whereas the poor man has no choice but to accept whatever is thrown at him. But then we agreed. This is how it is now and always has been. The rich can afford the finest lawyers to nitpick the detail and get off on a technicality, whereas the less well-off are stuck with some callow youth fresh out of law school who can't tell his torts from his tarts. Notwithstanding, the issue here is serious. It is absurd that the wealthy can exploit the considerable talents and resources of this country to make their profit and then legally avoid paying their due taxes by basing themselves offshore where the tax regime is practically zero. I am delighted that this case has forced thirteen of Spain's largest businesses to repatriate their fiscal arrangements and play their full part in accepting that they cannot have profit without responsibility. Spreading the word that these practices are morally unacceptable should encourage every company to support their country, not just the shareholders. Take them down."

Everyone stood and the judge left the courtroom.

El jefe turned and shook hands with Phillip and Prado. "Please accept my sincere thanks," he said. "And pass them on to Amanda for all her hard work during this marathon. I wish you both well with your forthcoming nuptials and look forward to working with you again. Now, excuse me, I have to confer with the judge. You should both go home and spend some time with your families."

Outside, on the front steps, as they waited for their driver, Prado and Phillip watched the prison van head off to Alhaurin with their prisoners on board. They would eventually be transferred to a more relaxed prison to serve their sentences.

Their driver arrived and they headed down a busy Avenida Andalucía back to the comisaría.

"So," said Prado. "It's done."

"Eight months of effort concluded," said Phillip.

"I wonder what will be next?" said Prado.

44

Silvano Furlan gazed out the steamy window as he savored his coffee in a cozy café just around the corner from the notary on Calle Pavaneras. Granada was bitterly cold. Several centimeters of snow had fallen overnight, and a biting wind was hampering the council workers clearing efforts. He checked his watch, drained his cup, left some money on the table, struggled into his coat, and pulled a woolen ski hat down over his ears.

"Hasta lluego," he said to the waitress as he heaved the café door open and shut it behind him as quickly as he could. He walked gingerly on the icy surface. He wasn't accustomed to this cold white stuff. It usually fell on the mountains over two thousand meters, not down here in the city.

The notary was located on the mezzanine of a modern, marble-clad, nine-floor block. He went into the lobby, climbed the single flight of stairs, and entered the spacious reception. He immediately spotted Anne's lawyer, Luciano Marín, a gray-haired man in his early sixties, sitting on a row of chairs outside one of the several glass-fronted notary offices.

He was busy checking the contents of a file.

"Buenos días, Señor Marín," said Silvano.

Marín looked up and smiled. "Ah, Señor Furlan," he said placing the file on the chair next to him and standing. They shook hands. "How nice to see you again. We're to go straight in, they're ready for us."

The notary was a medium height, thick-set man in his late forties.

They exchanged pleasantries and Silvano presented his passport.

A young female secretary took it out for copying, returned within minutes, and placed both copy and original in front of the notary. He picked up the original and compared the photo with Silvano, nodded then picked up the file in front of him. He scanned it then read the principal document out loud. It was a list of Anne's assets, except no mention of an envelope. Silvano agreed to accept, he signed, the notary then did the same on each page. The document was stamped and dated. They waited outside while the will was registered.

When the secretary delivered it, they both stood, retrieved their coats, and went down into the lobby appraising the weather conditions.

"What am I going to do about the brother?" said Silvano as they stood near the exit.

"He won't do anything in Spain," said Marín. "But he can be extremely effective in challenging your rights to the property over there. You'll need a sharp probate lawyer and a medical report in English from Anne's doctor confirming her mental capacity at the time the will was changed."

"Do you know her doctor?" said Silvano.

"No, but I can contact him, prepare the necessary

documentation, and have it officially translated."

"Then please do that. Could you also find me a good lawyer in Washington?"

"I will inquire at my bar association, I'm sure a colleague will have such a contact."

"Tell me about this envelope," said Silvano.

"Anne lodged it with me last year," said Marín. "Her instructions were to hand it to you personally after you had accepted her inheritance. It's in my safe. You are to open it on your own and not show the contents to anyone."

They went out, crossed the road, and headed around the corner toward the lawyer's office. It was only thirty meters to a door squeezed between two shops. Luciano opened it and led the way up the stairs to the first floor. Black capital letters stuck on the outside of a frosted glass door announced the incumbents as 'Luciano Marín e Hijo. Abogados'.

Luciano opened the door and ushered him inside. There were two rooms. In front of him were two desks each with computer screens. Huge, open, metal filing cabinets lined both sidewalls. A glass-fronted office was to the rear with an open door. Two chairs by the entrance formed a waiting area next to a coffee table scattered with out-of-date magazines.

A mature, smartly dressed woman, with gray hair pinned behind her neck was sitting behind one of the desks. She looked up and stood as he entered. "Can I offer you a drink, Señor Furlan?" she said.

"Thank you, but no," said Silvano.

Luciano escorted him into his office and closed the door. They took off their coats and hats then hung them on a stand behind the door.

The lawyer went over to a large safe in the corner

behind his spacious timber desk laden with piles of files. He twiddled with the dial, opened the door, and picked up an envelope. He passed it to Silvano and closed the safe door.

"I'll leave you alone," said Marín going out to talk with his assistant.

Silvano sat down, his heart thumping. He felt the contents, but the shapes meant nothing to him. He read the front, but all it had was his name written in Anne's hand. He turned it over. The flap was sealed with red wax indented with the circular stamp of the lawyer. He ripped open the flap and turned the envelope upside down over the desk. A large stainless-steel key landed with a clump followed by a credit card. He picked them up.

The key was just a key, nothing special or fancy about it other than its size. It was sturdy, made of steel, and nearly ten centimeters long. The card was a standard Visa credit card in the name of Silvano Furlan. Expiry date in two years.

Silvano scratched his head. What the hell does all this mean? He placed the card in his wallet and key in his jacket pocket. He struggled into his coat, then said his farewells to the lawyer and his assistant.

He almost ran down the stairs, wanting out of there. He slipped on his hat, opened the door, and went out onto the pavement. It was snowing again. He breathed the cold air deeply. The panic subsiding.

He needed help and he knew exactly where to find it.

It meant a taxi to the bus station.

45

Amanda and Phillip had just awoken from their siesta when her phone rang. She yawned, stretched over to the bedside table, picked it up, and swiped the screen without checking the caller ID. "Hello," she said.

"Amanda," said a male voice in English with an unmistakable Italian accent.

"Silvano?" said Amanda sitting up. "Is that you?"

"Yes. Sorry to disturb you but I have a problem and have no idea where to start solving it."

"How can I help?"

"I'm in Granada and have just come out of Anne's lawyer's office. I came to accept my inheritance, but that's not my reason for calling. The lawyer gave me an envelope addressed to me from Anne. I was instructed to open it on my own, which I did, but the contents mean nothing to me. I am convinced that Anne is trying to tell me something important, otherwise, why go to all this trouble? Could you help me work out what she is trying to tell me?"

"Can you find your way to Nerja?"

"Of course, I'll take the next bus. Can you

recommend a pleasant hotel?"

"You can stay with us. We have a guest bedroom with en suite."

"Where do you live?"

"I'll text you the address."

***

Silvano arrived by cab. They met him at the front door went inside and shut the door behind them. Phillip indicated that Sasha was asleep, and they should keep the noise down. Amanda showed Silvano to the guest room where he dumped his overnight bag, spruced up in the bathroom, and joined them in the kitchen closing the door behind him.

***

A silver car went to the end of the road, turned around, and headed back up to the main road. It stopped just outside Phillip's gate. A woman got out and checked the cars parked in the drive. She climbed back in, closed the door and they drove off into the darkness.

***

The terrace was a little chilly, so Amanda suggested they sit in the lounge. Phillip poured them a glass of wine as Silvano related his morning's adventures.

He then placed the key and card on the coffee table.

They both picked them up and examined them.

"I have no idea if these are genuine," said Phillip. "But I think your initial thoughts are correct. Anne is trying to send you a message and these two items are to guide you to it. Tomorrow morning, I suggest that we visit a locksmith and my bank, to see what we can learn."

"Meanwhile," said Amanda. "I suggest, if you can face it, that we regurgitate your years together and consider anything Anne may have done that was out of the ordinary."

Silvano looked stumped and took another sip of wine as he thought about their short time together.

"Did she have a laptop or smartphone?" said Phillip.

"I have both, but she was paranoid about anything technical and always used the landline."

"What about when you traveled?" said Amanda.

"She arranged everything with a local travel agent."

"Did she drive?" said Phillip.

"Never, we always used private hire with the same driver."

"Did she go shopping on her own?" said Amanda.

"The staff took care of the weekly stuff. The only time she went shopping was with me when we were traveling but she hardly ever purchased anything. She had wardrobes full of stuff and that seemed to be enough."

"So, for three years were you in each other's company the whole time?" said Phillip.

"Almost four if you include our courtship. And yes, we were hardly ever apart, except for when she took the paintings to be cleaned," said Silvano.

"Which paintings?" said Amanda.

"The muses. She started the process before we married but every six months or so, our driver took her off to Málaga for three days with one of the paintings.

Six months later, she took another and brought the previous one back."

"And was it cleaned?" said Phillip.

"More than that. She had the glass upgraded to non-reflective, along with new backing paper and fiberboard. The timber frames remained the same, but the hanging wire was replaced."

"Did they need cleaning?" said Phillip.

"Most were over a hundred years old," said Silvano. "They looked tired and shabby, so yes."

"Did she say who cleaned them up?" said Phillip.

"Some Belgian chap, she never mentioned his name."

"Did you ever hear her talking to this Belgian?" said Amanda.

"No, she must have done it when I was out walking or in the bath."

"Didn't you think that odd?" said Amanda.

"Not really, to start with we never discussed each other's business. It was not unusual for us to make business calls out of earshot. She preferred to leave the past behind and concentrate on our future. It wasn't until just before Salome and you visited that I learned that the house and all its contents belonged to the Steinman Foundation. Before that, I'd assumed it was all hers."

"Do you have the number of this driver?" said Amanda.

"Yes, in my contacts."

"Then tomorrow we can call him. Find out where he took her," said Phillip.

***

"Never seen anything like it," said the locksmith on Calle Cristo in Nerja old town. "But by the size, strength, and the complicity of the bitting, it's for a strong box or small safe. There's also something stamped onto the shaft." He took down a powerful magnifying glass from the shelf above his workbench and peered through it, moving the glass until he could identify what was there. "Make a note on your phone," he said then waited for Phillip to prepare his device. Phillip nodded; finger poised above his keyboard. "Plus sign, 350540673VB," said the locksmith.

Silvano tipped the man five Euros and they headed for Phillip's bank.

***

A woman followed them, her long dark hair fluttering in the cool breeze. An open three-quarter-length light gray coat over a black skirt, sloppy pink sweater, and black woolen leggings keeping her warm. Large black framed glasses disguised her plain features.

There was a queue for the manager's office, so Phillip and Silvano slipped next door for a coffee and a pitufo. The woman sat at the next table and played with her phone while she listened to their conversation. There was still a queue when they returned so they sat and waited for the first admin assistant to be available.

It took ages but they were eventually shown into the manager's office.

They shook hands and sat down opposite a smartly dressed blond woman in her late thirties.

"Please, don't get too excited," said Phillip. "But this is a most unusual request that will hopefully help us track down some assets of this gentleman's late wife."

The manager shrugged and sat forward. "Anything to assist a valued client, Señor Armitage."

Silvano took out the envelope and handed it over.

The manager spilled the contents onto her desk and picked up the key.

"This is a safe deposit key," she said. "The depository will likely also have one. It usually needs the two to open the box along with an account number and various passwords."

"There's a code stamped onto the shaft of the key," said Phillip. "Is that usual?"

"They vary," she said peering at the key. "Sorry, it's too small to read."

Phillip showed her the code from his phone.

"Could be the box number," she said picking up the credit card and examining it thoroughly. She slid her keyboard toward her and tapped in the numbers 3614-5353-1214-4396. After a minute or so, she shook her head, slid over a card reader, and inserted it.

"Sorry," she said but this is unreadable, there's no hologram, and the brown stripe on the back is purely for visual effect. There are also five numbers for a card verification code instead of the usual three or four. Having said that, the VISA graphics seem genuine but the hyphens between the numbers would never appear on a real card. It could be something produced by the depository as part of the identification process. These numbers probably mean something and may point to the location where the key can be used."

"Most helpful," said Phillip.

"Thank you," said Silvano.

They stood, shook hands and the two men left.

They sat straight back down at the same café table

and ordered up two more coffees. The woman was still there talking quietly on the phone.

"Do any of the number sequences ring any bells?" said Phillip in English. "I would have thought that if it were a message from Anne, she would want to be helping you solve the puzzle not confuse you."

"Nothing jumps out at me," said Silvano. "I'll have to write everything down on a large piece of paper and absorb them for a while."

"Then I suggest that we return to my study, call your old driver and use Google," said Phillip. "If there are any patterns hidden there, it might edge us further forward."

"So, all we have to do is break these codes," said Silvano.

"Any good at crosswords or number puzzles?" said Phillip.

"Useless, but you should try my Spaghetti Vongole. I'm a cook Phillip, used to dealing with real ingredients. Anything abstract leaves me cold."

"Then let's go play with these numbers and see what they are trying to tell us."

The woman watched them go, lifted her phone, and made a call.

46

"What did you learn?" said Amanda looking up from her computer as Phillip and Silvano entered the study and sat down next to her.

"Nothing much," said Silvano. "It confirmed what we thought last night but at least we have more detail to work on. Phillip, show me that code on the key please so I can write it down. Then I'll go for a walk and think about it."

Phillip passed over some paper and a pen. Silvano copied it and stood.

"Before you go," said Phillip. "Try the driver."

"Well remembered," said Silvano taking out his phone, flicking through his contacts, then pressing dial.

"Hello," he said. "Is that Pepe? No. Could I speak to him? He's what?" There was a brief pause. "Do you have a number for him, or know where he went? OK, thanks. Listen, if he does contact you, could you ask him to call me, my name is Silvano Furlan. My wife, Anne Pennington, and I were regular clients. Right, thanks again. Goodbye."

"What was all that?" said Amanda seeing the

disappointed expression on Silvano's face.

"Pepe sold his vehicle and client list at the end of December and went back to Argentina," said Silvano. "The new owner doesn't have any contact details."

"When did you use him last?" said Phillip.

"Early December. We went to Sevilla for the day, sightseeing."

"And Pepe told you nothing about selling up?" said Amanda.

"No."

"What about the exhibition?" said Amanda. "How did you manage?"

"The hotel kindly offered their car and driver."

"Then it looks like that avenue is closed," said Phillip.

"I'll go for my walk," said Silvano. "The fresh air usually inspires me."

They watched him leave the study. He looked sad and desperate.

"The credit card is unrecognizable by the bank," said Phillip turning back to the workstation. "The bank manager thinks it's a pointer to the depository. Let's follow Silvano's example and write out all the numbers and pin them up in front of us."

Phillip prepared two bits of A4 paper with a list of the different codes and clipped one to each of their vertical page readers.

"If the card is trying to tell us a location," said Amanda. "Try the numbers in an online map. They could be GPS locations."

"Or Longitude and Latitude."

"In which case, they will need decimal points inserted somewhere. I'll play with the first eight numbers; you try the second."

The office door burst open.

"Switzerland," said Silvano, eyes gleaming. "The plus sign on the key. Could it represent the Swiss Flag?"

"Did you travel to Switzerland?" said Phillip.

"For a few days last year but we were never apart the whole time."

"Switzerland could have something to do with it but look here," said Amanda. "See. The first four numbers on the card are 3614 the second 5354. If we convert those into 36.14 and -5.354 it gives us the Latitude and Longitude for Gibraltar."

"Hence the hyphens between the numbers," said Phillip.

"The remaining numbers on the card don't relate to any map references," said Phillip.

"On Google no, but see if there is a local map," said Amanda. "It might point to a street."

"St. George," said Phillip. "The cross could also mean the saint, the British Ensign, Malta, or the Red Cross."

"Here is a three-dimensional map of the rock," said Phillip staring at his screen. "Hand-drawn by a local artist. And look at the grid reference twelve down and fourteen across."

"George's Lane," said Amanda looking over his shoulder.

"Let's have a look at what businesses are there?" said Phillip zooming in on the street. "Only three. A bar on the corner. Spirit of the Rock, distillers of Campion Gin and the Valletta Bank."

"Does the bank have a website?" said Silvano.

"I'm looking now and guess what the telephone number is?" said Phillip.

"Plus sign, 350540673?" said Silvano.

"Correct, +350 is the international code for Gibraltar," said Phillip.

"And VB are the initials of the bank," said Amanda.

"Then there are only two groups of numbers unused. The CVC and last group on the card," said Phillip.

"A PIN perhaps?" said Silvano.

"Or an account number," said Phillip.

47

Phillip picked up his phone and tapped in the bank's number. He switched over to the speakerphone and handed it to Silvano.

"Bank of Valletta," said a male voice with an English accent.

"Good morning," said Silvano. "My name is Silvano Furlan."

"Mr. Furlan. My name is Steven Hall. Great to hear from you, we've been expecting your call."

"Really?"

"We didn't know when you would contact us, but your wife told us you would eventually. I assume that she has passed away?"

"Yes, on January second."

"My condolences."

"Thank you."

"I guess you must be wondering what this is all about?" said Steven.

"You could say that."

"I'm not permitted to discuss this matter over the phone, Mr. Furlan but you will need to come to the bank personally and bring the death certificate, your passport, the key, and the card."

"Just a moment," said Silvano muting the phone. "Can we go tomorrow?"

"Can your sister take Sasha for the day?" said Amanda.

"Pass me your phone and I'll ask her now."

Phillip tapped in the message. 'Urgent business in Gibraltar tomorrow, can you handle Sasha?'

'Yes', came the reply within seconds.

"Hi, Steven," said Silvano. "Sorry, just checking travel arrangements. Can I come tomorrow? Around eleven in the morning?"

"Certainly, we look forward to meeting you."

***

The top of the rock was covered in cloud as they wound their way around the many roundabouts in La Linea de la Concepción, the frontier town that lived off the crumbs of Gibraltar. Over twenty thousand workers crossed the border every day to build, clean, repair, or administrate the British Protectorate seemingly glued to the bottom of the Iberian Peninsula. The morning queue had thinned. It was still long but moved reasonably quickly. After half an hour of stopping and starting, they held up their passports and were waved through both sets of customs and immigration controls. A large white car was three vehicles behind them.

Phillip pointed out the distinctly British red buses and telephone kiosks to Silvano while they waited for a plane to land, then crossed the runway into the town itself. Phillip parked in the lot on Corral Road and they walked toward Casemates Square where they paused for coffee and a late breakfast of eggs and bacon.

Main Street was bustling with shoppers, many wearing group stickers from their cruise ship as they haggled with the traders for tax-free electronic goods and booze.

George's Lane was a narrow street with a slight upward incline. There was a small crowd gathered outside the distillery listening to a tall, gray-haired man with a goatee beard and glasses giving an eloquent preamble to a tour and tasting. It seemed Campion was a small flower unique to the rock and the distillery the only manufacturing business. The bank was a little further up on the opposite side.

It was an old, three-floor building solidly built with limestone blocks and barred windows. It wasn't the sort of financial services facility open to the public and there was no ATM outside. The well rubbed brass sign informed them that this was the Valletta Bank. Established in 1805. They rang the bell.

"Please look into the camera lens and identify yourself," said a male voice.

"Silvano Furlan with two friends." The heavily armored door buzzed open. "Please wait at the bottom of the stairs," said the voice.

They went in and the door shut automatically behind them.

There was only a short space some two meters long before the bottom steps of steep, narrow stairs. The staircase was then blocked by a metal door on the fourth step. To the left was a plain white plastered wall, to the right another armored door with a small window at head height.

"You are about to be scanned," said the voice.

"What is this," said Phillip as they all followed the instructions, "Fort Knox?"

"Oh no," said the voice. "We are far more secure than that. Stand still now."

There was a whirring sound in the ceiling and the armored door buzzed open. They went into a small rectangular room with no furniture except for a metal cabinet. The single window that faced out onto the lane was barred on the inside. They were met by a short thin man in his mid-thirties dressed in a smart pinstriped suit.

The man turned and extended his arm. "Mr. Furlan?" he said Silvano moved forward and they shook hands. "Steven Hall," said the man.

"These are my friends," said Silvano indicating Phillip and Amanda. "Is it OK if they accompany me?"

"Of course. Did you bring the items we discussed?" said Steven.

Silvano handed over an envelope.

"I just need to authenticate these and then we can go down to the depository," said Steven extracting a piece of folded paper from his inner jacket pocket. He unfolded the paper and compared the key and card with images on the paper. Then checked Silvano's passport and the death certificate. "That's fine," said Steven reinserting the items and returning the envelope. "You'll need the numbers on the back of the card to open the dial after we have both used our keys simultaneously. The last four numbers on the front of the card are your PIN to exit the depository. Before we enter our welcome lounge would you please turn off your devices."

He waited while they all did so. He nodded. "Follow me please."

He led them through yet another armored door. This one was controlled by a dial pad and a fingerprint scanner. They entered the lounge which was comfortably furnished with sofas, coffee tables, and table lamps. "We only one client or related group at a time in the depository," said Steven. "Occasionally, they take a little longer than anticipated, those following wait in here. Today is unusually quiet, so we can go straight down."

He pressed his index finger onto another scanner mounted on the sidewall at the far end of the lounge next to a metal sliding door. The door slid open and they entered a small square unfurnished space lined with painted portraits and photographs, some in black and white, others in color.

"These are the presidents of the bank since it started in 1805," said Steven. "Please don't be alarmed but this room is the elevator, it's old, slow, and noisy but extremely reliable."

"Two hundred years is a long time to stay in business?" said Phillip.

"We are a small bank still in the hands of the founding family," said Steven. "Many of the original settlers in Gibraltar were from Malta. They wanted a safe place to keep their valuables when they were traveling. It started as a depository and added private banking services as clients requested more from us."

He pressed a button and they descended into the depths of the earth and stopped.

"We are now ten meters underground," said Steven. "The hole was hacked out of the solid rock with picks and shovels. Over the years the security has been increased and sophisticated ambient controls installed. Today, the outside of the vault is made of solid steel and lined with sensors. Any attempt at tunneling will be identified immediately. The inside is lined with Titanium and yet more sensors. I'll try and put this delicately but please try to avoid any sudden noises, the alarms are hair-trigger sensitive."

The lift door opened.

They walked into a brightly lit rectangular room some ten meters long and four wide. Every wall was stacked from floor to ceiling with different sized stainless-steel deposit boxes. In the center was a rectangular table some two meters by one also in stainless-steel. An aluminum step ladder leaned against the far wall. The temperature and humidity were perfect. Steven took out his key. Silvano likewise.

Steven led them over to the far end and inserted his key into a small box about halfway up and a meter in. Silvano inserted his key into the other slot and they both turned simultaneously. The door opened revealing a dial pad on the front of another steel door.

"This is when I leave you," said Steven. "So, you may enjoy your box contents in private. When you are done, please close the inner door and twist the dial then push the outer door until it clicks shut. After that, you have two choices. You may call the lift and press exit. The lift will stop on the first floor where you can take the stairs directly down to the door you arrived at. The PIN from the card will let you out onto the street. Or, if you wish to talk to me about anything, press the office button on the lift. It will deliver you to the top floor."

Steven returned to his office.

The three of them gazed at the box wondering what could be inside. Silvano advanced, right arm extended, and grabbed the dial. Amanda read the numbers from the back of the card. Silvano turned the dial until all five numbers had registered. The door sprung open revealing a metal drawer with a handle on the front. Silvano jerked it to test the weight and was surprised by how light it was. He pulled the drawer out and placed it on the table. The drawer had a hinged cover.

They all stared at it.

"Amanda, please do the honors," said Silvano. "I can't bear to look."

Amanda flipped open the lid to reveal two white envelopes. One standard folded letter size, the other was much larger. Amanda looked at Silvano. Go on, he indicated. Amanda picked up the large envelope and slit open the flap with her fingernail. She reached inside and extracted a pile of documents. They were seven separate piles. Each pile was clipped together.

Amanda flicked through the top pile. "The first item," she said. "Is an invoice from Sotheby's Fine Arts in London dated over twenty-nine years ago for one point two million US Dollars. It's addressed to Anne Pennington at her house in Granada. The next is a copy of the payment made by bank transfer from this very bank in full settlement of the invoice.

"The next item is a colored print of a painting.

"Then comes a typed, physical description and title of the painting, with the artist's name followed by several supporting papers listing the previous owners of the work along with the galleries and auction houses that had been involved in the sale. There is also a letter from the artist himself describing his relationship with the subject.

"The subject was Fernande Olivier. The artist was Pablo Picasso. These papers are the official provenance of the painting."

"That means," said Phillip. "That Anne Pennington was the official owner of a Picasso Muse, not the Steinman Foundation."

"And the other papers?" said Silvano.

Amanda thumbed through them.

"They are all here," she said. "Anne purchased and owned all seven muses with her own money."

"What does that mean?" said Silvano.

"Best to read the other document before jumping to any conclusions," said Phillip.

Silvano picked up the smaller envelope and ripped off the sealed end. He scanned the text and as the realization of the contents sunk in, put his hand to his brow, and leaned against the table.

"You, OK?" said Amanda.

"What an amazing woman," said Silvano passing the letter to Amanda. "It's all here, could you read it out? It's too emotional for me."

"June 2018," said Amanda "Gibraltar. My Dearest Husband. Thank you for our wonderful time together. It may have been a brief encounter, but every moment was precious, and I treasured them all. I hope this finds you recovered from my passing and with a new friend in Siena.

"I'm so sorry to lead you on such a wild goose chase, especially as I know you hate puzzles of any kind. However, this was the only method I could think of to protect the paintings from the Foundation bully boys.

"They have probably worked out by now that the muse paintings they collected from me are not the originals. I had a competent Belgian gentleman in Málaga, who shall remain anonymous, make extremely plausible copies of all seven. You recall that every six months or so I would disappear for a few days under the pretext of having them cleaned. Whereas, I was having them copied and inserted into the original frames as well as updating the glazing and packaging.

"The truth is, I never needed Godfrey's money. I had plenty of my own. I inherited everything from a wealthy aunt and also from my parents and set up a trust fund in this bank before I even moved to Granada. Several generations ago, my mother's side of the family were migrants from Malta. One of the portraits in the elevator is a distant relative.

"My brother was, and still is, irresponsible with money and his wife was most untrustworthy. I helped him out by leasing him my house at a peppercorn rent. He even struggled to pay that. Do with him what you will. He is no longer my concern.

"With most of my inheritance, I purchased the muse paintings. There is some capital left that is in the original trust account in this bank. If you have a chat with the director, it should be Steven, and sign some papers, it is all yours. Best to keep it here and use the bank's credit cards for your expenditure. Undoing a trust fund is an expensive and complex exercise and for what is left, it is not worth it.

"The other documents track the history of the original paintings and include proof of purchase. Any art expert will recognize their authenticity, so before you leave the premises today, have copies made of everything and ask the bank to authenticate them with their official stamp.

"You're probably wondering what I have done with the original paintings. I have bequeathed them to the Picasso Museum in Málaga. They are already in the safe hands of the director, Joaquín Martínez. I took them there personally. Until you deliver the provenance documents to him, they will be kept in storage and under wraps. When all is out in the open, they will hold an exhibition of some sort. Oh, to be fly on the wall in the Foundation offices when that hits the fan.

"Finally, my darling man. It was divine to have been your wife and I thank you from the bottom of my heart for your love and tenderness. You made my remaining years an absolute delight. With love Anne."

Tears streamed down Silvano's cheeks. Amanda put down the letter and hugged him. Phillip patted him on the shoulder then went over to the drawer. He closed the lid, replaced it in the box, twisted the dial back and forth a few times, and shut the outer door with a solid click. He summoned the elevator, and they went up to the office. Steven Hall was waiting for them.

"The papers are ready for your signature, Mr. Furlan," he said leading Silvano to a desk in the far corner of the office by the barred rear window.

Silvano's head was in a spin as he half absorbed what Steven was showing him and explaining. While he pretended to read the terms and conditions, Steven copied the provenance documents, stamping and signing each one with a flourish.

"Are you ready to sign?" said Steven.

Silvano signed where he was told.

"Congratulations," said Steven shaking his hand. "You are now the beneficiary of a trust fund worth just over one million British Pounds."

"Thank you," said Silvano. "I have no idea what to do with it but I'm sure my sister will know exactly."

Steven bundled up the papers into a large envelope and passed them over to Silvano with a new credit card in his name and a PIN that he would never forget.

The last four numbers of the card that came with the key.

Steven escorted them to the exit.

"Thank you again, Steven," said Silvano shaking hands.

"My pleasure, call me whenever you want any help or advice."

Phillip and Amanda shook hands, and they all went out on to the street.

"Mr. Silvano?" said a male voice as they turned away from the door to head back down to Main Street. Two burly men dressed in beige overcoats and were facing them.

"Who is asking?" said Silvano.

"Detective Inspector Chilcott of the Royal Gibraltar Police," said the elder. "And this is Detective Constable Thirkettle. Can I see your identity papers?"

Silvano extracted his wallet and showed them his EU ID card.

Chilcott looked at the picture, compared it with Silvano's face, and nodded at his colleague.

"I have an arrest warrant for you," said Chilcott. "You are charged with art theft and you are to accompany us to Police Headquarters."

Chilcott looked at Phillip and Amanda.

"Are you accompanying this gentleman?" he said.

"Yes," said Phillip.

"Then you better come as well."

All four of them walked to the top of George's Lane where an unmarked black saloon car was parked illegally just around the corner. The three of them were ushered into the back seat. The policemen climbed in the front and they headed off to the Police Station.

48

It was only a six-minute drive to cover the two kilometers along narrow streets to the granite stone-built Police Headquarters on Pavilion road. All three were escorted straight into the same interview room without being searched or having their identity confirmed. They were asked to sit together on one side of a large table. The two detectives came in looking embarrassed and sat down opposite.

"Sorry that we had to haul you off the street like that," said Chilcott. "But we thought it best to bring you somewhere quiet to explain what is going on. No charges are being brought against you, and should you answer our questions satisfactorily you will be free to go."

"How may we help you, Inspector?" said Phillip restraining Amanda and Silvano from their obvious indignation.

"Our foreign office received a call only half an hour ago from the American Embassy in Madrid informing us that we had a wanted art thief, and two associates inside Valletta Bank. They suspected you were collecting seven valuable Picasso paintings that purportedly belong to the Steinman Foundation and that you should be prevented from leaving Gibraltar until said paintings had been examined by their experts."

"Did they say exactly which paintings?" said Phillip.

"We're expecting a list imminently," said the constable. "However, we can see that you are not carrying any paintings. However, it would help us assuage our foreign minister if you could throw any light on this matter. Do you even know what we are talking about?"

"Oh yes," said Amanda. "But someone, somewhere has their wires completely crossed. The seven paintings concerned are the property of this gentleman, Mr. Silvano Furlan. They were left to him by his late wife Anne Pennington. May we show you some documents that will verify that?"

"Please do," said the inspector.

Amanda extracted the two thick envelopes from her bag, opened it up, and passed the originals over to the policemen.

The inspector picked them up and flicked through them. "Sorry," he said staring hard at them. "I know nothing about art, and this means nothing to me."

"Let me explain," said Silvano glaring at the policemen his cheeks white with rage. "Every original painting has a history, or provenance as it's called in art circles. Who painted it, who bought and sold it? What galleries or auctioneers were involved? A description of the work and the payments made between buyers and sellers. The seven paintings concerned here have all been bought and sold several times over their hundred or so years since Picasso created them. The first thing that any buyer will look for before spending sometimes millions on acquiring any piece of art is evidence of its provenance. You wouldn't buy a car without checking out the logbook, or property without understanding the deeds. It's the same with paintings. These pieces of paper are the logbook of the paintings concerned and show quite clearly that my late wife purchased them over thirty years ago with money from her account in the bank you so rudely dragged us away from. Sadly, you have been unwittingly involved in a spiteful attempt by the Steinman Foundation to impinge on our freedoms. The Foundation has never owned these paintings but for some ludicrous reason assume that they have a right to them. That is a civil matter, not a criminal one. If they want to sue me, they are welcome but unless you release us immediately, I regret that I must inform the Italian Consulate and lodge a formal complaint against the Gibraltarian Government for false imprisonment."

The inspector looked sympathetically at Silvano absorbing his words. "May I make copies of these?" he said.

"Of course, take as many as you like and send them to whoever asks," said Silvano. "But if we are not out of here within five minutes, I shall be making a telephone call."

Three minutes and twenty seconds later, they were standing on the front steps of the police station with the two policemen.

"Sorry about that," said the inspector. "We were only doing our jobs."

"I understand," said Silvano. "I apologize for such bullying tactics. It is not normally in my nature, but once again these fucking Americans have pissed me off for no reason other than greed."

"That I can believe," said Chilcott. "The constable will drive you wherever you wish."

They shook hands and walked over to the same saloon they had arrived in. The constable opened the door, they climbed in and shut the door. They were just about to drive off when the inspector knocked on the window. Phillip opened it a fraction.

"Just one last thing," said the Inspector. "Are the paintings in the Depository?"

"I give you my solemn word that they are not in Gibraltar," said Silvano.

"May I inquire where they are?"

"You may," said Silvano. "But that is none of your business."

The inspector nodded and the constable drove off. "Anywhere in particular?" he said.

"Yes," said Phillip holding Amanda's hand. "The Registry Office, please."

49

The Registry Office in Gibraltar is located within the former library in a quiet area just off Main Street. They were shown around and reserved a date for the end of February. A little under six weeks away. They would have to arrive the night before to sign the papers which meant an overnight stay.

They walked down to the Sunborn Yacht Hotel in the harbor and booked the Bridal suite and five other rooms for their guests for three nights. It took them longer to choose the reception menu and then there were the rings. They chose a simple band each at a small jeweler on Main Street and eventually by midafternoon, they were ready to head home.

Fifteen minutes later, they had only just joined the motorway, when Amanda sniffed. Phillip glanced over to see if she was OK and spotted tears streaming down her cheeks. He looked in the mirror. Silvano had his eyes closed. He reached out and grabbed her hand.

"What's wrong, my love?" said Phillip. "Come, tell me."

"I'm being silly, ignore me."

"Humor me. Just imagine that I can magic away any problem that you have."

"Now you're being silly," she said almost smiling.

"All right, we're just a couple of idiots pretending that everything is fine, but you never cry. Aren't you happy about our wedding?"

"I'm delirious, but that registry office. Well. It's not exactly the sort of place where I've visualized committing myself to the man of my dreams."

"And the yacht hotel?"

"That was fabulous."

"We could try and arrange a church in Gibraltar."

"But it's such a long way for my parents and all my friends. Some of them don't even have passports."

"Would you prefer us to wait and arrange everything in Spain? The paperwork could take a year at least."

"That's why I'm crying. I want everything to be today and perfect. The place, the reception, the honeymoon but it's so expensive and we are always so busy."

"What do you want me to do?"

"You can't do anything. I just have to make a decision."

"At least you've stopped crying."

"I know, I'll be OK. Just give me a day or two to think it through."

"My darling. Take as long as you like. My only concern is that you want to marry me not give me the elbow."

"Now you're being stupid."

Silvano smiled, then went back to sleep.

***

Four days later with Silvano long gone, Salome summoned them to see her now completed house in Vélez-Málaga and to tour the convent for an update on how the refurbishment program was proceeding.

It was a Saturday, so they took Sasha with them.

The house was transformed. Vicente guided them around, explaining his design concepts. They couldn't help but notice the loving glances between him and Salome. Amanda looked at her. She winked and shrugged.

The convent hadn't been touched, but the church was starting to take shape. The roof was being reinforced; the walls replastered, and a start had been made on the cloisters and garden. Nobody was working but the pace of progress had been phenomenal.

"We have a huge team," said Salome. "Thanks to the donations from the exhibition. There is also an incredible amount of interest from the townspeople, the construction industry, the Bishop of Málaga, and the media."

"When do you think it will be ready?" said Amanda.

The hotel part will take another year or more," said Salome. "But the church and cloisters, around two to three months. Now I've reserved a table at La Mangoa for lunch and it's my treat as a thank you for all that you've done for me."

"That's…"

"Amanda, shut up. I insist," said Salome.

Amanda conceded.

They left the car in the convent car park and walked to the restaurant. Several people were sitting at the table waiting for them: Silvano, the Mayor of Vélez with his wife, Amanda's parents, their former business partners Richard, and Ingrid. Prado and Inma were chatting with Phillip's sister and nieces. Sasha was delighted and immediately ran over to them.

After hugs and kisses they sat down, and Salome ordered Cava. After it was poured, Prado stood and waited for everyone to settle down. "Before the toasts begin," he said. "I just have a quick word to say on this special occasion."

Amanda and Phillip exchanged puzzled glances.

"It was only some eight months ago that I had the pleasure of meeting these two. Since then, we've been working together on a complex conspiracy case, which I'm happy to say, thanks largely to their input, has recently been satisfactorily resolved."

He stretched out his hand to Inma. She passed him from below the table a thin, rectangular package wrapped in brown paper.

"Now," said Prado. "I'm sure that you are all aware that police salaries are somewhat pathetic and expense budgets extremely tight, yet my colleagues and I wanted to express our thanks to Phillip and Amanda in some meaningful way. Everyone in the office, including el jefe has contributed and we bought this at a special price from the evidence store before it was taken away for auction. I know that Amanda isn't a great fan of Picasso, but we discovered this original sketch of Fernande Olivier among the possessions of an evil man who is now deceased. For some reason, his sister declined it. But what that means is that this rare artwork comes with a most unusual provenance that connoisseurs will drool over for centuries. We've had it professionally restored and reframed. On behalf of el jefe and all of us at the National Police, I am happy to present it to you as a small token of our gratitude."

Prado walked around to them and handed it over with hugs and cheek kisses, to enthusiastic applause from everyone.

Prado returned to his seat.

Silvano stood and said in Spanish.

"Listen, I'd like to propose two toasts. First to Salome for this lunch invitation but secondly to two special people who have helped both of us recently. Phillip and Amanda."

Cava was sipped. Phillip was about to reply but Silvano held up his hand. "I'm not finished yet. Traveling back from Gibraltar the other day, I overheard how dissatisfied that Amanda was with their choice of a wedding venue and it made me think. So, I called Salome. Together we resolved to find a better alternative. This meant that we had to inject some urgency into the Spanish bureaucracy. A daunting task. Normally, arranging a marriage license in Spain takes ages and that's for Spanish people. For us foreigners, and I know because I've been through all that, it's far worse. This morning, with the help of the mayor, we have resolved all that. Mr. Mayor."

The mayor stood and extracted an envelope from his pocket. "This isn't my parade, so I'll be brief. This is a wedding license in the names of Amanda Salisbury and Phillip Armitage. It's dated for the end of March. I also have another permission to announce. From the same date, the church at Las Claras Convent may hold weddings and the cloisters may be used for receptions. Should you wish for a civil ceremony, I will be delighted to officiate for you. If you prefer something religious, we can arrange for the denomination of your choice."

The mayor walked around to Phillip and handed

over the license, then to Salome with the building permit.

Everyone applauded and exchanged approving glances.

Silvano stood again. "Just one more thing," he said removing an envelope from his pocket. "I haven't been back to Italy. First, I was at the Picasso Museum and handed over the provenances for all seven paintings. After that, I was back in Gibraltar to arrange for this." He walked over to Amanda and Phillip and handed her the envelope.

She ripped it open and help up a credit card, she looked at it more closely. It was in her name.

"There is more than enough on there to pay for the biggest wedding you can imagine, a lavish honeymoon, and plenty left over to treat yourselves to whatever you want. Thank you both for all your help."

The whole table stood and cheered. Sasha went and stood between his Dad and Amanda. He took their hands then looked lovingly up at them.

Tearfully, they returned his gaze and ruffled his hair.

The Author

Paul S Bradley blames his Andalusian Mystery Series on ironed squid. Otherwise, he'd still be stuck in London failing at this, that, and the other. As discerning diners know, calamares a la plancha should translate as grilled squid. Then he noticed bad translations everywhere. He quit the rat race, moved to Nerja, Spain, and helped the owner of this gastronomic gaff prepare his menu so that foreigners understood he was offering food, not laundry services.

During the following thirty years, this tiny translation evolved into a lifestyle magazine for the Costa del Sol, along with guidebooks and travelogues in English, German and Spanish. He's lectured about living in Spain and bullfighting but is keen to emphasize that he never dressed in a tight, fancy suit or waved a pink cape at anyone; especially if they weighed 600 kilos and carried a sharp pair of horns. He has also appeared on local radio and TV, but extremely briefly.

More recently, educated groups of posh American and Canadian Alumni have enjoyed his tour director services apart from the terrible jokes and occasional temporarily misplaced client.

Paul's books blend his unique taste of Spain with intriguing fictional mysteries. Learn more at paulbradley.eu where lovers of Spain can sign up for free short stories, blogs, and videos.

What did you think?

Reviews, good or bad fuel this independent author's continuous efforts to improve. If you enjoyed this book, please leave a comment on my blog, or your preferred retailer or follow my social media.
See the website for more details. Thank you.

www.paulbradley.eu

Darkness in Córdoba

What's in a name?

In the ancient city of Córdoba, it's *Semana Santa* – the Holy Week of Easter passion and processions. On the morning of Palm Sunday, the body of an eminent priest is found in suspicious circumstances in a private chapel within the magnificent Cathedral, the hub of the religious celebrations.

An elderly man is found sitting on the marble floor gazing intently at the corpse.

All he would say is three words in Spanish.

"Sólo hablo árabe."

"I only speak Arabic."

With a perfect weather forecast, the crowds are already jostling for the best positions in the narrow streets. Nothing will stop or delay the processions. Not even murder.

In the fifth stand-alone case of the Andalusian Mystery Series, Detective Inspector Leon Prado, with interpreter's ex British soldier Phillip Armitage, and American videographer Amanda Salisbury are summoned to assist with the investigation and translation.

Due out in January 2022.

Printed in Great Britain
by Amazon